His Revenge

By John W. Howell

Published by Keewaydin Lane Books
Copyright © 2015 John W. Howell
Published in the United States by
Keewaydin Lane Books Port Aransas, Texas
ISBN: 978-0-9969115-0-4

Dedication

His Revenge is dedicated to Molly Dwyer McCormick, who continually provides support and counsel, on all things connected with my writing. She is the one person who encouraged me to pursue my interest and passion in the first place. She is always ready to support the effort as days turn into months of concentration that produce the novels continuing to flow out of my imagination. It has been over three years since I started writing full-time and I cannot imagine where I would have finished were she not there providing the advice and encouragement all authors need. I count myself a very lucky man indeed.

Acknowledgements

His Revenge is a piece of fiction written out of the author's imagination. Port Aransas is a real place with real people, but the events described, characters developed and places visited are purely fictional with no intent to depict reality. I want to thank Bette A. Stevens for the kind words on the back cover and for reading the book in its initial stage. I also want to thank Mark Crosslin for providing insight into the location descriptions of Ecuador and for reading my story in its early stage. A thanks also to Bethany Drew, who has been patient in reading very rough drafts and providing valuable advice.

Chapter One

The water rushes over my head. I'm sinking and don't know why. With my breath held, I have trouble stopping the air from escaping since the pressure drives the air up and out. I try to keep my mouth closed, but the water pressure pushes the air out more and more. Will I pass out? In the distance, the light is dim. To rise to the surface in time might not be possible—I need to breathe right now. Toward ending the pain in my chest, my rambling mind rationalizes taking a deep breath—even knowing it will end my life. In conflict with the irrational thought of ending it, my body won't let me suck in the water, as it fights to retain the little bit of oxygen left to fuel my brain.

The despair is nearly overwhelming, and my mind considers other ways to battle the feeling. What more could I have done with my life? The pressure becomes more intense, and I'm about to lose it all, and I decide I've lived the way I wanted and have no regrets. I close my eyes and hear only the roar of the sea. I'm so tired. Exhausted. Sleep will fix everything, and I want to give in.

***

I snap to awareness, not hearing the doctor's question.

"I'm sorry, Doctor; my mind was a million miles away."

"Understandable, John," he says. "You've been in a horrific explosion at sea. Your mind can drift while you try to explain to yourself what happened."

"I remember hitting the water and then a large explosion, but that's about it."

"You know you're in the naval hospital, right?"

"Yes, I know, and you're Dr. Samuels. It's just ... this nightmare that I keep having over and over is so real."

"It's real because you lived it. You almost got killed. You and Jason Savard did the country great service. Those terrorists were going to blow up the Annapolis midshipmen along with the Intrepid Museum and you stopped them."

"They had explosives below deck on my boat My GRL. She was blown to bits by those bastards."

"Yes, but you got them to blow her up in the middle of the Atlantic and not on at the pier in the port of New York."

"Yeah, I think we were lucky to survive. I thought I'd only be a few days in the hospital. I feel like I've been lying here for a month."

"You have some serious injuries. The water blast bruised your eyes, and right now you have no mobility in your arms."

"How about Jason. Is he okay?"

"Let's worry about you for a minute and then consider Jason. I'll need to remove the bandages from your eyes before you go home."

"Can't I go home and then come back?"

Doctor Samuels' shoes squeak on the highly polished floor when he moves around the bed and perches on the end.

"It doesn't work that way. I'm your doctor, and we do it my way. I need to go now, and will be back later. Try to relax."

I hear Samuels get up and walk away. I want to call out and ask about Jason one more time but wait instead. There must be something wrong, or the doctor would have given me more information. Relaxing isn't one of my better traits.

So, I lie here and have nothing to do but think about how Jason and I swam away from my boat but still got caught in the underwater explosion. I also think about the terrorists who tried to blow up the midshipmen from Annapolis and the Intrepid Museum. I'm glad the government got those involved in the actual attack. The fact that Matt Jacobs, who funded the whole operation, is still a free man upsets me. With my eyes covered in bandages, there's little left to do but go over and over the events with the objective of trying to figure out a way to change things. Matt Jacobs is a son of a bitch and deserves punishment for underwriting an operation whose purposes were to destroy human beings and America's faith in itself. He also took a nice person like Sarah Barsonne and turned her into a traitor.

I can't change the fact that Sarah worked for the other side, but wish change could happen in how I feel about her. When I think through my last few days before being kidnaped by the band of terrorists, I remember that I just about told Sarah where I'd be at all times. She must have told the hit men I would be heading to the Police station, and probably the route as well. I'm not sure if she knew they'd shoot at me, but have to assume she did. She was the one who told the chief I was alive when everyone thought I'd died, so I assume she must have really been a part of the group since she knew. I can't kick the feeling we could've had a nice relationship. Then to find out she's part of the group who murdered poor Gerry Starnes and who were about to murder countless others including me. I need to quit thinking shoulda, woulda, coulda and get back to wondering how to get Matt Jacobs.

My senses have already adjusted a little for not being able to see, and I now hear footsteps in the hallway, which stop at my door. The door opens. "Hey, guy," Ned says.

"Ned?" My voice gives away the excitement I feel. "It sure is good to hear your voice."

The last time I'd seen Ned was before being kidnaped. Blind, I settle for trying to remember his face, and the vision comes forward slowly. He has the look of a cowboy in great shape. His face has a nice tan and is a little on the reddish side. It could be because he has snow-white hair and mustache, and the contrast may be too stark. As police chief of Port Aransas, he's used to wearing Hawaiian shirts and khaki shorts with his gun concealed not too well underneath.

The first time I saw him, I thought he was an ex-wrestler or football player. He was investigating Gerry's murder and since I was found unconscious next to her body, he thought I was involved. Yeah, I was involved, but innocent of harming her. He and I became friends and were trying to find out who killed Gerry when I was kidnaped by the terrorists to be used as a scapegoat for their horrific crime. The worst part was they were using my boat as a weapon with me tied to the wheel.

Ned comes through the door and makes noise with his shoes as he approaches my bed and grabs my hand. We shake (at least Ned shakes), and he lets my hand slip back onto the sheet.

"How are you feeling today?" Ned says it a little too loudly.

"Pretty good. I wonder when I'll be getting out of this place." I decide not to tell him my hearing is fine.

"The doctor told me you should be ready in a couple of days. They're going to take your bandages off tomorrow."

"What about the fact I can't move my arms?"

"Oh, yes, your arms," Ned says. He handles the subject a little too casually as if he wants to change the subject.

"Yes, my arms." There's too much peevishness in my voice.

Ned doesn't seem to notice. "The doctor told me you'd regain the use of your arms. The condition is temporary and, in fact, you should see some improvement over the next twenty-four hours."

"Well, as comforting as it sounds, I'm not too sure, since right now these things seem useless."

"He'll be coming round tonight. I guess around seven, which is about two hours from now. I do have something we need to talk about, and it's not going to be a pleasant conversation."

What could be wrong? I go for the direct approach, "It's about Jason, isn't it?"

Ned doesn't answer, which leads me to believe the news that Jason would be fine has changed. He clears his throat and mumbles to the floor, "I'm afraid Jason didn't make it."

Ned sounds genuinely upset, and I immediately want him to feel better, so instead of saying out loud my thoughts on the unfairness of the world, I ask him, "Tell me what happened."

"I'm real sorry for letting you believe Jason would be all right. I hoped it would go well. It was always a touch and go situation, and the doctor didn't feel it would be in your best interest to upset you about Jason's lack of recovery. So we all decided to tell you everything was fine, even though Jason had to fight for his life."

"Why were his injuries so life threatening?"

"Jason took several hits from the strafing of My GRL. He lost a lot of blood, and the explosion more or less put him over the edge. The doctors tried everything they could, but the damage was too severe. He did manage to hang on for two days, but in the end his heart gave out."

"Damn."

"Jason left a message for you." He pauses, and when he begins again, his voice sounds as if he's coming down with a cold.

The fact that Jason wanted me to have a message is too overwhelming. The tears rise behind my bandages. "Please, give me the message."

"Jason wanted you to know." Ned's voice gets heavy, and he stops to clear his throat. "He wanted you to know he very much enjoyed serving with you and hoped you'd be able to witness bringing Jacobs to justice." Ned stops, and I believe he's choking back tears. Ned is quiet, and I don't want to interfere with his moment, so I stay quiet as well. After about a minute, he says, "I know you had no idea, but I always thought of Jason as the son I never had, and I'll miss him so much. He continually made me proud, and I'm sorry I couldn't have taken his place. It seems so unfair; a young person in his prime has to die when a perfectly suitable old man is available for the taking." Ned sobs in earnest and I try to reach out to him to provide comfort; my limbs stay dormant, so I use my mouth instead.

"Ned, I'm so sorry for our loss. You're right, I had no idea how close you were, but now I understand why Jason was so brave. He had you behind him, helping to accomplish the unbelievable. You should be proud of him and yourself as well."

Ned seems to take comfort in my words and stops crying. He lets out a large sigh and is still for a moment. Then he says in a clear voice touched with humor, "Jason also asked me to look out for you. I guess he thinks you need some help."

We both laugh at the thought, but then turn quiet again. Would that there were words to tell Ned of my sorrow, but none is easy. Jason, no doubt, saved my life and now, sitting here with Ned, who knew him so much better, I can't help but feel guilty for surviving.

"I sure wish I could do something."

Ned touches my hand again. "You just get better. I think it'll be a tribute to Jason to have you walking around, perfectly normal. That's what he would have wanted." He stops for another moment, and then changes the subject. "You'll be ready to go home tomorrow. You'll need some help getting around, but I think you'll be okay. Oh, I almost forgot. I got a call from the White House this morning—"

"You get a call from the White House, and you forget? Sounds to me like an old man trait."

"It's just a saying, you twit. Do you want to know what the call was about or not?"

Glad to hear the humor back in Ned's voice, I say, "Yeah, of course, I do."

"Well, they want you to come to Washington to receive an award from the President. They think the best time will be after the memorial we've planned for Jason in New York."

"Memorial? When?"

"Next Tuesday. Jason's sister has planned a service at her church in Manhattan. She invited us to go."

"I'd love to attend, but I'm not sure I can handle all the arrangements and the travel. I can't even open a door."

"Aw, come on. I'll go with you. It'll be a piece of cake."

"Well, I need to make reservations."

"All set. I called the airline today, and you and I are confirmed on a flight to LaGuardia next Monday. We leave Corpus Christi at eleven and get there by six."

"It sounds good. Do we need a hotel?"

"I got us into the Pierre. We have a small suite."

"Sounds expensive."

"I got a real good deal. The manager owes me a favor."

"Notice I didn't offer before, but if it's a good deal, let me take care of it."

"Okay, I'll let you get the hotel, and I'll get the airline tickets."

"Ned," I put some firmness in my voice. "Jason saved me, not you; let me treat for the whole trip. I'm good for it."

"You know what? I never thought of it that way. Okay, you're on."

Ned becomes silent and I'm wondering what's on his mind.

"You sure are quiet Ned."

"Yeah, I know. I wanted to ask you a question about Matt Jacobs but don't want to upset you."

"You won't upset me. I hate him but would be glad to answer any question that might lead to his arrest."

"Well, it's not that kind of question but did Jacobs talk about his family when you were his prisoner?"

"Yes, he said his parents were dead."

"Hmm. That's all he said?"

"About his family yes. Why? Is there more?"

"I'll say. His parents, wife and children, I think his parents were killed in the Six-Day War and his wife and two kids were killed by a rocket during one of the skirmishes between the Palestinians and Israelis. He barely escaped with his life and was forced to leave Palestine with his brother."

"Man, no wonder he hates the West so much."

"He said he hates the West?"

"He is making it his life's work to see the West suffer for not allowing Palestine an independent country. At least that's what he said. I can see it is more personal. He wants to avenge those deaths."

"Makes a pretty powerful reason to behave the way he does." Ned gets up to leave. "I'll be back in the morning when they take the bandages off. I also want to take you home."

"Given the circumstances of me looking like third base, I accept with many thanks."

"Goodbye, kid. Oh, and thank you for your kind words when I lost it earlier. See ya." His footsteps tell me he is already on the way out.

The door swishes back into place, and I wonder just how well he and Jason knew each other. When I'd asked Jason if he knew Ned, he tossed it off as not too well. Yet, by Ned's reaction, they were fairly close. The door to my room opens, and a sweet voice tells me it's time for dinner. Frustrated, I try to imagine who this person is, but she takes the mystery away by introducing herself. It seems I'm eating courtesy of one Constance Mayfield, who's a candy-stripe volunteer. Apparently, she's been working in this hospital since the eighth grade.

"What's your current grade?" I ask.

She announces, "The eleventh," and sounds proud.

"You've been a volunteer for four years? You must be a great person."

"I like doing this because the patients are wonderful."

"I hope you think the same of me after we finish."

"I do and probably will."

She continues to chat about school and her life as she feeds me one forkful at a time. She doesn't hurry and seems to arrange the arrival of the next fork just in time. Also, she asks if I would care for a drink of milk periodically. Before long, the meal is finished, and Constance goes off to her next patient. As she leaves the room, I think that her parents must have set a great example of caring for others as exemplified by her cheerful approach.

Another sound at the door heralds another arrival, and in walks someone with a deliberate step. Given the heavy footfall, I guess it to be a male, and also just maybe Dr. Samuels—given the sense of urgency around the pace. "Good evening, John," says Dr. Samuels' voice. "How are you doing tonight?"

"Dr. Samuels," I say with some surprise at being right in my guess. "I didn't think you would be back so soon. By the way, I never got to ask before. What are you doing here? I thought this was a naval hospital."

"Yeah, well, I happen to be a naval reserve officer, so they let me practice here. I convinced them I would be perfect since I've had some experience with you in the past." He takes my left wrist off my chest and checks my pulse. "I think we're going to take your eye bandages off tomorrow. Have you been able to move your arms?"

"No, and I'm not sure how to get them to move, so I've not tried to do it."

"I see." Samuels pauses. "Try lifting your right arm. Send a message to your arm and command it to lift, and then think hard about lifting."

Even though I believe the good doctor has lost a screw somewhere, I play along so he won't get too anxious about his mental state. I think hard and order my right arm to rise from the bed, but don't feel anything happening. Dr. Samuels cheers me on as if we're at a little league game. He encourages me to keep thinking about raising the arm.

All of a sudden, I feel the arm move, and in my mind's eye have the vision of it lifting off the bed and raising it straight up into the air. "Is anything happening?"

"You have moved your arm about two inches above the bed." Excited, Dr. Samuels talks way too loud. "You're doing great."

Sweat forms in droplets on my upper lip. I can't hold the arm anymore and release it from my mental vision, then feel it fall to the bed. "Whew. Hard work." I say this more to myself than to Samuels.

"You bet it is, but you need to do the same exercise as many times a day as you can. You'll regain the use of your arms, but you need to encourage your body to get used to the fact your arms are for working, not lying there uselessly. These exercises will help you to become stronger."

"How long do you think it will take for full control?"

"I think by this time next week, you'll be fully restored. I'm going to recommend you see a therapist at least twice a day for a week. They'll be able to help you more. Your injury isn't permanent, but to be on the safe side, I think a few sessions will do you good."

"You're talking physical therapy, right?"

Samuels lets out a big laugh. "Yes, I'm talking physical. The little mind game I taught you was to wake up the pathway. You've opened it, and now the therapist will show you how to strengthen the muscles, so they're as good as new."

I ask him if there are any other injuries, and he lets me know that with the exception of my eyes, everything else is normal.

"What about my eyes?"

"The explosion pushed water at a high rate of speed into your eyes, which resulted in severe bruising and swelling. I believe that once the swelling has gone down, you should be able to see again. I hope the last week has been enough time for the eyes to return to normal and that they'll function once we remove the bandages. We will see tomorrow." He pauses, and then says, "I guess I should say, we will see tomorrow, hopefully."

He gets up and tells me he will be back after breakfast. "Keep doing your command exercises," is the last thing he says as he leaves.

I lie back on the bed and try a few more exercises. It seems to be getting easier to do them. However, not seeing where my arms end up, there's no telling if I'm raising them higher each time. I think so, but who's to tell?

Chapter Two

The morning comes and, still able to lift my arms, I decide to surprise the nurse with my newfound abilities. The door opens, and I prepare myself to spring the surprise upon hearing her footsteps entering the room. She will say a happy good morning, and when she does, I'll raise my left arm and say something clever. I wait and, sure enough, she says, "Good morning, Mr. Cannon."

At the first sound of her voice, I raise my left arm and knock the chart clipboard right out of her hands.

"Oh, my gosh, I'm so sorry for hitting your board," I say.

"Don't be silly. The fact you can move your arm so well is a wonderful thing."

She makes no noise as she bends over to pick up the chart and then comes close to the bed. "You've made amazing progress. The doctor is going to be pleased to read your chart today."

"Yes, he was the one who told me how to regain my arm movement."

"Well, it looks as if he knew what he was talking about."

The nurse takes my wrist and checks my pulse. She puts an automated thermometer under my tongue and mutters, "Ninety-eight point six degrees." Next, she takes my blood pressure and records the measurements on the chart. "Had any bowel movements?"

This question always makes me wonder what these people think I've been up to while confined to this bed. I answer the question truthfully, "I have no idea."

"What do you mean, you have no idea?" Her tone has turned to irritation.

"Well, I haven't been out of this bed since I got here. I believe someone came in and pumped me full of bowel moving liquids, but I'm not sure anything came of it. If I could get out of this bed, I could supervise the process and then answer your question with some knowledge and authority."

"Very well," she says in cool tones. "Why don't you get up and go over to the bathroom, and then we'll all know."

She takes a hold of my left arm, puts her hand under my armpit, and sort of yanks me to a sitting position. Then she swings my legs around, so they're dangling over the edge of the bed. "Okay, slide off the bed. Don't worry; I'll hold you so you won't fall."

Her strength surprises me—with the firm wrestler's grip around my waist, it's a sure thing she has my full weight on one arm. We shuffle to the bathroom and, as we move, the cold air hits my backside. Anyone standing behind me will get mooned to the fullest. We make it to the commode, and she turns me around and eases me down to a sitting position. Already, she's grabbed a fistful of gown, so there's no fear it'll get in the way. She then turns on the fan that I'm sure turns on the light as well. I want to make a crack about the fan being necessary, but hold on to it.

"Take your time, and I'll be right outside the door. Call if you need any help." She closes the door.

So, now alone in a bathroom, I feel a little light-headed from the activity, but overall good about getting up out of bed. I take advantage of the situation and allow my body to have its way with the ceramic throne. I'm about to finish when the thought of having no way to do the cleanup work strikes me. To raise my arm in a half-assed salute is one thing, but completing the delicate maneuver of unrolling tissue, tearing off a quantity, and hitting the target effectively to facilitate a clean sweep is, at this moment, impossible. Still, I attempt to take a run at it, and start by reaching out to where the roll should be and finish by hitting it quite hard with my knuckles. With my hand on top of the roll, I realize my estimate of impossible was optimistic.

"Nurse Williams."

"Here I am," she says. She opens the door. "Have you finished?"

"Yes." My face is hot. "I can't do the cleanup, though."

"Not to worry. I'll get you squared away in no time."

She grabs the gown and raises me off the commode. To my surprise, she does a complete job and, without too many cringing moments, we make it back to the bed. She asks about the bowel movement again, and I respond in the affirmative. When she turns to go, I thank her for her help.

"Oh no, Mr. Cannon. You don't need to thank me; I'm just doing my job. It's for me to thank you. You went way beyond your duty and, as a result, a lot of people owe you a debt of gratitude. My dad was at the pier in New York showing my son the Intrepid Museum. Without your help, God knows what would have become of them if the terrorists had been successful in blowing it up. Thank you, John Cannon."

My face burns; I don't know what to say, so I remain quiet. She goes out the door as the doctor comes in. "Morning, John." He sounds cheerful.

"Good morning, Doctor," I say with less cheer.

"Aw, come on, John; this is the day for optimism."

"I just hope to see again. I'm not sure if this is an optimistic thought or not at this point."

"Well, in a few minutes, we'll know one way or another. I want you to remember, as we discussed, there may be a period of adjustment. So when I take the wrappings off, there could be a few days where you may have some difficulty."

"I do remember." I pause to choose my next words, so they don't sound as if I'm afraid. "I'm nervous about this."

"I understand. Let's get started since waiting around isn't going to help you get un-nervous, so to speak."

The doctor goes to the door, calls a nurse to assist, and then heads back to the bed and has me sit on the edge. The nurse comes in with a roll-away cart filled with instruments that make a metallic sound when they rattle against each other while the cart rolls on the tiled floor. The doctor takes off the wrappings and describes to me what he's doing. I don't listen, due to anxiousness to get to the end of the procedure. He finally has the wrappings off. "Well, the only things left are the two gauze patches over your eyes."

"I guess I'm ready."

"John, keep your eyes shut for a few minutes until I tell you to open them."

He lifts the gauze patches off each eye. I'm not sure, but believe I can see some light. The doctor wipes each closed eye with some wet cloth. "I'm removing some of the dried fluid your eyes produced while bandaged. Just keep them closed for another minute."

I can hardly stand it another second, let alone a minute, but follow the doctor's orders. I'm not in a position to do something that could jinx my sight.

"Okay, you can open your eyes now."

The approval has come and now I'm reluctant to open them. My talk was big, but this is a moment of truth.

Slowly, I open them and feel the upper lids rise with a little stickiness. They both break free, and I believe they're wide open.

"I can't see a thing." Although I want to scream, I say the words softly.

"Just wait until your eyes adjust to the room. They need to get used to the relatively bright environment."

Even after blinking several times, I still see nothing other than a hazy glow of light and wavy images.

"Doctor, I don't think they work. I have a little sensation of light, but that's about all. I can't make out anything in the room. It looks as if I'm underwater."

"As I said, John, it may take a while. I can assure you, your pupils are behaving normally. They're contracting when I pass a light near them."

"Then what's the problem?"

"Similar to your arms, your eyes need to make the connection to your brain. You'll need to do the same kind of exercises with your eyes as you did with your arms. You'll need to think about seeing, so the pathways can open. In the meantime, I think you're okay to go home."

"Think about seeing. That's a new one. I wonder how you set it up."

"You need to have someone describe something in your presence, and then you need to think about seeing it. It's helpful if it is something you've seen before, so you have an accurate picture of it in your head. Let's try it with a well-known item. Can you remember what a Coke can looks like?"

"Well, I think I can remember a Corona bottle better."

Samuels gives a little chuckle. "So, I have a Corona bottle in my hand. Why don't you describe it to me?"

I describe the bottle right down to the slice of lime and the frosty rivulets of moisture running from the cold glass in the warm, humid air.

"Excellent. When you described it, could you see it inside your head?"

"The bottle's vivid and it seems to be floating in my brain."

"Let's not get too carried away, and with some practice, you should get your sight back."

"How long do you think it will take?" I ask the question trying to take the anxiousness out of my voice.

"I won't lie to you, John. It may take weeks. You'll need to be patient. By the way, Ned asked me to give him a call when you're ready for discharge. You okay with me calling him?"

"Yes, by all means. I'll need to have him get me home. Is there anything special I should do with my eyes?"

"I've written down some instructions, but it's real easy. Just make sure to keep your eyes lubricated. I'll give you some drops. I would wear sunglasses as well. They'll keep your eyes safe from stuff blowing into them. When we can see, we get clues about dust and sand blowing around. We unconsciously turn away or shut our eyes. When you're sightless, you don't have those clues, so you'll have to protect yourself when outside especially."

"Is that all?"

"Well, be careful with shampoo, and don't rub your eyes even if you get an itching sensation. We don't want you to damage them."

"Okay, Doc, I think I have it. I want to thank you for everything you've done. I hope I didn't seem ungrateful."

"Not at all. You've been a model, patient. I understand you'll be going to Jason's service and also to the White House. When you fly, you need to keep your eyes moisturized. A couple of drops each hour ought to do it."

Samuels gets up and takes my hand. We shake, and he says, "Best of luck, and congratulations."

I frown. "Congratulations?"

"You're getting the highest civilian medal from the President of the United States. I think you should be congratulated not only for the medal but for what it stands for—honor and integrity."

Beet-red, I mumble something about not deserving, and anyone would have done what I did.

Samuels expresses his opinion over his shoulder as he makes his exit, "Okay, if you think so, but I don't agree."

I lie back on the bed and imagine watching Dr. Samuels leave the room. I have his steps down good, but can't seem to get a fix on how he looks. The last time I saw him, I'm not sure I ever noticed him leave the room. While I'm trying to conjure up a vision of the backside of the doctor, the door hisses open, and a familiar voice calls to me.

"John, it's me, Ned. I was real close when Dr. Samuels called, so here I am to take you home."

"Sounds real good. Do me a favor and go out the door and come back in real slow."

"What? You want me to go out and then come back in?" I hear "John has lost his mind" in Ned's voice.

"Yes, exactly." I try to sound as sane as possible. "Also, when you come in, walk one step at a time and continue talking as you walk."

"What should I say?"

"It doesn't matter; you can even whistle. I'm trying to visualize you walking across the floor to the bed. It's an exercise Samuels gave me to do."

"Oh." He sounds relieved. "Okay, here I go."

Ned goes out the door and then comes back in, lifting each foot carefully and putting them down with more noise than needed. I admire his flexibility in putting up with my request. He also describes raising each foot and walking step by step. It reminds me of an old Abbott and Costello movie where they said out loud, "Slowly, I turned. Step by step, inch by inch." Ned reminds me of Abbott. I try hard to visualize Ned coming across the room, and maybe letting my imagination run away with me, but I swear I can see him as if he's walking in a mist. When he lifts each foot, I see the movement and shout out with excitement. Ned finally reaches the bed, and I can see a shadowy form leaning over me.

"So, what's happening?" he asks.

He sounds as if he's a kid watching an experiment in school.

"I think I'm beginning to see shapes and forms. I'm sure I saw your feet rise and fall, and I see you standing by the bed, although you look fuzzy; sort of like a ghost."

"Well, that's wonderful. At least you can see shapes and movement." Ned sounds genuinely pleased. "We need to get out of here. I brought you some clothes, and Uncle Sam is picking up the hospital tab, so all we have to do is get you dressed and sign out."

"More than ready to go."

He hands me the clothes and asks if I need any help. I fumble through the assortment of things and feel some underpants, a t-shirt, some shorts, and a pair of deck shoes. "I'm good to go. All you have to do is let me know where the label is on the t-shirt so I won't have to redo it if I get it backward."

"Do you want me to leave while you get dressed?"

"I'm not ashamed to be seen naked in front of you. On the other hand, if my being naked bothers you, then you can go."

He stays, and points out the label. I drop the hospital gown and pull the t-shirt over my head. Next come the underpants, and finally, the shorts. Ned says, "I forgot a belt."

"No worries. I hardly ever wear one." His chuckle tells me he's pleased with my response. When I've slipped into the deck shoes, I put my arms out to my side and say, "Well, how do I look?"

"Like a million bucks, kiddo." A telltale huskiness laces his voice. He clears his throat. "You ready to go?"

"I'm ready."

Ned takes my arm and steers me to the door. I try to visualize the door opening, but I'm not successful. We walk out of the room and into the hallway. As we take a step, a cheer goes up all around us. All the staff on this floor clap and cheer, and I can make out wishes of good luck and well-done sentiments in and around the noise. Ned trembles while he holds my arm, and I realize he's crying, as are most of the people on the floor. Their cheers come through their tears.

I whisper to Ned, "What's this? Why the cheering and tears?"

"They love you, son," Ned whispers back. "Folks are pleased you're walking out of here."

"I'm overcome. What should I do?"

"Just wave and give the old V for victory sign. It usually works well."

So, I raise my arm and give the victory sign, and more applause and cheering comes my way. Ned must've done this before. We make our way to the elevator and get down to the lobby. In the lobby, a serious sounding man takes my hand and thanks me. He lets my hand go, and Ned describes for me the motion of a two-star admiral shifting from a handshake to a salute.

"It was my pleasure to command the personnel responsible for your initial treatment, and I wish you God's speed on a full recovery."

I reach out for the Admiral's hand and say, "You have a dedicated team, and I'm fortunate to have been under your care. Dr. Samuels and the rest of the team have been wonderful."

"Thank you very much. Yes, Commander Samuels is one of our finest."

Ned and I say our final goodbyes and head out the door. As usual, Ned has his SUV parked right at the curb. We get in, and I let out a sigh of relief. Ned lets me know I had better get used to the fuss since it'll be some time before people get over the idea I was instrumental in thwarting Jacobs' plan. "Let's not forget Jason," I say.

"We won't forget him, but he's not here, and now people only have you to place on a pedestal. And they're happy to do that."

"It's a strange thing, but I have this feeling we'll eventually get Jacobs, and we'll do it for Jason. In fact, when I get a boat to replace *My GRL,* I'm going to name her *His Revenge* as a tribute to Jason."

"I think you ought to concentrate on getting well and leave the vengeance up to the authorities. Besides, this isn't your fight anymore. The matter of terrorism is for the authorities to get cleaned up."

Ned's right, and maybe my thoughts are because I feel guilty as a survivor, and this fantasy of getting even is a way to get over the guilt. Before I know it, we're back in front of my house in Port Aransas.

"Did I sleep?"

"You were quiet, so it could be you were. Here we are."

I stare out the window and look hard at the house. "Let me sit for a moment and try to visualize the entrance. I think I can make out the front door. On second thought, I don't see anything, other than what appears to be a large blurry outline."

"Let me guide you inside," Ned says. He seems as if he didn't hear me about seeing the house. Perhaps he hasn't bought into the exercise. He's probably the smarter of the two of us. "Sit there and wait until I get the house unlocked." He walks to the front door, and in a few moments, he's back. "All set. Here, take my arm, and I'll lead you. Don't ask to be carried over the threshold; I'm too old."

"Too old for carrying or too old to be married?"

Ned laughs. "You watch out there, sonny. You're totally dependent on me. Get cute, and you're on your own."

Ned takes me into the house and, even though I can't see too much, certainly the scent of home is here. It feels so good to be in a familiar space. Ned plops me down on the couch.

"I meant to ask you at the hospital, but forgot. Are your parents staying in town?"

"No. I sent them back to Indiana. They need to take care of some things, and I told them I would give them a call if and when they might need to come back."

"They will probably want to go to Washington. We'll give them a heads up when it's time."

"Oh yeah, the doctor mentioned a medal."

"Yes, so I hear. By the way, I've stocked the refrigerator. I also think it's a good idea for me to take you around the house room by room so you'll have an orientation to where everything is. We'll do it in a minute, but for now stay seated while I get us a couple of waters."

When he mentions the water, I realize I'm thirsty, not sure of the last time I had something to drink. He gets back and puts a cold bottle in my hand. I shake and bring the bottle to my lips, or should I say, just above my lips. Some spills under my nose, but I make a quick adjustment and fill my mouth with cold, delicious water. I drain the bottle.

I look Ned's way. "Thanks for saving my life."

He laughs. "It's just water."

Out of the blue, I ask, "How's my FJ?"

"I'd say you have a lot of work to do. When those guys shot at you, they didn't hit anything vital but made a mess of the body and windshield." Ned pauses to think about what he just said, and since I got wounded when some of Jacob's thugs were shooting at me and hitting the FJ more, I'm sure he now thinks he may have hurt my feelings. "Let me rephrase that. They hit nothing vital on the FJ."

"I knew what you meant," I say with a chuckle. "Even if you were referring to me and the FJ, I think you weren't too far off the mark. Is there anyone around here who can fix her up?"

"There is a place. Let me call them and see if they're up to the task. It'll mean hauling your FJ to Wimberley, which is about eighty miles from here. They're the only ones in South Texas who might know anything about a Toyota FJ 40."

"That would be okay. I don't think I'll be driving for a while, so they can keep her and take their time."

"I'll call them in the morning. I don't think they are working today. They resemble doctors the way they take off work. I believe they used to be doctors with the prices they charge." We share a chuckle. "You ready for a walk around the house?"

"Yeah, I'm ready. And don't worry about the price. Having the repairs done right is the main thing."

Ned and I take a slow walk around the building. He helps me into each room and describes it in detail. For the most part, remembering the placement of furniture and the general layout of the rooms visited is easy. He also walks me to the back door and up and over the beach walk. The smell of the salt air and sound of the waves cause me to inhale deeply and want to go in the water. Ned lets me know this will be something we can finish tomorrow. I don't put up a fuss and think maybe I'll go out again after Ned leaves.

After the tour, Ned takes me to the refrigerator and has me touch everything inside. He names the item, and it's an amazing exercise. I feel as if I could be on my own without worrying about the simple things. I could eat on my own if need be. He also has me touch the items in some of the cupboards and drawers so I'll be able to find plates and silverware. Finally, he takes me to the microwave.

"This is going to be tricky, but unless you want all your food cold, I'm going to teach you how to use this puppy without your eyes. You willing?"

"More than willing." I'm beginning to think Ned doesn't believe I will see better anytime soon.

He takes my hand and tells me to ignore all the buttons. He tells me all the settings are on high power, so there's no need to change them. "The only thing you'll have to do is judge how long the food will take, and then hit the start button once for each minute."

"I don't get that," I say.

He lets my hand go, and I hear him open a cupboard. He runs the water and then comes back. "Here's a glass of water. Let's assume it'll take a minute to heat." He opens the microwave, puts the water inside, and closes the door. "Do you remember where the start button is?"

I reach out to where I think the start button is and Ned guides my hand a little further to the right. "Touch the button once. If you need two minutes, then twice, and so on for as many minutes as you need."

The microwave starts after touching the button once. After a minute, the thing beeps, and from memory I know it won't stop until I open the door. "Go ahead and open it," Ned says.

The beeping stops after I open the door. When I reach inside, I feel the heat of the water. "How do I get it out?" I ask the question with a junior-high student sound to my voice.

"I left a mitt right on top of the counter. Find it and pull the glass out."

I move my hand along the counter and, right beside the microwave, my hand brushes the mitt and knocks it on the floor. "Damn, that's not good."

"Go find it," is Ned's only advice.

I need to get down on my knees and do a sweep of the floor. I find the mitt next to the cabinet base. "I found it." I say this as if Ned isn't standing right here. When I stand, the movement causes me to get a little light-headed. I hold onto the counter and find my way to the microwave, pull on the mitt, and with my other hand as a guide, wrap it around the glass. A simple act of getting a hot glass of water out of a microwave has taken on the proportion of enormity to the point I want someone to give me an award for getting the thing out.

"Well done," Ned says, and I smile. "Now, take it over to the sink, pour it out, and get another."

"What is this, kindergarten boot camp?" I ask the question to try to cover my trepidation since this next task won't be easy. It's good for me to try, so I turn and walk toward where I remember the sink to be. Lucky for me, it's still there. I dump the water and feel around for the faucet handle. When I find it, I fill the glass, being careful not to get it too full. With even more care, I walk back to the microwave and try not to spill any. With a trick learned from the movies, I put one finger on the rim of the glass. I can feel the water moving and make a correction if a spill is imminent. Successfully placing the glass back in the microwave, starting it and taking it out again, I'm pleased with myself.

Ned lets me know he's pleased as well and decides we ought to go out for lunch rather than his original plan of forcing me to make it. I'm glad my lesson will be suspended for a while because I'm hungry. I didn't eat anything before we left the hospital and am now starving.

"We'll continue your self-sufficiency lessons when we get back. I'll teach you how to make dinner. If you don't mind, it'll probably be a good idea for me to stay over tonight just in case you need anything."

"That would be great," I say with some relief, not being sure I'll be able to make it on my own, and Ned's offer is welcome indeed. We get ready to leave the house, and it occurs to me I no longer have a wallet. I'm not sure where it is, but mention this to Ned.

"Your wallet was in the FJ, behind the driver's seat. I guess it somehow came out of your pocket while you were dodging bullets and bouncing along on 11th Street. It's in your bedroom on the bureau."

"Would you wait a minute?"

"Sure, take your time."

I make my way to the bedroom and find the bureau. The wallet sits on top along with the FJ keys. I put the wallet in my back pocket, and the keys in the side pocket on my right. It feels somewhat normal to have my wallet, credit cards, and ID back. The keys will be handy to lock the house on the way out. I return to Ned, and we make our way to the front door. Ned goes first, and I pull the door closed after me, then pull out the keys. With some fumbling, I find the key that fits the deadbolt. I try to put the key in upside down, but make the correction, and again feel satisfaction when I hear the clunk sound of the bolt hitting the strike in the doorjamb.

Chapter Three

Ned and I have a great lunch at a new, little place on Beach Street called Café Paradise. We both have the Reuben sandwich with fries and a Corona.

"Is it okay for you to have beer on duty?" I ask when the beers arrive.

"I've taken a leave of absence from the police force."

"What? Why did you do that?"

"I'm back in the FBI, but no one is supposed to know. I'm working undercover and currently taking a two-week vacation. I want to be free to travel and make sure you're doing okay before I go back to active duty."

"I appreciate your thoughtfulness."

"It is nothing," Ned says. Shyness lowers his voice, and I imagine he's blushing.

While we have lunch, I hear people whispering. "What are they whispering about?"

"They're some tourists who wanted to come over to the table, but I waved them off."

I have a conflict, since I don't want people to think I don't want to talk to them, but also I'm deeply embarrassed when they thank me. I guess Ned's way of handling it is the best, since I don't know these folks.

When we've finished our lunch, I ask, "Can we go to the AT&T store in Corpus tomorrow to pick up a new phone?"

"We need to go to Corpus, so while we're there, I'd be glad to stop by the store."

I miss having a phone. I can't imagine where my old one is. Jacobs' thugs most likely took it from me on the way out of Port Aransas when they kidnaped me. Might be at the bottom of the ocean for all I know. While I sit and contemplate the phone sinking slowly in the blue water, the waiter brings the check. "I got it, Ned," I say with as much authority as I can muster.

Ned kids me, "Can you find it?"

"It's not a problem." I proceed to pat the entire table. Ned must have picked up the check tray already, because I can't seem to locate it. Then it occurs to me that this place probably puts the check on the table without a tray. When I brush the table instead of patting, sure enough I find the bill.

"Well done," Ned says with a smile in his voice. "You found it; you pay it. Do you know what kind of money you have or how you'll pay?" he asks as the waiter comes back over. I tell the waiter we'll pay by credit card and reach for my wallet. I pull out a card but have no idea which one. I give the bill and card to the waiter.

"You'll need a system for keeping track of spending," Ned says.

He's correct: I have no idea on how to tell the different bills and also no idea how long this lack of vision is going to be with me. Ned shows me how to mark my paper money with a little bend in the corner. He tells me to turn down the corner on the twenties once and the hundreds twice. He suggests the tens I fold in half, and the ones have no fold at all. "What about fives?"

"Fold them long ways." I suspect he just made his answer up.

"You should go to the bank and ask the teller each denomination and make the fold right then and there. Also, I would carry only one credit card, so there's no mistake on the one used. In addition, I would trust the waiter to add the tip and to point where you sign. You have no choice when you use a credit card, but to believe the amount put on it is the amount the waiter says it is. I wouldn't be so comfortable in New York, but here in Port Aransas everyone knows I'll kill anyone who cheats you." He laughs heartily, but I suspect he's half serious.

With all this instruction, I reckon Ned doesn't believe I'll regain my eyesight anytime soon. I hope he's wrong since I am not cut out to be a sight-challenged person the rest of my life. I have to adapt for now, but hope it is a temporary situation. The waiter returns with the card and credit slip. I ask him to tell me how much the bill is and where to sign. He seems a little uncomfortable but tells me lunch is thirty-two dollars. He tells me he has not added the tip yet. I ask him to add a tip of six dollars and sign the credit card slip where the waiter is holding his finger. He does and gives me my copy and thanks us for coming to lunch at Café Paradise.

We get up and make our way to the front door. People are patting my shoulder as we pass them. I keep a smile on my face, but have to admit it is a little creepy to be touched by those you can't see. We finally get outside and into Ned's SUV.

"Will you be turning in this police vehicle?"

"I plan to do that after my vacation period. All police officers on my force keep their cars even on vacation. Studies have shown crime statistics is low in areas where police officers live. It's not as if they all live in super great places, but the presence of a police vehicle in a neighborhood tends to dampen the crime spirit, so to speak."

In short order, we're back to my place. I want to impress Ned with my ability to open my door, so I open it as soon as Ned stops. Then I jump out and go straight to the front door, intending to put the key in the lock correctly. The only problem is that the front door is missing. My feeling around for the lock is useless since there's nothing there. I finally feel the door on my right—it's wide open.

Ned comes up behind me. "Don't to go in, and please, excuse me, but get the hell out of the way." I move to the left when I feel Ned push by me. "Stay there until I come get you." I hear him go into the house and move from room to room, and he finally returns to the front door.

"No one's here, but they certainly have made a mess."

I grip the doorjamb. "What kind of mess?"

"Your house has been ransacked. Someone wanted to find something and took no care in how they searched."

I'm speechless and don't have a good question to ask, so I blurt out, "Who do you think did this?"

Ned's laugh comes out strained. "Believe me, I wish I knew. I think it's safe to go inside. Try not to trip over all the stuff on the floor."

As Ned says not to trip, it's what I do. Ned catches me before I fall. He suggests I wait until he finds a chair and orders me to stand still.

"I'll just sit on the couch."

"You can't sit on the couch." Ned leaves for a moment, and comes back.

"Here, sit on this. It's a kitchen chair."

"What happened to the couch?" I ask.

"It's in shreds," Ned says. "Someone used a knife to cut all the upholstered furniture. All the drawers are out of the bedrooms and dumped on the living room floor. The kitchen drawers have been similarly pulled out and dumped in the kitchen. I don't think you'll be able to stay here until the place gets cleaned up." I'm about to protest when Ned adds, "They've shredded the mattresses as well. The people who did this also took all the food out of the freezer and apparently used an ax to chop it into a pile of little melting pieces. Can you think of anything this important which would require the wrecking of the house to find it?"

"Ned, I have no idea what they might be looking for and not a clue as to why."

"Did any of those thugs give you anything while you were being held prisoner?"

I've got to love Ned's ability at being the investigator. Thinking hard, I can only remember being given a cotter pin by Winther while he mocked my attempt at escape. I'd intended to use the cotter pin I'd found in the bathroom to try and unlock my handcuffs. When I lost it, Winther found it and gave it to me, daring me to try and escape. "The only thing I can think of is a cotter pin from the sink in the bathroom."

"Where's the pin now?"

"Might be in the clothes I wore at the time. Do you know where they are? They would be the ones I had on when they pulled me out of the water."

"This may come as a shock, but you weren't wearing any clothes. I think they got blown off you in the explosion."

"Well, then I'd say the pin is at the bottom of the Atlantic Ocean."

"Even if you had the pin, why would someone want to find it?"

"I'm not sure, but as we're talking, I remember Jacobs giving me one of his business cards."

"A card?" Ned's voice sounds as if this is something meaningful.

"Yes. He handed it to me when I met him for the first time. I didn't think much of it at that moment since I'm sure he gives out those cards to everyone he meets."

"True, but don't you see? The card places Jacobs with you on the container ship where they held you."

"I could have picked up the card anywhere, don't you think?"

"Yes, but if you were on the stand testifying that you met Jacobs, and then produced the card with the explanation he gave it to you when you met, you would have a powerful story."

"Wouldn't someone ask why he would give me a card that ties him to a terrorist act?"

"Yes, and the answer would be just as powerful. Because Jacobs thought you were going to die."

"Wow. Now I understand what you're saying. Well, I can tell you the card is in the same place as the cotter pin. I put it in my scrub pocket and forgot about it until just now."

"I think these guys wanted to make sure it wasn't here. I don't know if they'll be satisfied you don't have it or not. We'd better take some precautions, because I can imagine Jacobs won't give up until he knows you can't produce solid evidence against him."

"Wouldn't it be easier for him to simply kill me?" I say with a calm sense of detachment, which comes from my academic study of the mystery.

"You said it, not me," Ned says. "I think we better get some protection for you. I'm going to make a couple of calls and see which agency wants to pick this up."

I sit in the chair while Ned makes his calls. He talks to several people and explains what's occurred. It's obvious he's being put on hold a lot. Each time someone comes back, he explains the situation all over again. Finally, he seems satisfied with the response on the other end. He thanks the person, and then speaks directly to me.

"A team of agents will be here in about thirty minutes. An advance force will arrive within the next five minutes. It looks as if they were on standby at Corpus Christi Naval Air Station. They're coming over in a Blackhawk."

"You're kidding me, right?"

"John, this is serious shit. We should have taken some precautions before now. We never thought these people would be bold enough to strike so close to the event. This Jacobs guy won't stop until you're taken out or silenced—which is one and the same thing, and we can't take any more chances. You and I need to sit here until the team arrives."

"Do you have your gun out?"

"Bet your ass I do. How did you know?"

"I heard it hit the phone when you punched in the numbers."

As we continue to talk, a low vibration increases in intensity until it becomes clear that a helicopter is making its descent to the beach behind my house.

Ned says, "They're here. I'll go open the back door. No use in having them break it down."

He gets up and wades through the mess in the kitchen. He reaches the door just as I hear the team on the back porch. Ned greets them and makes sure they know he has his gun. From what I can understand, he has his gun over his head and, in the other hand, his ID. He's not taking any chances on confused messages leading to a firefight.

The team enters the house, and they go about checking and securing the building against any intruders as well as preserving any evidence that might have survived the visit of Jacobs' guys. The team members are quiet while they move around. Someone I don't know acknowledges that they've secured the house and authorized the helicopter to return to base. A high-pitched whine assaults my ears when the turbine fires up, and the rotor blade turns. Before long, the vibration returns and the helicopter lifts off. Silence resumes.

An unfamiliar voice asks me a question, "Mr. Cannon, will you be able to tell us if anything is missing?"

"I doubt it. I didn't have much here, and I just got to the house today. I've been sort of indisposed. Sorry, but I don't recognize your voice."

"Oh. Please, let me apologize. I'm Lieutenant Michael Hargreaves, and am in charge of this SEAL squad."

"Nice meeting you, Lieutenant. I cover it up quite well, but I can't see a thing. It's real hard keeping people straight. I need to rely on voices."

"Sir, you don't have to explain to me. I should have introduced myself up front. I'm embarrassed."

Ned comes up so quietly I don't hear him until he interrupts. "Embarrassed about what?"

The Lieutenant explains that he'd spoken to me, and I'd had no idea who he was. Ned tells the Lieutenant he understands. I break out laughing with the recognition that Ned's putting the Lieutenant on horribly. It's not a good idea to mess with Navy SEALS, so I finally speak up, "It's okay, Lieutenant. No harm done."

"Thank you, sir." He sounds relieved. "My men and I have secured this crime scene and will remain here until we're pulled out. The forensic team is right behind us in a van. They'll be here in about twenty minutes. We're thankful you're fine."

"Thank you, Lieutenant. I wasn't here when whoever it was showed up."

"Do you have any idea who would do this?"

Ned speaks up again, and his voice is aimed away from me, so I assume he's speaking to the Lieutenant. "Let's you and me go outside for a minute and I can give you a briefing. John's a little tired, and he needs to relax a bit."

Ned tells me to sit in the chair and try not to walk around. He hands me a bottle of water and says he'll be right back. I get the feeling he wants to tell the Lieutenant something out of my earshot. I can't imagine what it is, but I'll ask him when he returns. My attention is taken by drinking some water and listening for the movements of the men in the house. Their job now is probably to guard the premises.

"Excuse me, sir," another unknown voice says. "Chief Petty Officer Ted Wreesman, here."

"Yes, chief."

"We won't be making much noise, and I thought I'd let you know we're guarding your house and won't move around a lot. Our orders are to make sure you're safe. Six guys are stationed at various strategic places. We have the front and rear covered, as well as the roof."

"The roof? What would you expect on the roof?"

"It is not what's on the roof, but what may land there. We keep an eye out for unusual air traffic. We have some neat ways of knocking the bad guys out of the sky should they try to get to you via that route. By the way, sir, can I get you anything?"

"No, I'm fine. You think these guys would come after me from the air?"

"Well, they tried to get you one time with those P51s, and we don't want to take chances."

These guys must have had a complete briefing before this mission, and most probably the information had been part of a mission due to take place at a later time. The fact P51 Mustangs strafed Jason and me, while we were on My GRL, had become part of the overall information that whoever is to protect me needs to do their job. I suppose they all know about Jacobs as well.

"I'll leave you now, sir. We're all right here, so don't worry about a thing."

"Thank you, chief. I'm honored to be in the hands of the US Navy SEALs."

"It's more of an honor for us, sir. Not a man here would trade this duty for all the money in the world."

Damn. These guys are the best fighters in the world today, and they're here in my house. Here as protectors, and glad to be here. It's setting in: the country does consider me a hero, even though I don't feel like one. I'll have to come to grips with this at some point. To be considered a hero is the furthest thing from what I know to be the truth. Jason was the hero, and I went along for the ride. Unfortunately, Jason's no longer with us, and the job falls to me to be a surrogate for him. I can live with the responsibility for the interim, but I'll have to find someone to talk to when all the ceremonies are over. For now, my duty is to carry on.

Ned comes back. "I have the Lieutenant all briefed on everything. He was unaware you'd met Jacobs and considered him the suspect. They didn't give him the information because it's speculative right now. In other words, until we can prove Jacobs' involvement, we need to consider him a person of interest. I told that to the Lieutenant."

"How long will these guys be guarding me?"

"They'll stay with you until a detail of the Secret Service can be set up. We need to have a less visible force watching you. We can't have a SEAL squad follow you around everywhere you go. Men carrying automatic weapons make people nervous."

"I can understand that."

"You and I need to find another place to stay. We need to wait for the forensic team before we go. Any suggestions?"

"I always found the Holiday Inn Express to be good."

"It may be too hard to set up a defense there. Besides, we'd have to involve too many people. We should go to my house."

"Your house? What about your wife?"

"I already called, and she'll go visit her mother in Alice, about thirty miles from here."

"God, Ned. I hate to put you and your wife out."

"She's been bugging me to go visit her mother with her. Believe me, you're a great excuse for me to skip the trip, and I'm grateful. Besides, you have no choice. You're a sightless hero with a price on his head, and I'm in charge of you. The agency just made me active, and my first assignment is to supervise your protection and make sure nothing happens to you before they pin the medal on you."

"Well, I appreciate your hospitality."

"I'm going to pack a bag and once the forensic team arrives, we'll go to my house."

"How will the SEAL squad get there?"

"The forensic team is bringing a vehicle for them."

"Where they will stay?"

"They'll be on duty twenty-four hours a day, and the team of six will rotate rest periods."

I still feel bad for them. "Where will the team rest?"

"These guys are used to working with the minimum of comfort. They'll probably rest in one of the spare rooms or, if they choose, in the backyard."

While we talk, I hear the sound of the forensic team arriving. Considerable chatter erupts about how soft the life of forensic members is, and how hard the life of the fighters is. Obviously, the teams know and respect each other. Ned tells me he'll be right back and then we can leave.

"Excuse me, sir," an unknown voice speaks. "Lieutenant Seriles is my name, and I'm with the SEAL forensic squad."

"Yes, Lieutenant." I pause, thinking he'll say something further. When he remains silent, I ask him, "What can I do for you?"

"Nothing, sir. I just wanted to meet you."

"Thank you, Lieutenant. It's nice meeting you."

He takes my hand and gives it a gentle shake. "We're all pulling for you, sir."

"I appreciate it, Lieutenant. Try to figure out who destroyed my house, and I'll be grateful."

"We'll do our best, sir." He lets go of my hand, and I manage to keep it from flopping down to my side.

Ned returns and tells me it's time to leave. He calls out to Lieutenant Hargreaves to let him know we're on the move. The sounds of equipment being picked up and shouldered permeate the room. Ned leads the way, and I follow with one hand on his back. We get outside, and Ned puts me in his SUV. It takes some time for the team to get into their transportation. Ned tells me that they're in a Humvee big enough to hold all of us.

Chapter Four

Once we get underway, the trip to Ned's house takes about five minutes. Ned pulls up and tells me we're parked in the driveway, which is on the side of the house. He also describes the house as looking as if it's a transplant from Florida. Apparently, it has three stories with wrap-around decks on the second and third floors. It sits on a corner lot, and the street makes a gentle curve around to the driveway. Ned describes the house color as grey-green with white trim, and yellow shutters and accents. He also tells me that white railings go around the decks and white picket fencing around the lot. He hits the remote, and I hear the garage door open. Ned pulls into the garage and shuts the door. I know it may be more of a feeling than a reality, but I believe I can see the light get dimmer once the garage door is closed. I don't say anything to Ned. I'll wait to be sure.

Ned opens my door, and I get out of the SUV. He directs me to an elevator, opens the door, and we both get in. I ask about the SEALs, and he tells me they've already deployed in the house, as he gave Hargreaves a key to the front door. The elevator stops on the second floor, and Ned pulls the door open. He explains this is the main floor and describes the open concept with the living room, dining room, and kitchen in one big area. He says that two guest rooms are on this floor, and takes me to the one closest to the elevator. He describes the room as having a pale yellow color and a queen bed. He also describes the en-suite bathroom, which has a glass block open shower with a rain head. I ask him about the sound of the ocean that I can hear whenever he stops talking.

"Oh, yeah. The Gulf is right out the front. We're about a hundred feet from it. A neighborhood dune walkover and a swimming pool are straight out the front door." Then, evidently without thinking, he says, "You can see the Gulf from the front windows."

Ned takes me to another guest room on the other side of this floor. He explains, "The guest room is set up with a double bed and a bunk. The spare room here is the room the drunken fishermen usually take. Would you rather have this one?"

"I think the room with the queen bed would be better so I can move around without stumbling into the bunk bed."

He agrees, and we go back to the bedroom. Ned explains that the room has a chair and bureau, which shouldn't be too hard for me to avoid once I become familiar with the layout. He takes me to the chair, where I sit down and find it comfortable.

"Tomorrow, we'll do a little shopping to get you a new phone and some clothes to wear to the White House."

"When are we going to Washington? We have to go to New York on Monday. In case I'm really messed up, this is Friday, right?"

"Yes, this is Friday. I suspect the White House ceremony will be after Jason's service. If I were to guess, I think it might be in a couple of weeks."

"Well, it gives us plenty of time. Do we have to go shopping for clothes?"

"Unless you want to go to Jason's service dressed as a beach bum, then, yes."

"I guess Mustang Island clothes won't look right on Manhattan Island."

"You can say that again. Too bad you left all your designer suits back in San Francisco."

"Well, I say we go to TJ Maxx and buy something similar to my Armani."

Ned goes out the door laughing, and I get up and go to the bathroom. I feel the vanity to my left when I pass the doorjamb, put my hand on it, and then turn to face what I hope will be a sink. With my hand out and feeling for the sink, I continue to move my hand forward until I touch the faucet handles. I take the right one for cold and left for hot and turn each in about equal proportions, and the water delivered feels pleasantly warm. With the stopper pulled, I let the water run for less than a minute and splash some on my face, then feel around for a towel, which I find on the vanity top. I run my hand along the vanity and come to another sink. This vanity is a double sink variety, and by its cool temperature, it's probably made of marble. Ned certainly has good taste in home furnishings. After I've finished drying my hands, I attempt to fold the towel back to how I found it. While turning the towel into a wad, I can see a blurry outline in the mirror straight ahead of me. The image is so indistinct, it's as if someone filled the room with smoke and then sprayed a mirror with clear lacquer. I run my fingers along the vanity top until I come to a wall on my left, and to the location of the door to the bedroom. My hand goes up the wall, and I come to the light switch and turn it on. I look back to where I think the mirror will be and can see the outline of my head. The image is blurry, but it is my head. I move to make certain it's not a cutout someone's mounted on the mirror as a cruel joke. Sure enough, the blur moves as I do. I can see. I can see poorly, but I can see. I'm so excited at the prospect of regaining my sight that I call out to Ned. In an instant, he's here.

"Everything okay with you?" he says with concern in his voice.

"Ned," I say, breathless. "I can see myself in the mirror."

"Wow! That's great. How much can you see?"

"It's blurry but more than I could see yesterday and, hopefully, not as much as tomorrow. I get a definite outline of my head."

Ned directs me out of the bathroom and back to the chair in the bedroom, saying on the way, "Well, let's hope it continues. Not to minimize this event, but I want you to know I got a call from the White House. The service for Jason is being changed from New York to Washington. Jason's final resting place is Arlington, and the President wants to attend the service. After the service, will be a medal ceremony and reception at the White House."

I sit forward in the chair. "Who changed the arrangements? Did Jason's sister? If not, did she agree?"

"I assume she agreed since she'll be there as well."

"How do you know she'll be there?"

"I know because we're taking a private plane to New York to pick her up, and then on to Washington."

"What private plane?"

"The secret service thinks it best not to go commercial. They'll send a Gulfstream to pick us up on Monday."

"A Gulfstream? To Mustang Island?"

"Naw, we have to go to the Naval Air Station because the Mustang Island airport runway is only thirty-three-hundred feet long, and the Gulfstream needs about fifty-five hundred for safety, especially if the weather's bad. The Naval Station is only a twenty-minute ride right on the other side of the causeway."

"I don't know what to say, but this sounds like a lot of fuss."

"It wouldn't be very good if the men working for Jacobs decided to take you out along with several hundred passengers on a commercial flight."

Despite the gravity of it all, I laugh. "You have a way of putting things into perspective, Ned. I see your point."

"The SEAL squad will stay with us until we're on the plane. Once we get to New York, the Secret Service will meet us, and will be in charge of security from then on. You and I are not in charge of our affairs in the next few weeks. The Executive branch is calling the shots, because they feel Jacobs' followers will want to take some covert action to make sure you never testify at any of the trials, including Grand Jury sessions. The Justice Department is still trying to figure out how to get Jacobs himself but has little to go on. It's in the best interests of the country to keep you alive."

"I appreciate all the efforts, and I'm not complaining. I'd sure be pleased to live long enough to be able to testify at Jacobs' trial." He pats me on the shoulder, and I take it as a fatherly sign. Ned doesn't believe Jacobs will ever come to justice.

Ned breaks the somber mood. "You hungry for some dinner?"

Now he's mentioned dinner, I notice how famished I am. "I'm hungry as hell. It would be my pleasure to treat the team to something, but obviously I can't go get it."

"Tell you what, there's a place named Shelly's which has a killer carry out. They have seafood and pasta, and the best part is that all their stuff can be packed to go. Sound okay?"

"Sounds wonderful. Here, take my wallet and make sure the team orders as well."

"I hate to break it to you, but these guys aren't going to put anything in their mouths they haven't personally certified as free of contaminants. I'll tell them you're buying, but please don't be offended if they pass."

"At least make the offer."

Before he leaves, he puts me through the money exercise by asking for a hundred. I feel the money and correctly pull a hundred dollar bill out of my wallet.

"Don't forget to bring back the change," I say.

He laughs loud enough for the neighborhood to hear as he leaves.

With Ned gone, I begin thinking of the latest turn of events. Being able to see is an exciting proposition, but seems a little anticlimactic given the fact I'm now under the threat of being eliminated by Jacobs. Sort of makes your mind start to put together macabre thoughts. Will they get me before I regain my sight or after I can see? The prospect of facing elimination puts a tentative picture on the normal aspirations and behaviors most of us have. It must be how people who get the news their illnesses are terminal view life from the moment they hear. Why not have another piece of the pie, since who cares if I gain a pound before I die? I guess the only thing limiting reckless behavior is the wish or belief that somehow the news is wrong.

I must have been in deep thought because I didn't hear Ned come back. He enters the bedroom.

"Dinner has arrived," he says.

"Did the squad decide to join us?"

"As predicted, they politely declined."

When I get up and walk with Ned to the dining room, the smell of seafood comes into focus and makes my mouth water. Ned leads me to a chair, I sit, and feel around for the eating utensils.

Ned chuckles. "They're still in the carryout bag."

Rustling commences when he pulls the meals out.

"Here you are," he says.

He places what I feel to be a Styrofoam container in front of me, and it seems rather heavy and hot.

"Here's a stainless knife and fork. I can't stand to eat with plastic. I don't mind the carryout container, but the plastic silverware gets to me. Also, use this cloth napkin instead of the paper ones. It's another quirk I have."

While I take the knife, fork, and napkin, I see Ned as a blur taking a seat across from me.

"Would you care for some wine?"

"Man, wine sounds good to me."

The dining room isn't well lit enough for me to make out details. I can hear him pouring into a glass. "It's a Chardonnay," he says. "So it should go well with the meal." He pours another.

When I open the container, the delicious aromas of fresh seafood and pasta blast my senses. I inhale deeply. "This smells great."

"The dish is called Linguine de la Mer. It's a white sauce with shrimp, scallops, crab, and snapper over fresh linguine."

He places my hand on a small carton to my left and tells me it's a salad, and then moves my hand to the wine.

"You should be able to take it from here."

I take my time eating the immensely flavorful pieces of seafood one at a time, which finally leaves me with only the pasta. I try twirling the linguini on my fork, but realize it takes better sight than I have to determine how much is on there. I finally figure out that by putting my fingers near the fork, I can just about gauge how much is on the fork and control the bite. In this way, it ends up in my mouth and not back in the container. A sip of wine and a mouthful of pasta and I feel as if I'm in heaven.

While we eat, Ned and I discuss what we're going to do tomorrow. We decide to get an early start, so we won't end up running into the Saturday shopping traffic that's a later-in-the-afternoon phenomenon in Corpus Christi. We figure we'll go to the mall then to the phone store and, with any luck, be back by lunchtime.

We finish dinner and, as a joke, I ask if I can help with the dishes. Ned gives me a big surprise by suggesting I'll be capable of handling the chore. He tells me the locations of the trash container and dishwasher. I pick up the carryout containers and make my way to the trash, which I manage to open and throw the containers away. On my return to the dining-room table, I hit one of the kitchen counter edges with my hip.

"Watch out," Ned says. "Those counters can be tricky."

"You have a warped sense of humor."

He laughs out loud, and I continue to pick up the silverware and glasses.

To be helpful, Ned says, "The glasses go on the top rack of the dishwasher and the silverware in the basket on the bottom. The dishwasher is to the right of the sink."

I move through the kitchen until I come to the sink, and then move to the right. Sure enough, the dishwasher is immediately to the right, and I open it easily enough and put the glasses and silverware in their appropriate places. I turn to go back to the dining room, but stop when I hear Ned's phone ring. He answers, but I can't make out who it is from the short responses. I walk quietly into the dining room and find my chair again. Ned is still on the phone but not saying much. He finally finishes the call, and I can tell he's thinking about whatever he discussed with whoever was on the call.

"That was the Secret Service. They want us to move up our departure for Washington to Sunday instead of Monday. The President's busy on Monday and wants to have the medal ceremony at the White House Sunday night. I don't know how these things get moved around, but I guess the head of state has other things to do. I told them we'd be ready. Wheels up at ten o'clock on Sunday."

"Does Jason's sister know about the change?"

"Stephanie? Yeah, they talked to her first."

"How about my parents? I haven't called them or anything."

"They've been informed. The US Government will pick them up too."

"Well, I have nowhere else to go this week and it sounds like everything's taken care of, so it's fine with me."

"I get a feeling the change has nothing to do with the President," Ned says.

Like so much these days, that throws me. "What do you mean?"

"I think the change is being made because the Service wants to keep the plans in flux so if someone wanted to create mayhem, they'd have a tougher time. The press published the fact Stephanie and you would be going to the White House after the service for Jason on Tuesday. This change won't be announced to anyone. The whole thing is under a need-to-know cloak of secrecy, and we're not authorized to tell anyone of the change."

"Who would I tell?"

"Don't you need to check in with your employer?"

"You're right. Damn, I completely forgot. I need to get authorization to continue my leave of absence beyond the original six months. Already, I've spent two months of it, and it takes a while to get the administrative wheels in motion. Ned, thanks. I could have spilled the beans easily." I try to look at my watch, and then realize my mistake. "What time is it in San Francisco?"

"Well, it's seven o'clock here, so it's near five o'clock there."

"Can I borrow your phone? I think I can catch Peters before he goes home. He's usually there until at least six o'clock on Fridays. In a law firm of our size, a general partner of Peters' rank is customarily the first to go home, so no one leaves until he does. Peters usually stays long enough on Friday to make it annoying for the rest."

"Give me the number and I'll dial it."

Ned's request causes me to pause. I'm not sure of the number, but I think for a second, and it comes back to me. I tell Ned the number, which he dials, and then hands me the phone. Peters picks up on the first ring.

"Hi, this is John."

"John, what a surprise. I'm glad to hear from you. I've been worried about you, and hope you know we want you back just as soon as your leave is up."

"The reason for my call is to request another six months." A significant silence descends on the other end to the point that I think we've been cut off. "You still there?" I ask.

"Yes, I'm still here." Disappointment colors his voice. "I'm not sure about granting you more leave. I fought hard for the six months originally, and I'm not sure how another six months will be received by the partners."

He's lying through his teeth. He didn't fight for anything. I originally asked for a year off, as per the policy, and six months is the best he could do. I'll play it as innocently as possible, "The policy says twelve months is an acceptable amount of time for a leave of absence." Okay, that was my intention, but I hit him between the eyes.

"John." He sighs and pauses for a few seconds to allow a little drama to build. "The policy says *up to* twelve months."

"Well, up to or not, I'm going to request another six months formally. You can deny it, of course, but consider this: it might make for some bad PR for the firm not granting leave to a national hero." I can't believe I just said what I did, and hold my breath for what I'm sure will be an unpleasant reaction from Peters.

"Submit your request in writing and we'll see where it goes." Peters' voice is as cold as he can make it without sounding uncooperative. "When will you be going to Washington? We heard the President is giving you a medal."

"The plans have been made for Tuesday." The press has already reported this timing. He doesn't seem too pleased to get the public answer but says no more. He leaves the call with the wish for a speedy recovery. I hand the phone back to Ned.

"That son of a bitch isn't going to approve another six months. I ought to resign from the firm."

"Easy boy," Ned says in a soothing way. "You don't need to go off half-cocked. What did he say?"

"To send in the request for another six months, but he doesn't think the partners will go for it."

"Just send in the request and worry about what to do if and when he turns you down."

"Thanks. Good, advice." Suddenly, I feel exhausted. I'm not sure if it's the glass of wine or the discussion with Peters, but I feel wiped out. "Would you mind if I hit the rack?"

"That's perfectly okay with me, and probably a good idea."

I make my way from the dining room to the bedroom. When I close the door, I can hear Ned back on the phone. I can't hear what he says, but I can tell he's not pleased with the other person. He finally stops talking and calls to me.

"There are extra towels in the drawer of the bureau."

I stop at the location of the blurry bureau and feel good when I'm right about its location. The drawer opens easily, and I feel two towels—one hand, and one bath—and pull them out. I drop my clothes to the floor, pick them up, and place them on the countertop of the sink. I go to the open shower and turn on the water. Lucky for me, the shower control is a simple dial, so I put it in about the middle, which should deliver lukewarm water. Once in, I can turn it more to become hotter. I let it run until I feel some warmth, step in, and then push the control further to the left, which causes the temperature to rise. The rain shower head is wonderful. The water drops gently onto my head and shoulders. It feels as if I'm standing in a summer rain and the soothing stream causes the tension in my body to melt away. After I've grabbed the shower gel, I use the spongy thing to build up a big batch of suds and soap my entire body. I rinse in the man-made rain and feel one hundred percent better.

On the shelf in the shower, stand two bottles. I assume one is shampoo and one conditioner. The labels are similar enough with print small enough that I can only guess. I open each and take a sniff, and both smell of almonds, so I get no help from my nose. I pour a little of one bottle into my cupped hand and feel it with my finger. It seems thick and creamier than shampoo. It must be the conditioner, so I take the other bottle and pour some into my hand and rub it into my hair. I think I guessed right since a bunch of suds break out on my head with a little rubbing. I rinse well and remember from my more sighted days that the shampoo directions say to repeat, so I do.

When I finish my shower, I realize I don't know where Ned put my bag. Did he put it on the bed? Only one way to find out. Yep, it's here. I pull out what I think is a pair of short pajamas and a t-shirt, and put them on. Then I find my toothbrush and some toothpaste and go back to the sink and take care of my teeth. After rubbing my hair some more with the towel, I'm finally dry. I don't want to hunt for a hair dryer, and I think my hair is short enough to handle with a towel, so I don't go to bed with wet hair. I find my comb as well, but decide to let the wild-man look stay put until the morning when I'll have to wet my hair again to make it behave.

With the pre-bed ritual finished, I get in bed, then have a thought. I should double check to see if the light is off. It seems so, but I can't trust my eyes to be totally accurate. Back out of bed, I find the switch. Two switches sit on the same wall plate. I take a chance and flip the one on the left and can see the room fill with light. My vision is still fuzzy, but I can tell the difference. I flip the other switch, and a cool breeze circulates from the overhead fan. It feels good, so I leave it on, turn off the light again, and return to bed. I pull the lightweight cover up over me, lay my head on the soft pillow, and immediately am off to another world.

Chapter Five

I walk through the desert and haven't had a drop of water for days. The sun is in a position in the sky where it hits me right in the eyes, and I have to squint just to see what's ahead, even though there's nothing for miles. Finally, I stagger and fall to the sand. This may well be the end. I roll onto my back and let the hot sun hit me full in the face, thinking that maybe being exposed totally to the burning rays will speed up the end.

"John, time to get up." I hear Ned encouraging me to fight on and not give up.

It takes me a second to realize that Ned isn't encouraging me not to give up but telling me it's time to get out of bed. The dream was so real I'm a little taken back to realize the sand is nothing but the sheets of the bed, and the hot sun is, in fact, the light streaming through the window. I get excited because I see the window and the sun shining through it brightly. Of course, I need to squint as I did in my dream, and realize this sun is the most likely reason for dreaming of the desert. My mouth is dry, which probably served as a supporting character in the little drama my mind made up just before waking.

"John." It's Ned again. "Are you awake? Breakfast in ten minutes, and then we need to head for Corpus."

"Yes, I'm up," I holler from the bed. Of course, I haven't moved a muscle yet, but at least I'm awake. I roll over and hit the floor standing. After making quick work of teeth and hair, I get dressed, since I'm not sure Ned is going to be too patient about getting moving. Best not to take any chances. With the door open, I take in the sweet aroma of applewood-smoked bacon, and walk toward the dining room, where I nearly run into Ned. He avoids the collision.

"How do you want your eggs?"

"Over medium."

"Take a seat and have some orange juice and coffee; the eggs will be ready in a minute."

When I find my place at the table, I need to focus before locating the coffee mug. It's to the right and full of hot coffee.

Ned calls from the kitchen, "I already put some half-and-half and sweet-and-low in your coffee. Be careful; it's very hot."

I lift the mug and, before taking a sip, look at it carefully. I can see some writing on the mug, but can't make it out. I'm improving because, when the bandages came off yesterday, I couldn't see a thing, and now I'm able to see the cup as more than a blurry image. With my first sip, I relish the rich taste.

"This coffee is good," I call out to Ned. "What kind is it?"

Ned startles me since he's standing right at the table, and I was so involved with the coffee I didn't see him come in. I make a mental note that I'll be able to see things better if I concentrate on one thing at a time.

He sets the plates on the table and sits down. "The coffee is a mixture of two reasonably priced brands costing about five dollars a pound. I just mix them together, and this is the result. Tastes more like Starbucks, doesn't it?"

I have to agree that the coffee does taste as if it's Starbucks. After I pick up my fork, I use my fingers to feel what's on my plate, and can feel two halves of an English muffin. Also on the plate are two fried eggs, three strips of bacon, and hash browns. "You run a restaurant?"

He laughs loudly. "My hobby is cooking and I enjoy it. There's honey or blackberry jam for the muffins."

I dig right into the breakfast as if I haven't eaten for a week, and think of my desert dream. Can dream activity make you hungry? In any case, I certainly appreciate Ned's thoughtfulness in preparing the meal.

After we finish, Ned clears the dishes. I ask, "Can I help?"

"Naw, that's okay. I got this. Why don't you get ready to go? By the way, your polo shirt is on inside out, but other than that you look good."

Embarrassed, I go back to the bedroom and take off the shirt, then turn it back to outside in and feel ready to go. I meet Ned in the living room. "We'll take the elevator down to the garage level and repeat what we did when we first came in." Ned slides the door open and pulls my arm to direct me onto the platform. The elevator moves downward.

"I put the elevator in so that when I'm old I'll be able to move around the house without taking the stairs. Right now, it's handy for getting groceries up from the garage to the kitchen level."

We reach the first floor. Ned again opens the door and directs me to the vehicle, while he makes a call and tells (what I assume are) the SEALs that we're ready to go. We get into the SUV with me on the passenger side in front, and when we're strapped in, the rear door opens, and one of the SEALs gets into the car.

"Set to go?" Ned asks him.

"Yes, sir," he says in a crisp voice. "All clear to open the garage door and start the engine."

"Okay, thanks." The garage door opens. "That mean-looking SEAL in the back goes by the nickname Witch," Ned says. The man laughs, and I tell him it's nice to meet him.

The Sunlight floods the garage. What a sweet sensation to watch light flood a previously dark place, and I feel grateful I can witness it. Ned backs the SUV slowly out of the garage once the door is fully out of the way.

"The rest of the squad is in a Humvee behind us. The ride to Corpus is to be as quick as possible, so if someone has a mind to interrupt our travel, they'll need to be quick about it."

"No one knows we're going to Corpus, do they?"

"I don't think so, but you never know. I haven't told anyone we're planning to be there today. The SEALs haven't said anything, either."

After going through Ned's subdivision's security gate, we reach the highway. Ned accelerates and turns left, and the rear fishtails a bit. It's clear that Ned intends to break the speed record to Corpus. He has the SUV floored, and since I can't make out the speedometer, I'm not sure how fast we're going, although I'm sure we passed sixty miles an hour within six seconds. Ned's had the accelerator on the floor for more than fifteen seconds, so we may be going as fast as a hundred miles per hour. Just when I thought I have it all figured out, Ned hits the siren, and I also hear the clicking of the lights on the top, so I assume they're in full warning mode as well. By the sounds of it, we're passing everything on the road. As each vehicle moves over to the right, Ned comments about moving over and then thanks each under his breath. I'm sure most of the folks passed had some concern, as being passed by a police vehicle followed by a military machine is an unusual occurrence. It must be doubly troubling to see the occupants of the Humvee armed to the teeth, and both vehicles traveling at a dangerous speed.

"How fast are we going?" I ask.

"A little over one-twenty," Ned says as if it's most normal to be barreling down the road at this breakneck speed.

"I didn't know Humvees could go this fast," I say, but not wanting an explanation.

Ned's only comment is, "Special modifications."

Witch is on the phone in the back, and I conclude he's getting some instructions from the leader, as he keeps acknowledging with "yes, sir."

Ned says, "We're coming to the end of the fifteen-mile stretch of highway 361 and will need to get on South Padre Island Drive. Our current speed will be impossible without an escort."

The SEAL says, "The escort will join us in about two minutes. They'll lead us to the mall, and we'll go a little slower due to the risk to the public."

"It'll be fine," Ned says. "Who's doing the escort duty?"

"Corpus PD. A pair of motorcycle officers. Supposed to be members of the elite force handling drug and SWAT duties."

"Sounds as if they'll do."

We ride in silence until Ned describes to me the fact that out of nowhere two motorcycles have passed us on the left and taken up a position in the front. When they passed, I could make them out, but without the warning from Ned I might have missed them, even though their engines are loud. They don't have their sirens and lights on. Ned mumbles that sixty seems as if we're standing still. He tells me we're not asking anyone to get out of the way because they simply have nowhere to go. The South Padre Island Drive is a two-lane road until after we get over the Kennedy Causeway. I can't even imagine the fear of those in front of us who must wonder what to make of this entourage as they spot us in the rearview mirror. Luckily, the causeway is short and, as I remember, the road widens to three lanes. I can feel the speed pick up, the sirens hit high wail, the lights begin clicking again, and Ned is happy to describe we have one of those lanes almost to ourselves.

In short order, we reach the mall, and I can imagine the startled looks on the faces of the people we pass as we pull up to the front door. I'm sure it's quite a sight with two motorcycles, one police SUV, and a drab, olive Humvee all sliding to a halt.

Ned says, "Sit tight until Witch, in the back there, tells you it's okay to leave."

Witch talks to one of the others over the phone, and then says to Ned and me, "Get ready. I'll exit first, and then Ned will get out and come around to your side of the vehicle. When I open your door, that's your cue to get out and make your way with Ned's help to the entrance of the mall."

Witch listens to his radio again. "Roger that. I'm getting out." At the same time, Ned opens his door and grunts as he steps down from the SUV. Simultaneously, both doors shut as if they were one. My door opens, and so I jump down as well. I can feel Ned's strong hand on my arm as he half yanks me in the direction of the mall entrance.

We both turn and walk. Something smacks me in the face. A loud noise comes from right beside me. It sounds similar to the way an automatic rifle does in the movies. "Shooter on the roof," Witch screams and grabs my other arm. He and Ned lift me off my feet and drag me the last few steps to the mall entrance. Both Ned and the SEAL scream at me to stay put as they drop me to the concrete in front of the Mall door, and then they run back the short distance to the exposed area by the vehicles. While I lie on the concrete, I hear directions being shouted back and forth between the squad members. The noise nearest me is Witch returning fire, and a couple of the other squad members open fire too. I look in Witch's direction and can see the bright flashes from the muzzle of his rifle.

I try to determine if the squad has been successful in getting the individual who decided to take a shot at us. On second thoughts, though, I need to amend my thinking to the question of who decided to shoot me. It's a funny thing, though; I didn't hear a shot—only the slap to the face. Except for the declaration by Witch, I wouldn't have known there was a shooter.

Now I have time to think, I wonder what slapped me in the face, so I reach up to the spot and can feel a thick liquid on my cheek. I pull my fingers away with the liquid and put them under my nose. No mistaking now that the slap to the face was blood. I reach back to my head to try and find the wound, so I can determine how bad it is. I should have known I wouldn't be able to find a wound because I can't feel any pain. The only thing I can surmise is that the blood isn't mine, but that just concerns me more.

Exactly whose blood do I have on my cheek? I fight the urge to take my sleeve and wipe the blood away, as I figure someone should know the shooter has hit either Ned or Witch. Of course, as I think about it, whoever is hit will know about it anyhow. I shake my head and then wipe my cheek with my sleeve. Just as I finish, footsteps approach. Hopefully, they're part of the good-guy team.

"Hey, John." I'm so relieved it's Ned.

"Yes, I'm over here," I say as if he's the one who has a sight problem. "Someone got hit with that first shot."

"I know. It's Witch. Looks as if the shooter hid up on the roof of the mall and had a sniper set up including a silencer. He caught Witch in the arm. Seems to me, the guy needs a little more training in the art of assassination."

"My God, is Witch okay?"

"Yes. He'll have a sore arm tomorrow. Luckily, the shooter used full metal jackets, so there's no fragmentation.

He probably figured that we'd all have vests, and he wanted to make sure he could get through them. You sure look a sight."

"Did you guys get him?"

"Oh, yes, indeed. Witch hit him before he grabbed you. After the shooting stopped, we went to the roof and there he was—a contract type. We're running his ID now, but I'm sure it'll take some time to find out who he is, as he probably had a fake identity."

"What now?"

"Well, first of all, we need to get you off the concrete and get you inside to wash up. Also, I'm not sure we should continue our shopping venture. I think we better go back to my place in case they had some backup plan."

"I agree. I sure do need some new clothes and a cell phone, though."

"Tell you what, while the guys are cleaning up the details on this crime scene, you and I'll go to the AT&T store for the phone. By the time we get back with the phone, the squad will be ready to go. I'll get all your sizes and have one of the Corpus community officers do the shopping. I figure it won't be hard to get a dark suit, white shirt, and black oxfords."

"That sounds good. I'll need a raincoat as well."

When Ned speaks next, he sounds like he has to dig for patience, "We'll get a list together. Come on, let me help you up."

Ned gives me his arm, and I get up. I didn't realize it lying on the concrete, but I feel a little shaky. Ned makes no comment but grips me hard enough to give me the stability needed to start walking. We go through the front door of the mall arm in arm. I can't see the people so well but can see them part to let us through. While we pass the assembled curious, a lot of murmuring breaks out. When I walk by folks on my right, gasps sound, and it's obvious they've caught a look at the smeared blood on my face. "It's not serious," I say, but I'm not sure anyone gives a crap.

"We're at the men's room," Ned says. We go inside. "No one's in the room with us." He takes me to the sink.

"I need to use the facilities as well," I say, then turn to find a stall. Ned doesn't say anything but guides me to the right place. I go in and lock the door. If I don't hurry, there may be a big embarrassment. I'm glad I thought of this when I did and not five minutes later. Fear does amazing things to the body. I can only imagine the fight or flight response also includes making the body lighter fast. I finish and go back to where I believe I left Ned.

He stands by the sinks. "You okay?" Ned says.

"Yes, I'm okay."

"You're as white as a sheet and have sweat on your upper lip. You may be in shock and ready to pass out."

"No, I'm fine." At the same time I say this, I have to use the sink to steady myself. I put my hand under the faucet and, to my relief, it's an automatic system. With my hands cupped, I collect some water to splash on my face. It feels good, and I splash a couple more times. I look over to where Ned stands. "Do I look better?"

"The blood smear on your face is gone, but the white-as-a-ghost look is still there."

That's probably the best comment I'll get. Ned hands me a paper towel, and I dry my face. Determined not to be put off, I say, "I'm ready to go get a phone."

Chapter Six

We leave the restroom and take the short walk to the AT&T store. When we enter the store, a pleasant voice greets us and asks if we need help. I want to be a smart ass and tell her the big guy with me needs more help than anyone but keep my comments to actual business. "I want to get a new phone."

"Yes, sir. Please, follow me."

We go to a computer station so she can check my account. I give her my phone number when she asks and wait while she brings up my details.

"According to our records, you're eligible for an upgrade. You can have an Apple iPhone Six S for a hundred and eighty-nine dollars. You have the right data plan for the iPhone, and there will be no additional charges."

"I would prefer to get the phone now." She then asks for my credit card, which I pull out of my wallet and, from habit, my Master Card. She takes my card and tells me she will be right back.

"Easy transaction," I say. Ned doesn't answer. "You still there?"

"I think I saw someone moving in the mall in a way that doesn't look as if he's a shopper."

The girl comes back and starts to explain the phone. Ned interrupts her and tells her to pack the phone and that we need to move out of the store quickly. I can hear the fear in her voice when she tells me the phone is in a case and will be active once I go and do it online. She grabs my hand and puts my credit card in my palm just as some shots ring out from the mall.

I pull the girl down to the floor, and Ned swears and returns fire. I can hear the chatter of the weapon and pinging of the copper shells as they hit the terrazzo floor. I pull the girl close to me and drag her behind her workstation. I'm worried because Ned is out in the open, and I'm not sure how he's faring against those hell-bent to do away with me.

One good thing is that I can only hear Ned's weapon, and haven't felt the telltale shards of lead, wood, or glass that signal the passing of bullets through the infrastructure in this direction. Just as quickly as the shooting starts, it stops. A momentary vacuum of silence follows the halt of hostilities. The sound of the last few copper casings when they hit the floor, the soft sobs of the frightened, and a most fearful moan, fill the silence.

"John." Thank God, it's Ned. "Don't move. The squad's cleaning up in the mall. There still might be a suicidal maniac who wants to complete his mission, and right now you don't need to make a good target."

I follow Ned's advice and stay down. When I shake the girl in my arms to let her know everything will be okay, I realize that she isn't responding. I turn her over and sense she isn't breathing. Immediately, I put my mouth on hers and try to give her breath. Each time I blow into her mouth, blood seems to gush through the buttons on her blouse. My mind isn't doing well right now. My rational mind tells me she must have a chest wound, but I keep blowing, trying to save her. Ned's hand rests on my shoulder.

"John, the girl's dead. She was dead when she hit the floor, and there's nothing else we can do."

"It's my fault that this girl got shot. I can't just let her go." I keep blowing and feel the little traces of blood in her mouth mixed with the tears that are running into mine.

Ned leaves me with the girl and goes to others in the store. Sirens approach from far away. I keep telling the girl that everything will okay, knowing full well that it won't. I feel a terrible hurt over this poor girl losing her life over something as stupid as a smartphone. I make a silent promise to her that we'll get the sicko responsible.

Ned returns, and I've come back to reality. I move gently out from under the girl and cradle her head as I lay it down on the floor, and whisper, "I'm so sorry." Ned helps me get up.

"You know, John." Ned's voice shakes. "None of this would have happened if I'd gone directly back home. I made a mistake, and I'll need to be accountable." Ned's usually strong voice sounds stressed.

"You had no idea these guys would try again."

"I should have assumed they would. The danger was my gut feel, and I should have acted on it."

I'm close to hugging Ned when I realize the tremendous amount of strain he's under.

I want to make Ned feel better, so I try to break the tension. "Well, these guys are bound and determined to eliminate me, aren't they?"

Ned sighs. "It certainly looks that way. I'm not sure how the Secret Service will deal with this, but they'll have their hands full. I killed two in the mall, and the squad killed another three who came to help the two I took out."

"I didn't know you carried an automatic."

"I have two. Those guys were outnumbered."

It feels good to hear Ned make a little joke. The EMS teams arrive. After a few minutes, we determine that the only fatality besides the shooters is the salesperson. Five other innocent bystanders received wounds. I ask to speak to her boss, and he tells me her name is Julie Preston, and she was one of the best salespersons. I ask if Julie had a family, and the boss tells me that she's single and lives with her mother. I turn to Ned. "We need to go there and let the mother know what happened."

"No can do. We need to get to a secure place immediately. Public service officers can handle that task."

I protest but know Ned is right. I ask the boss if it would be okay to give me her mother's number so I'll be able to give her a call and express my condolences. The manager seems a little reluctant until Ned gives him his card and tells him it will be okay, and if his bosses have a problem, they can call him. The manager goes away to get the number, and I thank Ned. He pats my shoulder, letting me know it's the least he can do under the circumstances. The manager comes back with the number.

"Thank you so much. I apologize for the trouble my visit has caused you and your employees."

He whispers, "I know who you are, and I pray you get the guys who're trying to kill you. You shouldn't feel responsible for the actions of a lunatic minority."

Tears well up, and I grab the manager and give him a hug, and thank him for the comforting words. He bends down and picks up the box with my phone inside. "You better take this," he says. I nod, and he finds a bag and places the box inside. I thank him again.

Ned takes me by the arm and pulls me toward the exit. I can hear people moving around and, for the first time, can see more clearly the shapes of people. I can tell the men from the women. It seems a little disingenuous of me to be thinking of my sight right now, but in some small way, I feel that if I can see again, I can get that son-of-a-bitch, Jacobs. I'll do anything I can to get him. Ned brings me back to the current problem by announcing we need to go around the guys lying on the floor of the mall. I slip on a shell casing and hold on to Ned more tightly. We continue until we break out of the relatively dark mall to the bright sunshine of the outside. Ned's SUV remains where he left it, and I tell Ned I can make it on my own. His voice sounds doubtful when he explains that he'll need to make certain we get into the SUV without any more drama. I let him hold me until we reach the passenger door, and he swings it open. With haste, I get in, and Ned runs around the back of the SUV and yanks the door of the driver's side so hard it rebounds and hits him in the shoulder. He jumps in and seems to be out of breath.

"You okay?" I try not to sound too concerned.

"Just ducky." His sarcastic reply is untempered. "I can't tell you when I've had a better day." He puts the key in the ignition and starts his vehicle. The back door opens, and Witch jumps in the back.

"Go! Go! Go!" Witch says.

Ned floors the SUV and puts all the noise and lights into action. I turn around and ask Witch, "How're you doing?"

He chuckles and says, "I've had hangovers cause me more trouble than this wound."

I haven't seen Witch well before, but right now I can make out that he is, indeed, big. I don't mean tall, and I don't mean fat—I mean large. He fills his side of the rear seat and would cause the GMC marketing folks some problems trying to say this vehicle could seat three of him across. Dressed fully in black, it makes it hard to see what he's carrying. I think I can see the front section of an automatic rifle more or less pointing at a forty-five-degree angle across his left shoulder.

I turn to Ned and ask, "Is there anything known about the guys doing the shooting?"

He doesn't take his eyes off the road and answers in a matter of fact way, "I'm not sure we'll ever find out who they are." He pauses for a moment, and then adds a little more, "If any of these guys has a record, they'll show up in the criminal database. I suspect the only thing we'll find out is that they all served in the military, but it will be about all."

"Why do you think they served in the military?"

"Although they were no match for our team, I have to say they knew what they were doing. If they'd struck without the warning we got from the sniper's first shot, I doubt we would all be here now."

Ned and I talk a little more about the shooters. We come to the conclusion they were probably mercenaries working for hire. Eventually, we stop talking and let the sounds of the siren rule the atmosphere in the SUV. We're in a hurry, and it feels as if the air around us is rushing to get somewhere as well. Even though I know it's the air conditioner motor blowing air inside the vehicle, the lights and noise of the siren make the moving air a co-conspirator in the perception that we're flying along above—rather than on—the highway. I get light-headed and think that maybe this whole episode has been part of a bad dream that isn't over yet.

"Please, wake up," I say aloud.

Ned turns to me and says, "What the hell, John—you asleep?"

"Just testing whether or not I'm having a bad dream."

"This is no dream. This shit is real life, my friend." Ned now sounds the same as a preacher in a tent. "We need to get right with this group of people and put an end to this shit." Ned just lost his preacher-sounding status.

I shake my head and mumble, "Yep, you got that right. How can I help?"

"The biggest way to help will be to stay alive and testify against all of them."

"I'll do my best." The pickup in speed indicates that we've cleared the two-lane causeway and are again racing along at over a hundred and twenty miles per hour. Vaguely, I can see the cars ahead of us behave in a tentative way as they struggle to get over in response to the flashing lights and siren. I'm sure some think they're about to get arrested and breathe a sigh of relief as we blaze by them. It only takes seven minutes to travel the fifteen miles to Ned's house. We slow down in anticipation of pulling off the highway at Ned's subdivision, and Ned executes a hard right turn into the gated entrance. He punches in his code on the keypad, and the large white gate slowly opens to the right. We go through, and Ned says, "We'll need to observe the speed limit of the subdivision—nineteen miles per hour. I don't want to get a citation for speeding by the Property Owners Association." Given that he was the police chief, I find this humorous. We pull right into the garage and Ned hits the control, and the door starts down before he turns the engine off. We sit in the dim light of the overhead bulb attached to the opener motor.

I break the silence, "What now?"

"We need to get in the house and make a few phone calls. We also need to get you some clothes, and I need to get some clear direction on the next steps. I'm going to recommend that you not attend the service for Jason. As far as the award ceremony is concerned, I think the Secret Service will put the kibosh on it for now."

Ned makes a move to get out of the SUV, and Witch and I follow suit. Ned and Witch make a lot of clanking noise with their automatic weapons when they come into contact with the SUV doors and, in Ned's case since he has two, with each other.

I make my way to the elevator, pull the door open, and wait until Ned gets on. He thanks me and I follow him in.

"Floor, please," I say aloud, hoping to get a laugh.

"Number two," Ned answers without giving me the satisfaction of any humor in his voice. Then he says, "So, can you find the number two button?"

"No problem, sir," I say the same as I think an elevator operator would respond. "Please, step aside and let the attendant take control." I more or less elbow my way past Ned and hit the button.

The car makes its ascent, and Ned says, "We'll grab some lunch and figure out what's next. I'll call the Secret Service and find out what they think. I don't particularly care for the fact Jacobs' guys seem so relentless. They must know where I live. I can't believe they're in the dark as to our location, so the longer we stay here, the more vulnerable we are."

We reach the second floor and get out of the elevator. Ned puts his weapons down on the bookcase in the living room. I ask, "With the SEAL squad here, don't you think it's safe?"

"John, this is the same group who sunk your boat with a couple of World War Two vintage P51 Mustangs. Don't you think they could get their hands on a missile if they wanted to take out this house with us in it?"

"Yikes, I never thought about a missile." I look around as if I can hear one coming in now.

He grins and rubs his chin, then says, "You'll never hear the one that gets you."

Ned doesn't make me feel safe right now. Which I suppose is his intent, and I'm not sure what I should do about it. When I raise the subject, it only seems to make him cross. I put my hand in my pocket and take out the piece of paper the store manager gave me with Julie's mother's number. It's a little hard to read, but I think I have it. I pull my phone out of the box and again feel sorry for Julie's death. I see a little dried blood on the side of the bag and wonder how it got there. I throw the thought and the bag away.

Chapter Seven

I go to my laptop, and call for Ned. He comes in and helps me connect my phone. Before long, it's configured and now shows that I have service. The act of getting my phone operational forestalled the call that I have to make, but dread doing. I grab the paper, hand it to Ned, and ask him to dial the number. A guy who sounds gruff, the way a person would sound if he is sick and tired of answering the phone, picks up on the first ring. I ask, "Is Mrs. Jenkins available?"

"She's not feeling well, but what do you want?"

"When they shot Julie, I was with her and want to offer my condolences to her mother."

"Hold on." He seems to drop the receiver on the floor. I can hear people talking, and imagine the house is full of relatives and neighbors trying to support Mrs. Jenkins. I hear a rustling sound and someone picks up the phone, and then a soft voice says, "Hello?" The woman sounds old.

"Hello, is this Mrs. Jenkins?"

"Why, yes, yes, it is. Who is this?"

"I'm John Cannon. I was with your daughter today. I was buying a phone and—"

"You're the man who stopped the terrorists. Aren't you?"

"Well, um, yes, I suppose I'm—"

"And these terrorists are still trying to kill you."

"Yes, they are—"

"Then why don't you stay home so others won't get in the way as my baby was."

"I'm sorr—"

The line goes dead, and I realize this poor woman didn't need to hear from me today. In fact, my arrogance and guilt didn't need to expose this poor creature to additional pain and suffering. I wish now that I could relive the last three minutes. If so, I never would have made that call. I'm sure a place in hell is reserved for self-centered pricks who have no idea how their actions affect the feelings of others. This woman lost her daughter, not an hour ago, and who calls? The asshole that caused it, that's who. Why did this asshole get on the phone with this poor woman? The answer is because, in his bull-headed way, he thought he could be of comfort. It clearly backfired. I need to accept the fact that I caused this girl to die. Also, I caused her mother to be forced to give me new learning in what would amount to be a lesson in basic good manners, among other things.

As I kick myself from one end of the room to the other, Ned comes in. He looks a little redder than usual. "I just talked to Homeland Security and the Secret Service, and they feel it best to move on to a different location. We need to go to the Naval Air Station in Corpus where a private airplane will pick us up. Grab some extra underwear and a change of clothes." He leaves abruptly and goes downstairs to alert the rest of the team.

I go into the guest room, open my bag, and throw in various things I'll need, which is everything I brought. I don't think I'll be coming back to Ned's house for a while. I take my stuff from the bathroom as well. It occurs to me that the guys working for Jacobs seem to have a good idea where we are at all times. I'm not sure, but I have a funny feeling and decide to check my clothes again. While looking closely at the clothes, it occurs to me that I see quite well. I don't have the time right now to celebrate and am thankful my sight is almost normal.

I look at all the items with a special eye to any funny looking seams or any bulges in the material of the shirts and underwear. Despite my care, I find nothing, then I hear Ned in the living room, so I stuff everything into my bag and look around to check for anything else I might have missed. Ned calls to me, and I let him know I'm ready. As I walk out into the living room, I see him just finishing another call. I ask if he thinks Jacobs' guys have somehow put a transmitter in my clothes since they seem to know exactly where I am. Ned looks somewhat interested in the concept. "Let's have a look." He grabs my bag.

"If there is a transmitter, it has to be in whatever I wore to the mall," I say.

He grunts and paws through the clothes in the bag.

"I checked the bag pretty well and found nothing."

He grunts again and pulls out his phone, then makes a call and asks whoever is on the other end to bring in a Hunter. "What's a Hunter?" I ask.

"A device to find any electronics that may be broadcasting. We keep several types on hand. In fact, we swept this place before you got here. Now that I think about it, the break in at your place may have been to place a tracking device on an article of clothing that you would be sure to wear."

"I'm confused as to how they would know what I would be wearing."

"I don't think they worried so much about what you would wear, but more about what you wouldn't go out without."

"Oh, I get it. So they may have bugged all my shoes, knowing I wouldn't leave without at least one pair."

Ned smiles and gives me a look. We wait a minute, and then hear one of the guys coming up the stairs. It's the driver of the Hummer, known to me only as Sampson. "I have the Hunter," he says and takes a step nearer.

"Great," Ned says. "Let's start with his shoes and work our way to his head."

The two of them pull out of a duffle bag what looks to be similar to the wand they use at airports. Sampson turns it on and waits a minute. He then asks me to spread my legs and starts on my right side. Knelt on the floor behind me, Sampson goes from my shoe, up the inside seam of my jeans, around my crotch, and back down again. The wand is quiet until it reaches the top of my left athletic shoe. There, it lets out an annoying tone that the operator would never be able to ignore. When Sampson moves the wand closer to the floor, the tone grows louder. Sampson gets up and asks me to take off my shoes. I remove them, and he takes them to the dining-room table. Ned and I follow and watch as he examines the shoes while the infernal tone keeps begging someone to kill it. Sampson, mercifully, turns the Hunter off and lays it on the table.

"Looks like a bug in the left shoe," is all he says. He then takes a knife out of his pocket and makes a gentle cut in the side of the shoe where the sole and body come together. He squeezes the shoe near the cut, and a small, round, flat thing that looks like a watch battery slips out and hits the table. Sampson pulls at the black thread-like wire still attached to the bug and the shoe. He pulls until about two feet of wire coils on the table. "That should do it," he says with a grin.

"What the hell is that thing?" I say.

"A transmitter, and the black thread is the antenna." Sampson holds up the thread.

"Can they hear us?"

"No, these just broadcast your position. They're too small to be useful as directional microphones."

"How did the intruders install the bug without me noticing the entry point on the shoe?"

Ned says, "The bug would have been installed at a factory and, in all probability, the pair of shoes will have been switched at the time of the break-in."

"How did they know what kind of shoe to bring?"

Ned gives me the chills when he tells me, "These guys have obviously kept you under close surveillance. I'll bet all your shoes have a transmitter in them."

"I only brought two pairs, so let's look at the others." I go back to the bedroom and bring out my bag. Sampson turns on his wand again, and when he approaches the bag, the tone begins. He pulls out my shoes, and the tone gets louder and more intense. He looks at the shoes and sets the left one down. The tone increases when he scans the right shoe.

"Looks as if they put this one in the right," he says.

"Why would they do that?"

Ned says, "It looks as if both pairs of shoes are the same, and these guys didn't want to miss anything. Let's say you switched the pairs. For example, maybe in the dark, you would grab the left from one pair and the right from another. If the transmitters are only in the left shoe, then quite by accident, you'd leave the transmitter behind. Worst case, they figure if you made the ultimate mistake; wrong left and wrong right, there would be two transmitters on your feet rather than none. Given your previous vision problem, this was brilliant." He chuckles.

I shake my head. "These guys seem to think of everything."

Ned agrees and adds, "You would think of everything if you had a boss named Jacobs. He doesn't play well with others."

"So what do we do now?"

Ned thinks for a moment. "Hey, Sampson, check everything we're taking to see if there are any more transmitters around. I suggest checking the SUV as well."

Sampson starts working on the rest of the clothes. Ned turns to me. "We need to leave the transmitters here and get on the road. Once Sampson's cleared our gear and the SUV, we'll pull out."

"The rest of the clothes are good to go," Samson says. "I'll just remove this other transmitter, and you can take both pairs of shoes. Sorry about the cuts."

"Don't worry," I say. "I'd sooner be free of the bugs."

Sampson finishes pulling out the antenna. He hands me my bag and the two pairs of shoes. I put one pair on and the other in the bag. Ned motions for us to follow Sampson down the stairs. We get to the garage and Ned describes the process, "Sampson's at the SUV. He's going over each compartment, front, and rear." Ned pauses for a moment.

I grin and say, "Actually, I can kind of see now." I feel sheepish all of a sudden.

Ned grins, and we watch while Sampson checks under the SUV. Then he opens the rear cargo door and checks the cargo space. "Looks clean," he says.

"Thanks, Sampson," Ned says.

We climb into the SUV, and Ned gets on his cell phone and talks to the squad leader. Witch jumps into the rear seat. I want to ask how come he's not in the hospital, but hold off because I don't want to call attention to his wound. If he needed to be in the hospital, he'd be there. Ned tells the leader we're all set to go, listens in silence, then signs off with, "See you there." He hits the remote for the garage door opener and, when the door rises, he engages the SUV. We back out of the garage. The Hummer waits down the block. Ned hits the remote one more time, and we pull away as the garage door settles home. We pass the Hummer, and it pulls in behind close enough, so it looks to an outsider like a weld holds the vehicles together.

"Doesn't it make you nervous having a Hummer on your tail so close?" I ask to make conversation.

"Naw," Ned says. I notice he doesn't look my way. "I figure those guys are some of the best fighters on the planet. If they don't know how to drive, then we have more to worry about than getting run into."

Ned makes a lot of sense now and then, and he doesn't seem to mind my questions. "I notice you aren't using the lights and siren this time."

"Yeah, we decided to go low-profile so maybe we can have a clean get away. The two transmitters are still stationary and, unless they have some visual surveillance, they won't know we're on the move. We have another car about a quarter of a mile behind us to see if we're being followed. Once we get over the Causeway, we'll take some evasive maneuvers to see if we have a tail."

"If there is a tail, they've probably reported where we are already. Wouldn't they?"

"You're right. It's just that we want to know if, in the end, there are going to be any more fireworks. If it were me, I'd have a car tail us and then sit on the end of the runway at the naval station and use a shoulder rocket launcher to bring our plane down."

I shudder at Ned's scenario. "I'm glad you're on my side then," I say with no humor intended.

Ned laughs. "It's always good to keep thinking about what the other guy is going to do and then try to outdo them."

I'm glad he and the squad are with me. Survival would have been impossible without them. Ned says, "Your eyes seem to be getting better nice and quick. The doctor told me that's the way he thought it would go."

"What about our travel plans?" I want to get off the subject of my eyes.

"We're headed to a hangar on the grounds of the naval air station, and we'll get on a Gulfstream Four, which is under guard there. Once we're on board, the hangar door will be opened, and we'll taxi and take off in the shortest distance possible. The takeoff will be scary, as we'll climb out on full power at about a forty-five to fifty-degree angle and will be doing some sharp turns until we get to cruise altitude. These are standard evasive maneuvers we use whenever hostile fire is possible."

"Hostile sure sums up the situation. Let's hope the 'fire' part is left out of the equation."

"That's good, John. I appreciate the levity."

I'm not sure if Ned is appreciative or being facetious, but it doesn't matter. I'll just take the comment at face value and let it go. I cheered myself up, which is what I was trying to do. We approach the causeway and, as Ned explained earlier, we make a sharp right turn after the causeway ends, and South Padre Island Drive begins. The Hummer stays close, and we take the exit at a speed that would have earned us a ticket under different circumstances.

Ned's phone rings and he answers with a grunt. He listens a minute, and then puts it away. "Bad News. We *are* being followed."

"They sure?" I say.

"Yup. We'll make a couple more turns to make sure, but our chase car thinks it's near certain. Why don't you grab the sissy bar?—I'm gonna do some hairy moves."

The reminder isn't needed, and I grab the bar above the passenger window. Ned whips the wheel, and the SUV drifts into what seems to be the longest slide sideways ever, as he attempts to catch a right turn onto a street coming up way too fast. I think we might just roll over on my side when the rear end whips around and we carom down the street. I don't think I have ever been in a vehicle going this fast on a side street, but Ned seems to know what he's doing. Just when my confidence goes up, Ned tells me to hang on, and he puts the SUV in another sideways slide. This time, we don't get any rear end whip. The SUV slides sideways until the drag coefficient slows it down. We come to a gentle rest against a curb, and Ned and Witch jump out onto the street. "Get out of the truck," Ned yells at me. "Stay down behind the engine area."

He is, of course, telling me to take cover in the front of the SUV, which is now sideways to the street. I jump out and go where Ned said. Ned and Witch position themselves behind the SUV with their weapons aimed down the street. The Humvee sits behind the SUV, and all the occupants spread out behind it. Ned leans over the hood, and I'm right beside him. Witch stays at the rear, where I can't see him.

"Here they come," Ned says to no one in particular. The squad leader yells for everyone to hold fire until he signals the okay. We all hope that the car following will simply give up. The car, a black Lexus, comes to a tire-smoking stop when the occupants realize they can't escape from this end of the street. The undercover chase car comes to a stop and turns broadside behind the Lexus, effectively blocking any route of escape. Sirens wail in the distance, and I breathe easier because reinforcements are on the way.

The Lexus sits with the motor running. The glass is blacked out, so there's no way to tell if the occupants are in a state of panic or not. They must be aware that life as they know it is going to change from here on out. They can give up and go to prison, or not and go to eternal rest. It's up to them. The squad leader has a bullhorn and tells them to turn off the engine, slowly open the doors, and place any weapons they have on the street. He tells them that if they don't follow directions, he is authorized by Congress to deal with them with extreme prejudice. Then he sums up the options with a short statement, "Give up or die."

Chapter Eight

The car sits there, still running. The guys inside have no wish to give up. The leader of the SWAT team shouts, "Prepare to fire. Make certain your target is the Lexus. Remember, the chase car is in the line of fire behind the Lexus and is in danger." He then aims the bullhorn at the car and says, "You have one more chance. Stop your engine, lay your weapons on the ground, and come out. This is your final warning. We *will* fire upon you."

The whole scene reminds me of one of those spaghetti westerns where the townsfolk all hide, and the hired guns wait for the bad guys to ride down the street. The only sound in town is the cry of a hawk or the flapping wings of birds scared up by the approaching gang. Right now, the only sound is the faint noise of the motor idling under the hood of the Lexus. The leader shouts, "On my mark." In unison, the sound of rounds being racked into the firing chambers of the automatic weapons seems to signal the need for action on the part of the Lexus. The car bolts forward, obviously aiming to ram Ned's SUV. Do the guys inside think they'll somehow get away with such a maneuver? Or do they just want to end the standoff? In any case, the automatics open up and pepper the Lexus. Each hit leaves a mark on the metal and glass until the glass implodes under the relentless pressure of the high-velocity bullets. The Lexus swerves slightly to the right, and then rams into a tree on the side of the street. "Cease fire," the leader yells. The resulting silence makes the sound of the approaching emergency vehicles seem all the more urgent.

Ned moves with care around the SUV and, with his weapon aimed at the Lexus, edges toward the car. The squad in the Hummer and the team in the chase vehicle accompany him. From my position, I see two police cars and an EMT vehicle come to a stop behind the chase car. I glance toward Ned, but he's looking in the other direction. I trot over to him.

"I wouldn't get too near if you have a weak stomach." Ned isn't trying to warn me off, but to give advice.

Inside the car is utter carnage. I must have an ugly look on my face, as Ned says, "You don't need to continue."

I say, "I'm okay." And then take another look into the car. On seeing what used to be human beings, I have some trouble not retching. These guys look as if they went through a grinding machine. The damage done by the bullets makes recognizing them impossible. Most of the shots from the team hit the glass, so the body hits are mostly from the waist up, and the occupants are all surely dead. My mind can't get over the fact that they look more shredded than shot. I turn away and struggle to retain whatever is in my stomach.

"Since you looked, do you recognize any of them?" Ned asks.

"I can't tell anything. Sorry."

"Don't worry. We'll ID these guys, and then maybe have some pictures you can view later, and we can see if these were some of the guys who kidnaped you."

I need a drink of water, and so I walk slowly back to the SUV, where I grab my bottle and take a long drink. The liquid helps me feel better. Ned talks to the EMT guys. The police put up the crime scene tape. Some folks come out of their homes and peer round cautiously. The squad leader makes announcements for people to remain calm. His force has fanned out and now looks up and down the block for any collateral damage. I doubt there will be any since these guys keep the focus on doing the job right the first time. It amazes me how soon things get more normal.

Ned comes up to the SUV. "We'd better get rolling again."

"Who's going to stay with the scene?"

"The local police will take care of it. There'll be lotta paperwork on this one, but the locals can handle it. I gave them my card and asked for a complete report." He signals to the rest of the team, and they return to their vehicles.

"Do you think there'll be any newspaper or TV people on this?"

"Well, if there is, the mayor and prosecutor will be able to handle it. We already have a gang hit cover story that the authorities will give out."

"What about all the people who work around here? Surely they know it wasn't a gang hit."

"Our people hand out the story that this action is a matter of national security, and we expect their co-operation. I'm sure a couple will try to tell a story about federal agents shooting up a car, but there won't be much evidence to back them up. Probably go down as some conspiracy story, 'cos who's gonna believe a bunch of Federal agents shot up a car full of innocent people. I'm just glad no innocents got hurt."

"I feel like we're in some kind surreal movie. Are you sure there's nothing we can use to go after Jacobs?"

"Well, let's just say, I'm as sure as the information I have now. Who knows? Maybe someone will be willing to talk before this is all over."

"Yeah. I saw how much these guys were willing to share."

"These are paid thugs. They're not going to get caught, and I'm sure they were well aware of the consequences. They probably thought it would be worth the risk to run for it." He jerks his head at the SUV. "Let's get going."

Ned goes around to the driver's side, and I get in on the passenger side. As Ned starts the engine, the rear door opens and Witch climbs in the vehicle. He doesn't say a word, but I can smell the cordite from his weapon, and my eyes water. Ned says, "Hit the window button and let in some fresh air." I open mine too.

We finally get rolling and, more or less, retrace our route back to the freeway. We stay on the access road because the exit for Corpus Christi Naval Air Station is just a few blocks away. The exit ramp climbs about forty feet into the air and has a lazy curve to the right. If the government should want to cut off the entrance to the air station, they could do so easily. Given the height of the ramp, foot traffic would be impossible if something barricaded the ramp entrance. We continue up the ramp, and restaurants and bars line the roadway, but I don't see side streets, which amazes me. Now I'm sure this ramp is designed for maximum control over entrance and exit to the base. We come to a stop at the gate, and a young man inside the gatehouse—dressed in camouflage fatigues—opens a sliding window and asks for our names. I'm quite surprised he doesn't seem to be worried about Witch sitting in the backseat with an automatic weapon on his thighs. Then I realize someone probably called ahead.

The young man looks at a clipboard, and then leans out further to give directions. "Proceed directly ahead for about a mile and make a left turn on the Alpha apron. You will find the hangar directly on your right. Pull around the hangar, and someone will meet you there to guide you in." He enunciates his words clearly and doesn't smile even once. Ned thanks him and we pull away. I look back and see the guard doesn't stop the Hummer and gives it a smart salute. While I'm wondering why he did, as if reading my mind,

Witch tells me from the back that the group comes here all the time, and the guard knows each personally.

After about a mile, we come to a sign indicating Alpha apron to the left. We make the turn and can now see a person directing us forward toward the front of a rather big hangar. As we get near, I can see it's another person in Camouflage Fatigues, but this time I think it's a female. Not sure why I think so, because the person's hair is under a cap, and the face is without makeup. The slight frame indicates a female, though. The fatigues don't flatter the form. She directs us with a smart hand movement to make a hard right turn that Ned negotiates nicely, and we find ourselves in front of a huge, closed hangar door.

Another uniformed person directs us to pull straight ahead, and then stops us in front of a smaller door, which forms part of the big one. Ned puts the SUV in park and starts to get out. Witch calls out from the rear and asks Ned to remain in the car. He pulls back in and shuts the door. The large hangar door rises slowly, and the personnel direct Ned to pull the SUV in as soon as the door is up far enough to let his vehicle pass. With care, Ned steers the SUV under the door and into a carnivorous space occupied by a few vehicles and a Gulfstream IV. The huge room is well lit, and another person—who stands next to the Gulfstream—directs Ned to pull up next to the plane, which he does. He puts the gear lever in park and turns off his SUV. Witch gets out first and, like he's trained to do, looks around suspiciously as if he has just landed in the middle of a terrorist camp. He seems satisfied this is a friendly situation, and then motions Ned and me to get out of the SUV, which we do quickly.

When he has the rear of the SUV open, Witch pulls out what little there is for the trip. Ned comes around the car and says to me, "Hold on. I expect someone will meet us." I nod. The Hummer enters the hangar, and the door moves down toward the closed position again. This feels like a lot of drama, but then the day has been filled with much more drama than is taking place right now.

Once the door has gone down, my attention turns to the gathering of military personnel. An officer approaches Ned. "Agent Tranes," he says. "My name is Major Hapson, sir, and I have been directed to welcome you and Mr. Cannon aboard."

"Nice meeting you, Major," Ned says with a nod. "Anything we should know?"

"Well, sir, once you and Mr. Cannon are safely on board the aircraft, we will be closing the cabin door. After that, your security detail will stand by as we taxi out of the hangar and onto an active runway. Take off will be in a matter of a minute once we are on the runway. When we get on board, a Mr. Montrose will brief you on the nature of events. Mr. Montrose is the White House liaison for public relations matters. Are there any questions so far?"

"Yes," Ned says. "We were in the process of getting Mr. Cannon some clothes to wear, something more appropriate than what he has now—"

"Yes," Hapson nods. "We have arranged for the clothes. They are on board the aircraft. Mr. Cannon can try them on once we are airborne."

"We? You coming with us?"

"Yes. This aircraft is a member of the 89th Airlift Wing and, as Aircraft Commander, I'll fly it to New York."

"New York, okay," Ned says.

Major Hapson smiles. "We are going to LaGuardia airport to pick up Ms. Savard. Because of the security concerns, it was agreed she would be safer in a military plane. Once we pick up Ms. Savard, we will fly to Andrews Air Force Base near Washington DC, and then ground transport to a hotel."

Ned presses. "Which hotel?"

"I'm not at liberty to divulge."

"I guess we should get going then," Ned says. He turns to me to check if I understand as well. I nod in affirmation and step back to wait for the Major and Ned to lead the way. Ned does the same, and the Major walks toward the aircraft and mounts the stairs. He disappears through the doorway, and Ned goes up the stairs next with me close behind.

Once on board, a pleasant, uniformed airman escorts us to our seats. The person I assume to be Mr. Montrose gives us a friendly wave from the rear area. The airman asks if we would care for something once we are airborne, and both Ned and I order a beer. The Major has already gone into the cockpit area and is behind the closed door. We sit, and the airman goes to the front of the plane, touches a button, and the stairs to the ground retract. Once the grinding noise of the retracting stair stops, the airman closes the door and takes his jump seat. The Major comes on the intercom and says, "Okay, folks, we are ready to roll. Please, fasten your seatbelts." Ned and I turn around and let Mr. Montrose know whom we are. He says it's his pleasure, so we turn back and buckle up.

The engines start one by one, and the plane rolls on the tarmac. We move past Witch and the Hummer, and then out into the bright sunlight. Immediately after we clear the hangar, the plane takes a hard right turn, and we commence the takeoff roll. I turn to Ned and raise an eyebrow. "Powerful machine," he says. "I don't think I've ever flown on a G Four before." He taps the arms of his chair. "This airplane is nice."

Ned's right. The interior of the plane is configured to seat maybe ten or twelve people. Although we face front in the forward part of the cabin, two chairs face aft directly in front of us. Ned and I each took a forward-facing seat, so we sit next to each other, separated by an aisle. Behind us is another forward and rear-facing configuration that would seat four, and behind those is a bench seat on the left side of the cabin. Two more people could ride on it if necessary. So, a total of ten places to sit. Montrose occupies one of the forward-facing seats right behind Ned. Forward, a galley separates us from the crew compartment. The head lies to the rear, along with some storage compartments. The chairs feel quite comfortable—soft, beige leather.

The plane lifts off gently, and then seems to sit on its tail as the full power of the engines presses my back into the soft chair. "Holy shit," I say. "Where are we going?"

"This is standard operating procedure in a combat zone," Ned says. "We'll execute a hard sixty-degree bank soon. These maneuvers are so anyone on the ground won't able to get a good fix on us with a rocket."

Just as he finishes, the plane takes a severe twist, and I can see the ground out of the window. Just as quickly, the turn ends and we stand on our tail again. "When is all this over?" I sound like a schoolgirl but can't help it.

"Another couple of turns and we should be pretty much on our way." Now Ned sounds as if he's trying to comfort me. After another couple of twists, we hightail it up into the rare air.

About ten minutes later, we stop climbing so radically, but still fast enough to feel the sensation of speed. The Major speaks on the intercom, "We will be reaching our initial cruising altitude of forty-one thousand feet on the way to forty-five thousand in about six minutes." When I learned to fly in high school, I had some basics of aeronautical training, and I realize this is about twice the standard rate of climb of one thousand feet per minute in a jet. This fast rate is also in the avoidance of ground missile assault. I wish I'd finished my training, but unfortunately, all I did was solo and then never got a license.

My stomach grumbles a reminder that it has needs. In all the excitement, we didn't get any lunch. I lean over and ask Ned, "Do you think they might have anything to eat on board?"

He smiles. "I'm sure they have something."

I sure have to admire the way Ned seems to take everything in stride. While he sits looking out of the window, I watch him. You could take him for someone's dad, possibly retired, or who works in a machine tool shop. An observer would never believe he's an agent for the FBI, although the automatic weapons in the chair in front of him give that away just a bit.

His white hair and mustache remind me of a kindly Santa character. His ruddy complexion and easy smile add to the vision. He doesn't, however, have the round belly one would expect, and, in addition, looks rather fit, as would a big former football player. His huge hands rest in his lap, and his arms stretch the black shirt above the elbow. One could think his arms are a little fat, but having had one of them around me, I know he's solid muscle. Ned sits straight in his chair and says little. When he does speak, I listen, as he usually only says what's worth saying.

Deep in my thoughts about Ned, I'm surprised when the airman stands in front of us with two beers on a tray. "Excuse me, gentlemen," the airman says. "Here is the beverage you ordered." He helps us deploy our trays from the armrests. While serving the beer, he says, "I'll be back with your lunch when it's ready. Today, we are having beef tenderloin medallions, au gratin potatoes, and spinach. I can also offer you a salad if you prefer."

Ned and I speak in unison and order the beef. The airman nods and moves on to Montrose before returning to the galley. Ned and I smile and raise a glass in the classic "now we are living" toast. The airman also brought us a small container of mixed nuts, from which I pull out a cashew and raise it to Ned in the same manner. He laughs out loud, which is a good sound to hear, given the day he's had.

"We should be in New York within two hours," Ned says. "I think you should go in the back after lunch and see if you can find anything to wear. I don't want Jason's sister to think you're a homeless person by your appearance."

"Trying to fix me up?" I couldn't help the jibe.

"Naw," he says. "I just don't want her to think I hang around riff raff."

"So you want her for yourself." When Ned turns a little redder, he gives me the reaction I'd been looking for. It probably never occurred to him to date Stephanie, but the mere idea that someone would think he would date a young girl causes him to have proprietary concerns.

He ends the discussion about Stephanie with two words, "Never happen."

Montrose comes up, and Ned removes his weapons from the seat. He sits and we discuss the arrangements for Washington. He details the agenda, which includes the meeting at the White House. "A meeting will be held tomorrow with representatives of the protocol team to brief you further on events. Any questions?" Both Ned and I look at each other and shrug. Montrose takes this to mean we have none and goes back to his seat.

We finish our beers and talk about the Washington arrangements. "A ground security coordinator will take care of the protection details," Ned says.

"Do you know what the details are?"

"I don't. I've got no information."

"That surprises me."

"All I know is that when we get to New York, we are to stay on the plane. I've been instructed to stand by and be prepared for armed interdiction if necessary."

"What does that entail?"

"I wait inside the door and shoot anyone who enters the cabin with a weapon. I won't have much time to think if anyone has his signals crossed."

"Signals crossed?" I say. "You mean if one of ours comes through the door and has a weapon, you have instructions to shoot."

"For a lawyer, you're smart." Ned smiles, and then looks out of the window.

Ned's job could mean making some split-second decisions, and any mistakes in those decisions could have some pretty dire results. The airman approaches and asks, "Would you gentlemen like another drink?" Ned and I decline, and the airman picks up the trays and returns to the galley.

"Ned?" I say. "Have you ever shot a friendly?"

"The subject is not something I care to discuss in detail, but unfortunately, I have been in situations where our troops have suffered from friendly fire."

I decide not to push it since this is a grim subject at best, and Ned doesn't need to relive any bad memories to satisfy my curiosity.

The airman returns with two trays. On each is a beautiful plate with tenderloin and potatoes. The spinach sits in a ramekin, and is creamed with a cheese top. Creamed happens to be my favorite way to have spinach. The trays also have a good-looking roll and pat of butter, a wine glass, a water glass, and silverware. After he sets the trays down, the airman asks if we want wine. Ned and I both order water.

"I would have wine if I didn't need all my senses," Ned says.

I nod. "I would have wine if I didn't need to watch you."

He laughs and cuts into his tenderloin.

The lunch is perfect. I don't recall ever having such a good lunch on an airplane. Ned tells me the caterer of the food is the Officers Mess back at Corpus. Then quotes the old expression used when food tastes unexpectedly fine, "Hunger makes a good sauce."

We share another laugh, and the airman clears the trays and asks about coffee or dessert. We both decline and I think Ned has the same idea of a nap that I have. I lean back in the chair and close my eyes for what I think will be just an instant.

Chapter Nine

It seems as if I no sooner shut my eyes than the Major comes on the intercom and announces that we're on a final descent into LaGuardia. I think Ned was asleep as well since the announcement seems to have caught him by surprise.

"I think we're there," Ned says. "I managed to catch a few winks. How about you?"

"I was sound asleep when the Major announced our arrival. I won't be able to get presentable, after all."

"When we land, you go to the back. It'll be a safer place. While you're hiding out, you can put on some decent clothes."

Ned sounds more and more like a father every day. I agree to do as he says, which seems to please him to no end. We both get ready to land and, just as I get my seat into an upright position, the plane goes into a nauseating dive. This maneuver has my seatbelt pressing against my stomach, which keeps me from hitting the ceiling. "More maneuvers?" I say.

Ned turns, smiles, and gives me a thumb's up sign that, I must say, is of little comfort. I have the feeling we're on a giant roller coaster, and someone has dropped the tracks into a deep hole. Just when I think I won't be able to take any more of the falling, the plane levels out, and the g-force flattens me as if I'm clay. My ears ring and I have to wonder if I will, indeed, pass out. When I finally decide I won't, the g-force reduces with a more normal attitude. The flaps descend, as does the gear, and the nose of the plane rises, which indicates the beginning of the flair that will break through the pressure made by the wings as we get close to the ground. A reassuring thump and sound of rubber on the runway tell me we've landed. The nose settles down, and I feel the pressure of the seatbelt again as we decelerate. I glance back at Montrose and see he is totally not affected by this kind of ride. He likely spends a lot of time in the air avoiding missiles.

When I look out of the window, I see flashing lights on vehicles. When the plane reaches the end of the active runway and turns to move onto the taxiway, the vehicles line up on either side of the apron. Major Hapson opens the intercom and says, "We will be accompanied by security vehicles while we taxi to the executive aviation area. Please remain seated until we have reached a complete stop." The intercom clicks closed.

"Some welcome," Ned says.

"This is all so unreal. I think it's a little overdone, don't you?"

Ned laughs deeply. "You won't think so if your friends figure out a way to get to you."

Ned's right, I suppose, and I should just shut up about the precautions. It's a little bothersome to know the government is spending a lot of money just to keep me alive. "I should just sit back and quit fighting it. Right?" I look at Ned for some response.

"Let's leave it at this. If you were to be somehow killed or kidnaped, the President would be totally embarrassed if he were powerless to keep you safe. If it makes you feel better, just think of him when you're getting uneasy about the attention being paid to you."

Ned makes sense. I nod. "Good advice. Thanks."

"We're near the terminal. I want you to stay in the rear of the plane. The Major is the only one who will get off, and he and Stephanie are the only ones getting back on. He'll escort Stephanie on board, and then we'll take off again right away."

"Yes, sir." I give Ned a modified salute, and he smiles.

"Good boy." Ned unbuckles his seatbelt, picks up his weapons, and moves toward the cabin door. He kneels facing the doorway, with one of the automatic pistols leveled in such a way that a strange face in the doorway won't have a chance once the door is open.

While Ned gets into position, the plane comes to a stop in front of the executive terminal. Three police vehicles sit bumper to bumper in a line between the terminal and the plane. As the engines wind down to a stop, the flight deck door opens, and Major Hapson steps out. He motions to the airman to open the cabin door. The airman is visibly uncomfortable getting between the door and Ned's automatic rifle. He does his duty, and the fresh-air-feel indicates the door is open, and the whirring sound tells me the stairs are being lowered. When the noise stops, Ned motions for the airman to get out of the way, and his facial expression indicates he is only too happy to comply. Ned gives the Major a sign that it's okay to go through the door.

The Major disappears from the cabin, and I see him again as he reaches the bottom of the stairs. He moves quickly to one of the police cars, the rear door opens, and a woman who I surmise is Stephanie places a leg out of the car. She follows it with another, and the Major takes her hand to help her with the final egress from the back of the patrol car. An officer comes forward with a roller bag and gives it to the major, which he handles along with Stephanie, and heads for the plane.

While the Major and Stephanie take the last few steps and start up the ladder, I happen to glance again at Ned. He has his finger on the trigger, as he reacts to the sound of shoes on the metal ladder. I have a brief thought about a mistake and Ned letting loose with gunfire, but forget it when the Major and Stephanie enter the cabin. Ned motions for Stephanie to take the seat next to me, and the Major opens the flight deck door and disappears again. The airman jumps up and hits a switch retracting the stairs. About thirty seconds elapse, and the stairs grind into their compartment. The airman then swings in the cabin door and at the same time the engines make the startup whine. In all the excitement, I never changed clothes, and now I feel a little self-conscious.

Stephanie makes her way to the seat and smiles at me as she comes down the aisle.

I give her a little wave. "Hello, I'm John."

"Hello, John, I'm Stephanie." She gives me the same kind of wave.

Well, we got the introductions out of the way. Stephanie waves to Montrose, slides into the seat next to me, and buckles her seatbelt. I look at her and smile. She responds back with a large smile, showing what have to be the most beautiful teeth on the planet. Her complexion is quite fair, and the redness of her lipstick is in sharp contrast. Stephanie is a stunning woman. Her blond hair is pulled tightly into a bun, giving her the look of a competent executive. She has on dark slacks and a blazer in the same color. Her periwinkle blue blouse lies open at the neck, and the first button is fastened well below her breast. When she moves a certain way, I can see the top of her bra on the right side, which has a white, lacy trim. A silver chain hangs around her neck, and a locket sits right between her breasts. She glances at me and I look away, so I won't be caught trying to catch a glimpse of more.

"We are about to roll, so make sure your seatbelts are secure," Ned says from the front. He then proceeds to the chair directly across and facing me. He puts his automatic weapons on the chair across from Stephanie, who doesn't seem to react to the guns. Her brother *was* a SEAL, after all. Ned looks at me and gives me a frown of disapproval that I assume is about my clothes. I give him a shrug that I hope he understands as the "no time" excuse.

The plane rolls on the taxiway, and then makes a sharp right turn onto the active runway, and we make our takeoff roll. In a few seconds, we are airborne once again. The Major takes the usual evasive turns, and again, Stephanie seems unfazed by the whole thing. She looks out of the window and seems interested in gazing back at where we've been.

"You flown with this airline before?" I say.

Stephanie looks at me and smiles. "Not on this particular aircraft type, but yes, I have flown with military air before."

I smile back; there's more to this story. I pursue more information, "What aircraft type have you flown on?"

"Flown on is a misnomer. I have flown several."

"Flown—?"

Ned chuckles and says, "Stephanie is a Navy combat pilot."

"Oh," I say. That'll teach me to be so nosy.

Graciously, Stephanie adds a little more to Ned's summary. "I'm checked out in F22's, F18's, F16s, F15s, and the Osprey. I also have a multi-engine commercial license. I've been flying since I could walk."

"She's also a graduate of the US Naval Academy and an aeronautical engineer," Ned says.

At a loss as to what to say to that, I settle for, "I'm in good hands then." Ned could have given me a little more information beforehand. I'm just glad I didn't give Stephanie some manly advice on how all us important people get used to flying crazy patterns in the sky and that she would get used to it in time. Shit. I could have made a real ass out of myself on this. The fact Stephanie is Jason's sister and was able to outfox her terrorist kidnappers should have given me a clue. Then again, she's cute and certainly doesn't look the part of a combat pilot. I'll keep my mouth shut from here on in, to avoid saying anything stupid. Also, since I look as if I've been working in the yard, I might do better to keep my thoughts to myself.

Stephanie leans over and asks me how I'm doing. I tell her I'm just fine now I can see and move my arms again. She seems genuinely pleased, and I can't help but be impressed by her concern. "I'm sorry for your loss," I say. She nods and turns back to the window. I'm not sure if what I said was inappropriate or not. I look at Ned, and he raises one eyebrow as if to tell me to shut the hell up. I sit back in my seat and close my eyes.

"Thank you for your expression of sympathy," Stephanie says, still looking out the window.

"Jason saved my life, and I'm sorry he isn't here to accept what's rightfully his."

She turns and looks at me. I glance at Ned, and he drops his eyebrow as if to tell me again to shut the hell up.

"Jason was doing his duty," she says. "He would be proud knowing you survived and are on the mend. You don't need to feel guilty. I'm proud I can stand in for Jason at the ceremony, and look forward to sharing this honor with you. You helped stop the terrorists, and you should be glad for the honor."

I'm embarrassed and look at Stephanie directly. Her eyes sparkle with the passion of someone who knows exactly how they feel and where their loyalties lie. I envy her because I'm not as confident. "Thank you," I say. I look back at Ned and can see he agrees with Stephanie. I smile weakly, and he returns a big grin that signals it was okay not to shut the hell up after all.

The airman comes aft and asks if we would like anything. Stephanie asks for water, and I do the same. Ned orders a beer and I guess he figures he's off the clock since we'll be landing at a government facility when we get to Washington.

The rest of the trip passes without a lot of conversation. Montrose again covers the details with Stephanie, and I check out as I've heard it before. Finally, he goes back to his seat. Stephanie and I make some small talk, and Ned finishes his beer then goes to sleep. He snores a little, and Stephanie and I trade some smirks. I explain that I don't normally dress this informally, but didn't have a chance to change. She tells me it's okay, and I believe her.

Before long, we're on the final approach to Andrews Air Force base. We land and have what has now become the usual escort. Our plane taxis into a hangar and the door glides down, which turns the day into dusk in the low internal lights. The airman opens the door. Ned is in his usual position forward, and the cockpit door opens and the Major steps out.

"I'll disembark first, and then you guys can follow with Ned," the Major says. He then disappears through the door. I undo my seatbelt and wait for Stephanie to start down the aisle. I follow her and give Ned a wink as we pass. I'm sure Ned appreciates my gentlemanly demeanor. He rolls his eyes and shakes his head. "Nice outfit," he says.

Stephanie and I reach the bottom of the stairs, and I'm quite surprised at the assemblage. Several cars are in line in the hangar, and a group of people all stand and look at us. Ned comes down the stairs, and a couple of guys dressed in black, and wearing earpieces, walk over to us. The first walks by Stephanie and me, and goes directly to Ned. "Thanks, Agent," the man says. "We will take it from here." He then turns to Stephanie and me, and introduces himself, "Special Agent McConnell of the Secret Service."

Somewhat clumsily, I tell him it is nice to meet him, and he introduces Agent Ramon. Stephanie introduces herself much more suavely.

"If you and Miss Savard would please follow Agent Ramon, we will get you to your hotel as soon as possible. Your things will be waiting for you when you check in."

I wave to Ned, and he gives me the "see ya" chin up motion. I'm not sure I'll be seeing him again this trip, so I call a goodbye over my shoulder.

Agent Ramon shows us to a black SUV, and Stephanie and I get in the second row. Two guys already occupy the back row, and by the looks of them, they are agents as well. Agent Ramon gets in the front with the driver. He talks to his shirt cuff, which puzzles me, and then I realize he has a microphone there. Even though no one could possibly know my thoughts, I still blush.

We move off at a slow speed and, as I look back, I see another SUV behind us. We approach the hangar door, and it rises to expose the brightly lit late afternoon. The sun hangs low in the sky and shines right through the doorway. I look at my watch and see it is half past six. Here in Washington, we're an hour ahead. I ask Agent Ramon how long a ride it is to the hotel, and he says it will be about a half hour.

A half hour is good news to me because I'm flat out of energy. This day has been one hell of a trip, and I want to see it come to a close. I lean back in the seat and, before I realize it, fall asleep.

Agent Ramon shakes my shoulder, and I pop awake. My first thought is how rude it was to fall asleep and leave Stephanie without the erudite and witty conversation I'm capable of sharing. My second thought is I hope I didn't drool, babble, or snore. Any one of those would leave a worse impression on Stephanie than I've already left.

I climb out of the SUV with some stiffness. The tension of being shot at has gotten to me. We're in the basement of a hotel. I still don't know which one, and am thankful I have no one who needs to know where I am, and no one to worry. "Follow me," Ramon says. He heads for an elevator on the sidewall.

Stephanie looks back as if to make sure I can walk, and I follow her and Agent Ramon.

"Nice nap?" Stephanie asks while we walk.

"Yeah, sorry about that," I say.

"Why be sorry? I know what you've gone through today, and if I were you, I would have had a couple of drinks and been G-O-N-E gone."

I smile at her comforting words. "Thanks. I thought I was pretty rude."

We reach the elevator, and Agent Ramon hits the button.

"You need to cut yourself some slack."

"Yeah, I know." The door opens, and we get on. The agent hits another button and, after a few minutes, the elevator opens to a hallway with a double door at the end.

"These will be your quarters," Agent Ramon says. "Through these two doors are identical suites. Miss Savard, yours is on the left, and Mr. Cannon, yours is on the right. Let me show you in." The agent opens the two outer doors and, sure enough, a door sits to the right at an angle and one to the left at an identical angle. I see the rooms number the same: 2000, but Stephanie's has an A after the number and mine has a B.

The agent opens Stephanie's door and directs her to enter. "I think you will find everything you need. If not, please call this number." He hands her a card and her key. Stephanie takes them and thanks Agent Ramon.

"Will there be any formal events tonight?" she asks.

"No," Ramon says. "We will begin with a briefing by the protocol personnel tomorrow at nine o'clock. You will find a schedule on the desk in your room. We won't be leaving the hotel until just before the service, so all the meetings will be in the hotel."

"John," she says. "Would you care to have dinner together?"

I look at Ramon, and he nods it would be okay security wise, but says, "It will have to be room service."

After a quick nod to Ramon, I give Stephanie a smile. "That would be nice. I look forward to it."

"Good. Come over at nine o'clock. I'll have everything ready." She closes her door.

Ramon unlocks my door, and I go inside. He gives me a card and key as well and wishes me a good evening. "There will be armed guards outside the two double doors, and I would appreciate it if Stephanie and you would refrain from opening them."

"You can count on us," I say. After all, I won't need to go outside the double doors. Everything I need is right here.

The suite resembles an apartment. An outer room holds a couple of couches, which sit parallel to each other, and a fireplace sits at the far end. Comfortable sitting and reading spots dot the room, and a full dining table takes center. I move around the couches to a door off to the left. I go through and enter a fairly large bedroom, which has a bathroom connected. I move to the bed, and across from the bed are a couple of doors. I walk around and open them to reveal a walk-in closet. In the closet hang a couple of suits, shirts, and on the shelves I see shoes. A tie rack holds a few nice ties as well. Will the suits fit? I pull one off the bar, throw it on the bed, and open the coat. The size is a 43 regular, which should fit. Will I be too formal if I put on the suit? With a shrug, I think that maybe I'll just wear a pair of pants and shirt without the coat and tie. Anything is better than how I look now.

I go to the bathroom and turn on the shower. I have about forty-five minutes before I need to knock on Stephanie's door, so a nice warm shower and a shave are on the agenda. Once I've stripped off my clothes, I step into the shower. While the hot water loosens my muscles, it works the same way on my thought processes. I read once that the action of a shower passing over the body produces some ion exchange, thus improving the thought process. Great ideas generate in the shower. I don't get a great idea while soaping my arm, but do manage to feel a little lump underneath the skin on the underside of my bicep. I keep feeling it and can't remember getting hurt. I would have never noticed it, as it's only a small, raised point in the skin—barely detectable. And it doesn't feel as if it's any kind of swelling, but just a high point on the skin. The shape is curious too. It feels sort of square—not natural. I'll ask Dr. Samuels to take a look at it. Tiredness and the soothing shower put the item out of my mind.

After the wash and shave, I pull on a pair of boxers, surprised they're my size, and finish dressing. I choose a blue shirt since I think it will look more casual. One of the pairs of shoes are loafers, and that makes me happy. At least I won't have to wear the oxfords and look the part of a businessman who left the casual wear at home.

Chapter Ten

The prospect of having dinner with Stephanie excites me. Obviously, she's a capable woman, and the thought of sitting in her hotel room causes some evil thoughts to run through my brain. I need to get rid of the thoughts and concentrate on being a gracious and interesting guest.

Finished dressing, I check the clock: I have about five more minutes. In the kitchenette, I open the refrigerator and find it empty, so I open the mini bar and see a split of Cabernet. I won't feel right showing up for dinner without something, so I pull it out and wrap it in one of the kitchen towels. Looks small, but oh well, nothing I can do about it now.

I glance at my watch: two minutes to nine. I'll wait until a little after, so I won't look as anxious as I am. I sometimes wonder why I get hung up on these little details, but the fact is I do. Personally, I don't think looking too anxious is a bad thing, but experience has taught me that others don't share the same opinion. If Stephanie picked up on my anxiety, her alarm system would kick in and would, in all probability, cause her to feel uncomfortable. I wouldn't want to start off on a bad foot.

One more time, I check my watch and see that the digression into my compulsive behavior took one minute. The hell with it; I pull my door open. The noise of the heavy door must carry into Stephanie's room, so I have no choice but to knock lightly on her door, losing the ability to wait any longer. Her door swings into the room.

"Hello, John," she says. "So glad we could get together. Come right in."

"Hello, Stephanie. Here, I brought a bottle of Cabernet. Sorry, it's only a half-bottle but I didn't have time to run to the store."

She laughs and takes it from me. "I see you had it gift-wrapped, though."

I flush and don't have a good reply. I look at her and am amazed at the transformation. On the airplane, she looked the part of a businessperson with her blond hair done in a bun and her dark suit. Here, she looks as if she's about to go on a date. She's changed her clothes and is now in a dress, perfect to wear to an expensive dinner. It has a slim skirt with a plain white blouse; she also wears heels. Her hair is down, and I have to wonder how she got it looking so smooth in such a short time. Her lipstick is the same as on the plane, but she's also put on some eyeliner and a pair of sparkling earrings. I'm not sure if they are diamonds, but they flash in the light of her entryway.

I step in and look around. Her suite is identical to mine. Plates, silverware, and glasses line the dining-room table, and what looks to be a room service cart covered with a white tablecloth sits off to the side.

"This is nice of you to invite me to dinner," I say. I'm trying to break the ice, but get a feeling I sound stilted.

"Not at all. We both have to eat, and why be alone."

She motions me to have a seat at the table and takes the one on the other side, near the room service cart.

"I hope you have a taste for Chateaubriand with twice-baked potatoes and French cut green beans because it's all I have."

The fact this will be the second beef meal of the day need not enter into this discussion. "Sounds fabulous."

She smiles; thank God, it seems I said the right thing. She opens the wine I brought and pours two glasses. "I have endive, escarole, and baby greens with a vinaigrette dressing," she says as she opens the cart, pulls out two plates, and sets them in front of her. She then makes a glass bowl of greens appear and pours some dressing from a silver carafe.

"Gotta love room service," she says.

With tongs, she mixes the salad then places some on each plate. When she passes mine to me, I'm surprised at how cold the plate is.

"Should have chilled forks, but hey, we *are* roughing it," Stephanie says with a grin. She then sits down, picks up her fork, and the meal gets underway.

"So, tell me about you and Jason and your boat," she says. She then takes a mouthful of salad and looks at me: I'm on.

I tell her about Jason and me being held captive on the container ship and both of us finding ourselves part of an attempt to blow up a ship carrying the Annapolis midshipmen on their summer cruise. She seems more interested in hearing about how Jason and I managed to thwart the mission of the terrorists. I try to tell the story without too much hyperbole, but it's difficult since Jason was effective as a leader. I get to the part where he and I are swimming for our lives, and I can see Stephanie is deep in thought.

"You okay?"

"What?" she says. "Oh, I'm sorry. Just thinking about when Jason and I were children."

"Tell me."

"I remembered when I fell into the pool at our grandmother's house, and Jason jumped in and grabbed me." She stops talking and seems to be watching the scene behind me on the wall across the room.

I fight the urge to turn around and look. "Do you mind sharing what happened then?"

"No, I don't mind. Jason held me close and told me not to worry, and everything would be okay."

"Was it okay?"

"Yes, it was. He pulled me from the pool and got me a towel. I was afraid he would tell mom, but he never did."

"Jason did the same for me. He talked me through the ordeal, and then when it was time to try and get away, he pushed me in the direction that turned out to be the safest. I'm sorry he gave his life for me."

"I don't think he gave his life for you. I think you both were in a dire situation and Jason got a little too close to the explosion. He'd also been wounded more severely by the strafing; that's all. He didn't stop to save you, did he?"

"No, I can't remember him stopping."

"You need to believe Jason was trying to get away the same as you, and he didn't make it. It had nothing to do with you. Together, you saved a lot of lives, and that's what counts. The lives you both saved are what the presentation tomorrow is all about."

While I sit and look at her, I'm amazed that Jason's sister has such an immense amount of compassion.

"Would you care for more salad?" she asks.

"No, thank you. Here, let me clear the plates." I get up, take her plate, and place it on the covered cart.

She turns to the cart and takes out three covered dishes. She prepares the plates as if a professional server, and places mine with the warning I shouldn't touch since the plate is hot. As we continue the meal, I ask her about being kidnaped by the terrorists. She shrugs the experience off and lets me know all along that she knew she would get away.

"How did they grab you?"

"I was walking down Fifth Avenue looking in store windows when someone came up behind me and put this bag over my head and dragged me to a van. I think it was a van because they threw me in the side. They gave me a shot to knock me out, and I never could remember being transported. I woke up in my apartment with a couple of guys with guns. I found out later that they'd called the super and gave him the story I was passed out drunk, and he let them in. I don't know why he left me with these guys, but he still believes they were friends of mine, so they must have had a good story."

"You would think someone would call the police on seeing you kidnaped. Did they ever hurt you?"

"I don't think anyone saw the grab. It all happened so fast. They never even tried to hurt me. They just waited for Jason to call my number and let me talk to him. I told Jason they had me captive, and I guess it was all he needed to co-operate."

"I can tell you that Jason never co-operated. He played the part but always stayed ready to take the offensive."

"Good information to hear. I was so sorry to put him in a bad position. I even told him to refuse what was being asked."

"Yeah, but he knew those guys would have killed you."

"I knew it as well."

Time to change the subject, so I complement her menu choice. "There's nothing nicer than a high-quality cut of beef, and this one seems especially good."

It might be the company, as this steak has been in a warmer for at least an hour, but I think it's one of the best I've had.

"Thank you, John, but I only did the ordering. The chef should get the credit. I want to thank you for the information you shared about Jason."

When I get up to clear the plates again, Stephanie tells me she didn't know what to have for dessert so she thought we could order up whatever sounded good.

I don't want to turn down dessert, and then have the evening end, and I figure coffee will take a while, which means I could still hang out here. "I'm all full up, so a cup of coffee would do me just fine."

"I have coffee here. I'm going to order a brownie sundae. Are you sure you don't want anything?"

Now, since she mentions it, I always have room for a brownie sundae. "Sounds perfect."

She picks up the phone and places the order. While we wait, we tidy up the room service items and roll the cart closer to the door. A knock sounds, causing us to jump. Stephanie goes to the door, "Who's there?"

A muffled reply sounds as if it's room service. Stephanie looks through the peephole. "I can't see anyone," she whispers.

Alarmed, I get up from the table and go over to the door. "Don't open it. We need to call Agent Ramon. Do you have his card? Mine's still in my room."

"Yes, it's in the bedroom. I'll get it."

Stephanie goes to the bedroom, and I look through the peephole myself. The view looks completely dark, and I suspect that someone has blocked it off so we can't see who's out there. Stephanie comes back with the phone and card. She has the phone to her ear.

"It keeps going to voicemail on the first ring," she says.

"Send a text, and then leave a message."

Stephanie thumbs out a text message, and then redials the number. "Agent Ramon," she says. "This is Stephanie. We need you to come to my room. Someone's outside my door, and I can't identify them. I've sent you a text as well.

Please, call me back." She looks at me and puts the phone on the table. "What do we do now?"

"I think we ought to move to the bedroom in case someone tries to break in."

Stephanie picks up her phone, turns, and walks into the bedroom, with me close behind. I can't believe right now I'm embarrassed to be alone in the bedroom of a beautiful woman. With all this going on, I need to get over it.

"This wasn't how I imagined you'd find your way to my bedroom."

"I don't even want to ask how you imagined I'd find my way here."

"That's wise, as I might get totally embarrassed revealing my fantasy."

"Can we revisit this discussion at a later time? I mean at a time that might be a little less tense."

Stephanie laughs. She has the courage of a lion. This situation doesn't seem to bother her at all. I, on the other hand, am real shaky thinking about who could be outside the door. I nearly make a noise when Stephanie's phone rings. She answers it and says a series of "uh huhs" and then drops the phone on the bed.

"That was Ramon. He says there's a guy out there with two brownie sundaes. He suggests we come and get them before they're soup."

"Oh my God," I say. "Are we paranoid or what?"

"I would say 'careful' is the word." Stephanie heads for the door and unhooks the latch. She pulls the door open to a nervous-looking room service clerk and Agent Ramon.

"Your dessert, ma'am."

"Yes, yes, come in," Stephanie says. "We also need this cart taken back. Thank you."

Ramon comes in and looks around. "Everything okay?"

"Yes," Stephanie says. "We felt concerned when we couldn't see out of the peephole. Also, getting your voice mail wasn't reassuring either."

"I understand. I was on the phone with the two agents outside the suite door. They'd reported the room service clerk and needed him checked out. Our communication system went out briefly, so I needed to use my cell phone. My apologies."

"I apologize, Agent," Stephanie says. "I just thought something was wrong when I couldn't reach you."

"You *should* think something is wrong. You did the right thing. No need to apologize. By the way, there was a tape over the peephole. I don't know why or who put it there, but I removed it and will be asking the hotel some questions."

The agent turns to go and reminds us to keep the door locked. Before leaving, he signs the tab for the room service clerk, and then follows him out of the room. Stephanie closes and locks the door.

"Something's not right here," Stephanie says. "Please, don't leave me alone tonight."

"What do you mean, not right?" I ignore the part about not leaving her alone.

"Well, for one thing, don't you think it funny an obscure piece of tape finds its way to our peephole? For another, don't you think it odd the communication system goes out? Finally, when you're on the phone and a call comes in, the only way the call can go to voice mail on the first ring is by pushing the ignore button, or there's no service. Don't you think it funny the guy who's supposed to protect us hits the ignore button when I'm calling?"

Stephanie looks at me as if I should have some rebuttal. I have to admit that she sounds right. Something's off here. "I have no explanation, and I think you're correct. I don't trust Ramon right now."

"Bingo," Stephanie says. She points her finger in imitation of a gun at my midsection. "What about those sundaes? And then what about not leaving me alone?"

"Count me in on both."

Chapter Eleven

I jerk awake so suddenly that Stephanie nearly jumps out of the bed. "What's wrong?" she says.

"Uh … Nothing's wrong." I rub my hair, which is a bad habit for me in the morning, and look over at the clock on the nightstand. "It's six-thirty; I guess I should be getting to my room, so we don't cause a scandal."

"You're okay right where you are."

Stephanie slides up next to me, and my natural instincts are to turn on my side so she can spoon me. She wraps her arm around my side and strokes my left nipple. Her breasts press into my back, and the softness of her legs press up close to my butt. Her breath on the back of my neck caresses the tiny hairs and causes slight chills to raise goose bumps on my arms.

All this attention causes something else to rise as well. Stephanie moves her hand from my nipple, down, and across my abs. This moment makes all those crunches in the gym worthwhile. Slowly, she continues to move downward and uses her long nails to rake the area from my chest to my abs. I'm about to turn over, but she whispers for me not to move. She takes my hand and places it on her thigh. I'm turned on and inch my hand down her leg. I move the back of my hand down her inner thigh. My fingers slip inside her with ease, and she's excited too. I concentrate on the sensation of my fingers and feel her gentle torturing moves with her nails.

"Take me," she whispers.

For the next few minutes, we are joined in mutual self-interest, benefiting the other. I've never had such attentive, self-satisfying sex in my life. The strange part is, I didn't care a whit for me but spent all my efforts on pleasing her. Our mutual climax is like the song of the whales. We both sing out in tones reminding me of an old Animal Planet episode on whales where they made recordings of the animals calling to each other.

"The song of whales," I say and flop onto my back.

She giggles and seems to understand the reference. Stephanie makes no effort to hide under the sheet and puts her arms behind her head, which reminds me of a move a guy would make after sex. I look at her and marvel at the beauty of her skin, breasts, legs, knees, arms, and stomach. She remains mildly out of breath, and the fact I'm responsible for her condition, as well as the lovely pink color in her cheeks, makes me want to sing as if I really were a whale.

"I'm afraid it's time for you to get ready," she says.

"I know, but I want to stay right here forever."

"I know what you mean, but I need to get moving as well."

I sit up on the bed, reach over, and give her hand a squeeze. She leans way over and gives me a gentle kiss. With a soft sigh, I get up and collect my clothes that are everywhere. She can't help but smile and gives me a little wave as I start my walk of shame to the next room. It doesn't dawn on me to dress before leaving since the double door protects the rooms. I look back and wave as well. She smiles, and I close her door.

Am I in love or what? What a night. I never knew a person could be as warm and giving as Stephanie. Most of the women I go out with are totally self-absorbed. They would never have thought to go to the trouble of putting on such a fine dinner, let alone taking me to bed for some of the most satisfying lovemaking ever.

I go into the bathroom and start the shower. When I look at my watch, I realize that Stephanie and I need to be downstairs in a little under a half hour. We must've spent well over an hour making love this morning. The time seemed to go in an instant. "Not sure if I'm in love," I say out loud. "But I could certainly get used to this."

I step into the shower, and the hot water feels so good. Goosebumps prickle my skin, and I think again of Stephanie's bed. I'm obsessing over her. I need to knock it off, as an obsession isn't good for any relationship. Of course, I have no idea how Stephanie feels. For all I know, she just needed a good lay, and it will be the end of it. I snicker to myself at my use of the term "good." She certainly didn't complain, and I've come to expect females never to tell you that you were good. There must be some unwritten rule that if you tell a guy he's good, he'll somehow get a big head and stop trying to please. Come to think about it, that has to be the reason. Have I just solved one of the biggest mysteries surrounding male and female relations?

I finish the shower, towel off, and get dressed. I put on a dark suit and white shirt, ready for the serious occasion of Jason's service. I'm not sure I'll have time to change after this morning's meetings. I decide to give Stephanie's room a call to see if she's ready to go. I dial the room, and she picks up on the first ring. "You ready to go downstairs?"

"Give me about two minutes; I'll meet you in the hall."

After I've hung up the phone, I go out into the hall, and thoughts jump in my head. I don't know why, but I half-expected Stephanie had already gone down. I thought that maybe she wouldn't want to be seen arriving at the same time. Obviously, this would be more my concern than hers. I feel a little embarrassed at my chauvinistic attitude. I could mask my feelings with the excuse I didn't want her to get a bad reputation, but such thinking only points out my double standard. We will go together, and there is nothing wrong with it. I square my shoulders, only half convinced. I also tell myself I really need to drop some of my old standards. This woman is single, a warrior, and she can damn well do as she pleases without any criticism from me or anyone else. Besides, the government put us up in the same place, so it's natural we would leave together.

"Miss me?" Stephanie says. I jump at the sound of her voice, as I hadn't heard her coming. She pokes me in the side, and I can't help but laugh. She looks happy, and I grab her around the waist.

"You look real nice," she says.

"Thank you, and you do as well."

Stephanie is in dark colors, and she chose slacks instead of the skirt.

"How do you feel about the service?"

"I'm a little nervous, and I know I'm going to cry. Jason was very special to me."

"Well, crying is normal and don't worry about the tears. Jason deserved them. I'll most likely cry myself. I have a couple of handkerchiefs just in case."

She smiles at me and I back to her. We walk through the double doors.

"Wait here," Ramon says. He holds out his arm, mimicking a crossing guard. Stephanie and I break apart and make an effort to stop smiling so we can get as serious as Ramon is right now.

Agent Ramon talks into a little microphone he has up his sleeve and acknowledges the conversation coming back to his earpiece. He nods and says a few more words I can't hear, as he's turned his back on us. I look at Stephanie, and we trade a look that conveys the thought Ramon is extremely rude. We also exchange a smile since we know he is only doing his job.

"Any info on the tape on the peephole?"

"Excuse me, sir?" he replies.

"Last night, you said you would look into the tape on the peephole. Did you?" I hadn't meant to sound as if I was trying to catch him not doing what he promised, but that's exactly how it comes out.

Agent Ramon looks at me and raises his eyes. He sighs. "We haven't determined anything yet. I'll let you know when we find out." He turns back to his conversation with his sleeve. Then nods at us. "Okay. It's safe to proceed."

Ramon walks down the hall and makes it clear that Stephanie and I should stay behind him. He approaches the elevator and looks right and left before touching the call button. The elevator takes about a minute to arrive, and during the time Ramon looks up and down the hall what must be twenty times. At the chime of the elevator, Ramon imitates a crossing guard once again. He has us wait while the doors open and he steps inside. He waves us in when he's satisfied the elevator is normal. The doors close, and we go to the meeting room level without talking. Ramon excuses himself and goes by us, so he faces the doors as the first line of defense when they open.

Ramon sticks his head through the open doors and again looks left and right. He motions for Stephanie and me to get off the elevator. We do, and meet some people who direct us to one of the conference rooms. We get an offer for coffee that I accept with relief, and then they take us to some nice looking chairs at an equally nice looking conference table.

"Shall we all take a seat so we can get started?" The person speaking is seated at the head of the table and has the appearance of a diplomat. He wears a dark suit with a white shirt and conservative tie. He has a leather folder in front of his place at the table. "Ladies and gentlemen," he says. "Please, have a seat so we may begin."

The room gradually falls silent with each of the participants in his or her seat. The diplomat looks pleased. He opens the session with introductions around the table. We have representatives from the White House, State Department, Secret Service, Navy, and Department of the Interior. His last three introductions are Stephanie, me, and him, in order. When I learn that the diplomat is the Chief of Protocol for the White House, I feel surprised.

The meeting goes fairly well and by eleven-thirty we've finished. The service for Jason will be held at Arlington National Cemetery at two o'clock, and the award presentation will be at the White House at six, followed by dinner. In between, Stephanie and I'll be able to come back to the hotel to change clothes and rest up a little. The service is to last no more than an hour.

In addition to the Secret Service agents, Stephanie and I are each assigned a protocol representative to hold our hands through the process. The rules of the protocol road are complex, and we're both glad to have someone who can keep us from making complete fools of ourselves. One representative is male and one female. I guess this makes a lot of sense. They seem cordial enough, and we join the two people for lunch in the hotel. Over crab salad, they tell Stephanie, and me to follow what they do and seem confident all will go well. Stephanie expresses some concern about being nervous, and the young lady assures her that it's perfectly normal to be so. I ask about Montrose, and the two let me know he is working another case.

After a rather rushed lunch, the couple tells Stephanie and me it is time to go. We get up and are immediately joined by Secret Service agents who seem to come out of nowhere. The entire entourage moves as one to the elevator. Agent

Ramon escorts us to our suite of rooms and tells us that we'll need to leave in an hour. Stephanie goes to her room and me to mine. We agreed to take a little rest in our separate places.

In what passes for a few minutes, but must have been almost an hour, Agent Ramon knocks on my door and lets me know it is time to leave. Stephanie comes out of her room, and we take the elevator to the lower garage to the car waiting below. When the door to the elevator opens, we all step on except for two of the agents. Ramon gets on last, and the two agents left behind take up a position in the hall with their backs to us while the door closes. Ramon punches a button, and then turns toward the door.

"Cozy in here," I say.

"Yes, sir," Ramon says without turning around.

I look at Stephanie, and she raises an eyebrow. I think I'll keep any more comments to myself, even though she did smile at my remark. The elevator reaches a stopping point, and the door opens to the sight of a large black limousine with a black SUV in front and the same behind. Ramon takes charge.

"You and Ms. Savard will be in the car along with me."

He points to the protocol people and tells them to get into the SUV behind the car. The front car is for more agents. As we climb into the limo, the sound of motorcycles invades the underground space, and a pair of mounted Washington police take up a position at the head of the line with two more behind. We couldn't be safer.

Agent Ramon holds the door for Stephanie, and she gets in. I go around to the other side.

Agent Ramon gets into the front seat. He says something into his sleeve and the driver starts the car. Agent Ramon turns around and talks above the noise of the motorcycles.

"We will raise the divider once we're rolling so you two can have some privacy."

Wonder why he thinks we need privacy? I ponder as the car and divider start to move at the same time. I look at Stephanie with a puzzled expression on my face, and she shrugs.

I'm dumbfounded because, when someone offers privacy, usually there is anything but privacy available. Agent Ramon probably has some listening device so he can record what we say. After all, this is a government vehicle, and there's no reason to believe anything is private in the government.

"So, what do you want to talk about?"

Stephanie looks at me as if trying to figure out what I mean. I raise my eyebrow to give her a hint that what I just said has no relation to what I want to say. I want to tell her that the two guys in the front seat can probably hear everything we say. Repeatedly, I glance to the front, and I think she gets it.

"Well," she says. "How about talking about how excited I am to be going to the White House?"

I decide to be the straight man. "Yes. So, how excited are you?"

"This is a very exciting thing for me. I never thought I would be invited to have dinner with the President. How about you?"

"Oh, yes. I'm excited as well."

I turn and look out of the window. We pass a sign indicating we're going in the right direction for Arlington National Cemetery. "Wonder how long the drive will take?"

"Shouldn't be more than ten minutes. I see the Capital from my side, so it's a short ride to the Arlington Memorial Bridge. By the way, we'll be passing the Smithsonian, the Washington Monument, and the Lincoln

Memorial on the way." Stephanie grins. "Unfortunately, they'll all be on my side. Want to switch places?"

"You sound like you've seen all these before."

"I've been to Washington many times. I spent almost two years at the Pentagon. So, yes, I have seen the sights. How about it, want to switch?"

"Yeah, sure. I'm still a tourist, so let's do it."

We do a switch maneuver that the big back seat of the limo makes possible, and I settle in to watch some of the monuments go by. "I wish we could stop and take a good look."

"Maybe some other time. Right now, you and I are not in control here."

That's all too true, I have to admit. To roll through Washington with a couple of secret service cars as an escort isn't exactly choosing one's destiny. Up ahead, I see the Smithsonian and the Washington Monument. It's a wonder how people go about their workday and think nothing of walking by these gorgeous symbols of America's history. The Lincoln Memorial comes into view, and I can also see the Arlington Memorial Bridge, which crosses the Potomac River. We make a left turn and start across the bridge. The day is beautiful, and as we approach Arlington Cemetery, I can't help but feel the sense of history contained on this sacred ground.

Chapter Twelve

The limo and SUV stop in front of the visitor's center. A military person dressed in the ceremonial uniform of the honor guard approaches the car. He tells the driver to follow the road until it jogs a little to the left and to park where another uniformed officer will indicate once we get there. The driver pulls away. I look at Stephanie, and I think I see a slight twitch of a muscle in her jaw, leading me to ask, "You okay?"

She nods and takes my hand. "I was just thinking of the last time I saw Jason. It was his birthday, and we went out to dinner. He was happy."

I give her hand a squeeze. "Keep the thought and remember him as always being happy."

"What's your last memory of him?"

I don't want to tell her about Jason and I swimming frantically for our lives and the look of tension on Jason's face. I'd rather tell her of the two of us hiding under the boat cushion and realizing we'd prevented a major disaster. Jason and I gave each other "atta boy" looks and a priceless smile. I tell her that, and can see it was the perfect thing to say. We finish the ride in silence but holding hands.

The car stops and breaks whatever train of thought we each were on. We separate our hands, and Ramon opens the door on Stephanie's side. Stephanie gives me a smile and slides out of the car. I reach for the door handle next to me, and then hear a sound of a whip cracking. Stephanie is pulled off her feet as if someone has yanked her with some invisible rope. Frantic, I pull the door handle, but it's locked remotely. I punch my seatbelt release so I can slide through the still-open door on Stephanie's side. However, before I have a chance to move, the car accelerates, and I'm thrown back against the seat. The door on Stephanie's side slams shut, and it's obvious we're leaving her behind. "Turn around," I scream.

I get up and look out of the back window. Stephanie lies on the street with Agent Ramon on top of her. He seems to be looking off toward Arlington House and has his weapon drawn. I turn to the driver and realize he can't hear me. I pound on the divider until I get his attention. He lowers the screen and shouts, "Mr. Cannon, I must ask you to put your seatbelt back on. Please, sir."

"We've left Stephanie behind. Turn around, goddamit."

"She's with Agent Ramon. He will take care of her. My orders are to get you to the Pentagon as fast as possible."

"What about Stephanie?"

"I don't have any information on her. She is now under the control of Agent Ramon. You need to buckle up. Now."

I look back again but cannot locate Stephanie or Agent Ramon because the car has taken several turns by now. We head out of the cemetery and onto the George Washington Parkway, and then move at speed toward the Pentagon. I pull my seatbelt over my shoulder and click it in place. I lean toward the driver. "What happened back there?"

"I don't have all the details but I think there was a sniper in or around the Arlington House, and Miss Savard may have been hit."

"Might have been? Is there any way to find out how she is?"

"I'll let you know when I hear anything. Right now, the teams are busy, and we need to get you to a safe place until we figure out what to do."

I'm about to ask the driver to pull over when I spot a Washington cop on a motorcycle coming up beside the car. "You see the guy on a motorcycle?"

"The police officer? Yes, I see him, but as far as I know the Capital Police don't know where we are. Hold on." The agent talks into a microphone. "Capital Dispatch, this is Special Agent McCormick, authorization: Whiskey Tango Foxtrot. I need an all-points for the Washington Parkway to break off the intercept. Do you copy?"

I can't hear the response because it goes to the agent's ear bud, but I do hear the satisfaction in his voice that someone understands his message.

"Do you think he's a real cop?" I ask and cast an anxious glance back at the motorcycle.

"As you heard, I called Capital Dispatch, and if he is real, he'll drop back."

"What if he doesn't?"

"I'll do a basic maneuver, and then, hopefully, he'll understand we need to be left alone. Let's give him another ten seconds."

I watch the cop and count down from ten in my head. He shows no sign of backing off and, in fact, pulls an automatic pistol from under his leather jacket. "He's got a gun."

"Hold on," Agent McCormick says. He warns me too late as I feel the G-force tear at me. Luckily, the belt holds, and my fear now is that we'll roll over. Agent McCormick obviously knows what he's doing and has put the limo into a sideways slide. The police officer opens up with his pistol. Agent McCormick applies a little power. The surge in speed snaps the front of the limo around and takes the cop off his cycle and over the hood. Now we head in the opposite direction, going the wrong way on the Parkway. Agent McCormick has his lights and siren on, but the way people are driving, a crash looks to be the next challenge to avoid.

The agent whips the car around one more time, and we are now right with the traffic once more. I can imagine some soiled underwear on a few drivers about now. "We need to go past the cop again to get back on route. I hope he didn't fare well on his fall," McCormick says.

When we reach the scene where the cop went over, it's clear something is slowing the traffic. The cars swing wide of what looks to be a bag lying on the roadway. It's the cop, and he isn't moving. Agent McCormick calls the position and requests Traffic Control, but like the rest, we swing wide and keep going. We pass the motorcycle, which lays on its side by the edge of the roadway. When I turn and glance at the motorcycle, I see for the first time some droplets of blood on the small carriage window on Stephanie's side of our car. The force of the wind smears the droplets, and they turn a more blackish color.

I grip my stomach against the pain. I pray the blood belongs to the cop and not Stephanie, but can't explain how they would get there from the cop, as he went over the front of the car. In my heart, I know the shooter hit Stephanie. The whip crack had to be the sound of the bullet. The way Stephanie fell off her feet meant a high-velocity round had struck her. The droplets can only confirm my fears. Please, dear God, make it okay. Please, dear God, don't take Stephanie. Please, dear God, let her live. The tears run down my cheeks, and I can't stop them.

"We're here, Mr. Cannon," Agent McCormick says.

I look around. We've gone underground. "Are we at the Pentagon?" My voice sounds like something is sticking in my throat.

"Yes, sir. We are in the lower reception area. Someone will be here to take us upstairs shortly."

"Any word on Miss Savard?" My voice comes back some more.

"I'm afraid not. I can tell you that she is supposed to go to Bethesda Naval Hospital, but it is all I know."

"Thank you. I hate to bother you but is she still alive?"

"I don't have any more information. I'm sorry. She must have been important to you."

My heart skips a couple of beats. "Must have been?"

"Poor choice of words. She *is* important to you."

I'll have to count on her being tough enough to make it.

Two men approach the car from across the garage— agents of some sort. You get a feeling about people after you have experience with a certain type. Agents all seem to walk and talk the same way. It's hard to explain, maybe it's the gun that gets in the way of a normal gait, but these guys approaching have the agent walk down pat. When they get nearer to the car, McCormick gets out and opens a discussion. I know not to move unless I'm told, so I watch as the three men talk in low whispers.

Do they know anything about Stephanie? My guess is they'll be too wrapped up in the event to be concerned about what goes on outside their purview. McCormick motions me to join them, so I open the door and step out of the car. The three look at me as I approach the front of the vehicle. When I get near, McCormick speaks, "Ms. Savard has arrived safely at Bethesda, and she is in surgery. There will be no further information until she comes out. I did get a report that she was talking to the attendants when she got to the hospital, which is a good sign."

A wave of relief rushes through me, even though he hasn't given me much information. If she's able to talk, then the injury might not be as bad as I thought. Maybe she just got nicked or something. Please, dear God, make it all okay. I thank McCormick, and he introduces me to the other two agents. My mind is still on Stephanie, so I don't get their names. I'm not even sure McCormick told them to me. One of the agents places his hand on my shoulder and says, "We'll do everything to protect you, and will get information on Stephanie as soon as it is available."

"Thank you, Agent. Where do we go from here?" I say.

"We will take a helicopter to the airfield, and you will go to a safe place until we find out who is behind all this and put a stop to it."

I wonder where a safe place might be and also why these guys can't figure out Jacobs is behind the whole thing. The agent motions me to proceed toward a gray elevator on the other side of the garage. I look back at the limo. The ugly blood trails still mark the window. My stomach turns, and I think I'm going to be sick.

"Just a minute, I need to bend over. I think I'm going to pass out."

The agent has me put my head between my knees and the feeling passes. I struggle to stand upright, and the agent cautions me not to move too fast. The other agent talks to someone on his radio, and I make out patches of conversation. He seems to be getting some instruction from someone on what to do.

"I think I'll be okay now."

"You've had a big shock," McCormick says. "You need to take it easy, or you will pass out."

"I understand, but I think I'll be okay."

The agent holding me helps me stand up. I feel better and thank him for his help. "What's your name?" I ask.

"Mathews," he says.

We walk toward the elevator, and Mathews keeps a tight grip on my forearm. I can understand why he doesn't want to let go. My legs still feel made of rubber, and I have this vision of some old man shuffling along in slippers and a hospital gown.

We get to the elevator and get on board. McCormick, Mathews, and the third agent take care not to crowd me as we make the ascent to wherever we're going. We pass about five or so floors, and the elevator door opens to the roof of the Pentagon. The sun all but blinds me, so I can't quite see the helicopter I hear idling in preparation for boarding. The rotors create a major wind vortex, which causes my hair and tie to blow every which way. I stoop down and follow the agent into the 'copter.

I'm quite surprised when it's relatively quiet inside the cabin. Two pilots sit above me, and it's obvious this is a military helicopter. These guys have on white helmets and drab, olive flight suits. The co-pilot smiles and gestures for me to take a seat. I flop down into one facing forward, and Agent Mathews takes the one next to me. Agent McCormick doesn't come fully into the cabin but tells me he won't be going with us and nor will the other agent.

"Agent Mathews will be your escort. We don't expect there will be any more trouble, but to be on the safe side, we are sending a couple of Marines with you as well."

Two combat-equipped Marines get on board and take the aft-facing seats. They look as if they mean business and give me a slight nod, but are not the smiling type. They buckle up, and with their equipment, the ride will be less than comfortable. Both sit in an at-attention posture with their weapons firmly in hand.

McCormick says his goodbyes, "I'm sorry about Stephanie. I hope you have a pleasant trip." Then he backs out of the cabin. Someone outside slides the door shut, and the powerful engines fire up. The craft shakes and then we're airborne.

The trip to Andrews Air Force base takes about ten minutes. We arrive and straight away receive clearance to land. The helicopter touches down close to a hangar. The pilots shut down the engine, and one of the Marines gets up and kneels in the doorway. It reminds me of the way Ned knelt when we arrived on the plane. Someone unlatches the door from the outside and slides it wide open. The Marine jumps out of the cabin, and the other follows. Agent Mathews motions for me to move out as well. I undo my seat harness and go rather clumsily through the door. Once I'm on the tarmac, I realize this helicopter looks to be the one the president takes when he flies from Andrews to the White House. I ask Mathews, and he confirms the President has ridden in this helicopter.

"By the way," Mathews says. "The President extends his apologies for this situation and wishes you safe passage, and Ms. Savard a quick recovery. The President is personally active in the concern for Stephanie's welfare and your safety. Stephanie is being guarded by the secret service, and I've been ordered to stay with you until you're safely undercover."

"Where we are going?"

He shrugs. "I have no idea. For safety, we won't know until we're airborne again."

A uniformed guard comes over and asks us to follow her into the hangar. We file in through a small door in the closed, larger door, and she takes us across the massive space to the waiting G4. "I think this is the same plane that brought us," I say.

"Quite right." Mathews nods. "You will also recognize Major Hapsin—the pilot who brought you to Washington from Corpus Christi."

Mathews stops at the stairway and motions for me to go on board first. I climb the stairs and an aircrew member greets me, "Welcome aboard, Mr. Cannon." He smiles.

"I'm happy to be aboard," I say. He surprises me by expressing condolences for Stephanie's injuries. The news media must be on to the story, as I'm sure no one would think to brief an airman on what happened.

"Thank you," I say. I finish climbing the last two stairs and enter the cabin. Mathews follows close behind me. I take the same seat as before, and Mathews sits in the one next to me, which was Stephanie's on the inbound trip. I feel like we're leaving her behind, and having Mathews take her seat is somehow a little disrespectful. I decide not to say anything and just let it go.

The airman retracts the stairs, and the first engine turns over. "I guess we're on our way," Mathews says. I look at him and nod, although I think it's obvious. I'll reserve judgment, but Mathews seems a little taken with the whole idea of the jet and riding off into the sunset without any knowledge of where we're going.

"You been an agent long?"

"Huh, what? Oh, did you say 'have I been an agent long?'"

Evidently, I caught Mathews thinking of something else, so rather than be rude I simply nod my head "yes."

He smiles. "Been with the Secret Service for ten years. Been on assignment for visiting dignitaries mostly. I did participate in helping guard the Vice President during the November elections. I hope to be able to join the elite White House detail on my next rotation."

"How do you get the job?"

"You have to be good at what you do and pass several psychological and physical tests. Being assigned to a Washington post is the first step, so I feel fortunate."

"So, the White House detail is the ultimate job in the Secret Service?"

"You bet. Number one assignment. It's winning the lotto; only luck has nothing to do with it."

"How do you feel about being assigned to me?"

"I'm proud to serve, and between you and me, any friend of the President is a friend of mine."

The airplane moves, and I keep quiet about the fact I've not even met the President. I'm sure Mathews knows, but don't want to give him any ideas that might cause him to pause on a protection decision down the road. Being the friend of the President is the exact position to be in right now. With my seatbelt buckled, I watch the crewmember pass us on his way to the back. The intercom comes to life with the major's reminder that we'll be starting our take-off roll, and all seats should be upright, and seatbelts fastened. Major Hapson welcomes me aboard, and then clicks off.

I look out of the window just as we pass out of the hangar. The plane takes a now-familiar sharp turn to the right, and we make the taxi to the active runway. We reach the runway in no time, and the thrust from the powerful engines once again presses me into my seat. The takeoff roll lasts mere seconds and the ground drops below us. The angle of takeoff is the same anti-aircraft fire-avoidance technique as before, but I feel a bit more accustomed to it this time. I look over at Mathews and can see he hasn't had many rides in what I would call "difficult circumstances."

"You okay?"

"Yeah, sure," Mathews says. His darting looks out of the window give him away.

Afraid of flying, it seems. I'm not totally certain what I think about someone guarding me who's afraid of flying. But then everyone is afraid of something. Hopefully, Mathews isn't afraid to shoot. Time will tell.

Once the evasive maneuvers are complete, the aircrewman asks if we want something to drink. Mathews orders a diet coke. I decide to go for the biggest water I can find. I feel dehydrated. The crewman goes to the back, and I look at Mathews, who's studying his cell phone, and I'm worried the device will interfere with the equipment and send us off course.

"You supposed to have it on?"

"Oh, this?" He holds the phone so I can see it. "I'm playing solitaire."

"Okay, I just didn't want us losing our way."

"Speaking of losing our way, I need to go up front to see where we're headed. I still don't know."

"You can't call anyone from here?"

"The Major is the only one authorized to have the information. Security is real tight on this one."

The airman returns with the drinks. He sets them down on the divider between Mathews and me. Mathews takes a sip from his, and then gets up to move to the flight deck. I take a couple of big swallows right from the bottle before pouring some over the ice. The water tastes good, and I finally have some wetness in my mouth. It's a wonder I could talk at all given how badly I needed a drink.

Mathews comes back to his seat. I ask, "Where'd the destination turn out to be?"

"Greenbrier in White Sulphur Springs, West Virginia."

"Where's that?"

"It is not a where but a what."

"A what?"

"Yeah. Greenbrier is a resort set in the Allegheny Mountains of West Virginia. Has every amenity a person could want: golf, swimming, spa, and even horseback riding."

"Why there?"

"The Greenbrier was used as a safe house for the President and Congress from 1961 to 1996 in case of nuclear attack. It has bunkers and accommodations for over a thousand people. Although it's now part of a hotel and a public place, the brass figured we would be safe to use the facility since it's remote and would be easy to defend. Brilliant choice, if you ask me."

"We can get there by air?"

"Oh, yeah. The Greenbrier Valley Airport has a runway big enough for Air Force One, so this G4 should have no problem."

"How long 'til we arrive?"

"The Major said it's about forty minutes more."

"Any word on Stephanie?"

"I asked, and apparently she's still in surgery, so no, there's no new word."

I lean back in my seat and think about what Mathews just said. If Stephanie's still in surgery, then she's still alive—unless they don't want to tell me the truth. At this stage, I'll go along with the charade, if there is one, because I can't think about the alternative. I feel as if the weight of the world is upon my shoulders, and am now so extremely tired I can barely hold my eyes open. Maybe I could just close them for a minute, and I might be able to recover. When I reach for the drink of water, I feel like I'm in a movie watching my hand go toward the glass. The problem is my hand hasn't moved. I thought it had, but it's still in my lap. I can't fight the weariness anymore. I must give in to the sweet feeling coming over me, and sink into a soft, billowy cloud of sleep.

Chapter Thirteen

I wake up with a lurch and a splitting headache.

"You must not move, Mr. Cannon," the airman says. "Stay calm, and you won't get hurt."

I'm so confused and don't know how long I've been asleep. When I look over toward Mathews' seat, I'm surprised to see him slumped against the window. "W-what's going on?"

"You and this airplane are now under the control of the Desert Wolves, and I would suggest you lean back and relax."

It doesn't help that I have to blink repeatedly to try to clear my eyes so I can see well. My brain isn't processing the information fast enough for me to get a handle on what's happening. The airman sits across from me and points a gun at my head. "Can we, please, not have a gun to my head?"

"Sorry sir, but I was told to shoot you if you move."

"I'll make a deal. I won't move. Promise. Please, lower the gun before we hit a bump, and I'm no longer here."

"Okay. I'll have to use it if you try anything, though."

"Don't worry, I won't. Can you tell me anything?"

"I can tell you that we're traveling to the San Francisco area and will be there in about two hours."

"Why're we going there?"

"Mr. Jacobs wants to see you."

Oh shit. "Great. What does he want?"

"Don't know."

"Who's flying this thing and what happened to Mathews, over here?"

"The Major is flying. The co-pilot is knocked out with the same drug as Mathews."

"How did this happen?—Jacobs bought you off?"

"I don't want to brag, but I'll never have to work again for the rest of my life. I think the Major is in the same position."

"What about your duty to the United States?"

"Fuck the United States. I need to take care of Taylor. Here, drink this."

"If I don't want to?"

"You die."

I take the glass of water from Taylor and drain it. No use arguing over something as stupid as getting drugged again. It's happened so often lately that I'm now used to it. While I try to figure out how a Major in the Air Force could be on Jacob's payroll, I fade out.

When I next come to, I'm no longer on an airplane, but lying on a bed. At first teary-glance around, it looks as if it's a hotel room.

A wave of nausea hits me when I make a move to sit up, and I feel as if I've been on a forty-eight-hour drink-a-thon. After a pause, I move a little slower and shift my right leg to the edge of the bed and allow my foot to fall to the floor. I then move around until I can get my left leg on the floor as well. When I've done this, I feel ready to raise my body to a sitting position. Once moving, I fight the urge to flop back to the bed and, finally, make upright. My head is splitting, and my stomach does a rolling boil. I might be sick, so I take a chance and lurch to the bathroom. The best thing to do is to flop down on the bathroom floor as close as possible to the commode. I grip the commode and feel like it will save me from going over a cliff.

The tile floor feels cool, and I realize I'm wearing only my underwear. The cool feels good. I may have a fever as well as the headache and upset stomach. I lift the lid and seat of the toilet and lay my head on the cool porcelain rim. I should concern myself with protection from an unsanitary rim of a strange toilet, but right now, a bullet to the brain would be a welcome relief, and besides, the cool rim feels comforting to my feverish face.

Did I fall asleep again? Now I'm lying on my back and looking up at the ceiling of the bathroom. I use the toilet as a brace, pull myself into a sitting position, and feel better. No longer thinking I'm going to be sick, I venture to stand. The process, although not graceful, has me holding the toilet until on my feet. Then I edge to the sink and run the cold water, in dire need of a drink. With cupped hands, I let the water fill my palms and suck them as dry as I can. Then I take some water, splash it on my face, and at last, realize I'll survive. I don't want to look in the mirror but can't help myself. My appearance is hellish, and I grab a towel to dry my hands and face.

Now that survival seems assured for the time being, and I have the presence of mind to wonder where I am and how I got here, I figure that this hotel isn't the Fairmont in San Francisco. The room looks out of character for the gracious hotel that is the Fairmont. The décor in this room is all about dark woods and heavy drapes, rather than the simple interiors I remember. The furniture looks heavy, and would be suited to a hotel that mostly caters to the convention trade. I'll take a look out of the drapes to see if I can get an idea of the surroundings. On the way, I glance around to see if my clothes are in sight. I don't see them, so I assume they're in the closet. At least, I hope they are.

When I pull back the drape, I give a start. The drape is over a wall and not a window. I make sure by pulling the other side as well. There don't appear to be any windows in the room at all. A tight feeling constricts my chest, and if I don't get control, I'll spiral into a deeper panic. I go to the closet and pull the door open. Nothing inside. Next, I go to the chest of drawers and check each drawer. Still nothing.

They've left me in just my underwear to discourage me from attempting to leave. I'm a victim of the worst-case scenario, being as Matt Jacobs' team got me here. The thought hits me that I haven't tried the door yet. Despite feeling sure it will prove to be locked, I rush over to the door and turn the knob—sure enough, it's shut tight. No way would it have been a simple matter of strolling out in a hallway and asking what was going on. I'll need to wait for whoever has me to come in and let me know what they want. I look at the keypad on the wall. It's supposed to be a security keypad, but it doesn't have any lights working, and when I punch a few buttons, I get no results.

In frustration, I go over and sit in one of the easy chairs. I pick up the TV remote without thinking and hit the power button. Like the keypad, nothing happens. Not that I expected the TV to work. I just wonder why these folks went to the trouble of having a TV in the room. Why not just eliminate it? I'm sure the phone is in the same condition but, out of curiosity, I pick up the handset next to the bed. A click sounds, and then a ringing tone.

"Hello, Mr. Cannon," a male voice says. "How may I be of service?"

"Hello." I'm momentarily out of breath but recover. "You can tell me where I am and how I got here. Oh, and another thing, where are my clothes?"

"Yes, sir," the voice says. "You're at the corporate offices of Jacobs Enterprises. You came by jet and car, and your clothes are being cleaned. Are you hungry?"

"No, I'm not hungry, but I do need to know what you people want."

"I'm not privy to such information. If you're not hungry, may I get you something else?"

"How about contacting someone who *is* privy to the information?"

"Yes, sir. In the meantime, please call if you need anything to eat or drink." The phone goes dead, and I wonder if whoever was on the other end will find someone who knows. I'm kidding, though. All these guys are on the same team. This guy is only playing a part, and won't call anyone.

Frustrated, I drop the phone in the cradle and try and think through this situation. Something in my drink knocked me unconscious. If that happened to me, what happened to Mathews and the co-pilot? Jacobs obviously bought off the Major and the airman. What did they do with the co-pilot and Mathews? They'd never let them go free. I shudder to think of the various alternatives.

No amount of looking around shows a way out of this place. There has to be a camera here, and I intend to find it. Even in the most arcane stories of a guy being held against his will, there's a camera in the room. I imagine the goons looking at their monitors, keeping notes on everything I do. With a sigh, I go to the bed, lie down, put my arms under my head, and close my eyes. Make 'em think I'm as relaxed as can be. While lying here, I scan the room through my half-lidded eyes. I can't see much, so I quit the charade and sit up to have a better look.

Sure enough, I'm not disappointed. A camera sits in the corner of the room. It looks like an infrared motion detector, which is probably part of a security system. Is it connected to the keypad at the door? The small lens, located in the front of the oval-shaped, white smoke detector, is shiny, and stands out from the matte finish. It's a clever place to put a camera. A person gets used to the detector without giving it a second look.

Where there's one camera, there's bound to be more. I get up and cross the room to the bathroom. I'll bet one's in there as well. I'll have to be discreet in looking. I don't want those guys to think I give a damn whether they watch me or not. I enter the bathroom and spot an imperfection in the large mirror over the twin sinks. It reminds me of those houses built with TVs behind the mirror in the master bathroom. You were only supposed to see the TV when it was on, but in reality, you could see what appeared to be a hole in the mirror when it was off. This imperfection is somewhat the same. I can't see the lens, but I'll just bet it's there. Do these guys get off watching people shower and use the toilet?—It's all clearly visible from what I think is the camera location. As a subterfuge, I turn the water on and splash some on my face, and then I pull up the stopper and allow the bowl to fill. After taking the wrapping off a bar of hotel soap, I give my hands a good wash. No telling where they've been while I was out of it. Just as I finish, the phone rings, so I grab a towel and hurry across the room.

"Hello?"

"Mr. Cannon, your clothes are ready. A person will be delivering them. Also, I suggest that you get dressed, as you'll be at a meeting in thirty minutes."

"Meeting? What kind of meeting?"

"The meeting of the senior managers, sir."

"Who the heck are the senior managers?"

"I'm not—"

"I know, I know. You're not privy to that information."

"Yes, sir." He hangs up.

Damn, these people are frustrating. A key turns in the door lock.

I cross the room and look through the port in the door. A big guy stands on the other side and gives me a glare.

When the door opens, I jump back, and the big guy holds a large gun. He waves it at me with the obvious message to move back. I immediately move back since I'm not in the mood to be shot by this thug. He smiles as if to say "good boy" and then steps inside the room. He looks around and then waves a bellhop in, carrying plastic cleaner bags. The bellhop nervously goes to the bed and lays them down. He turns to go and, of course, I cannot resist asking the big guy to tip him. The big guy scoffs and the bell hop scurries out of the room. The big guy turns to go and tells me he will be back in a half hour. He grabs the door, and I hear the lock thrown back to a secure position again.

I go to the bed and pick up the first bag. It is a suit I have never seen before. The second has a shirt and tie and a small bag on the hanger with shoes and socks. This set up is crazy, I think as I pull the plastic off the suit and pull the shirt out. I put on the shirt and pants and can see they fit very well. I don't see a belt but since the pants fit so well, I don't think it is going to be a problem. I go to the mirror and get the tie squared away. I look as if I'm going to a manager's meeting. The shoes are well-made Italian cap toe oxfords, and I slip them on my feet. They feel wonderful. Someone spent a lot on this wardrobe, I think as I pull on the suit jacket. The material is fine wool, and I can tell by the fit, it is custom made. The fact everything fits brings to mind the thought someone must have measured me while I was out. I don't remember anything if someone did measure me.

Hearing the key in the lock again, I know better than to rush the door this time. The door swings open, and the big guy enters, not smiling. He looks around as if something or someone had somehow entered the room since he last visited. He gives me a wave of his hand, indicating I should go out the door. I follow his direction and move into the hall. I don't see his gun, but I'm sure he has it, and you only have to see it once for the effect to last. I'm not sure which way I'm supposed to go so I look back, and the guy points down the hall to the right. I walk along and see an elevator a short walk further.

We reach it, he pushes the down button, and we wait for the doors of the elevator to open. They finally do, and he motions me to get on board. The doors close, and we go down a few floors and then stop. I look up and see the floor indicator shows we are at floor number two just as the doors open again. I'm dumbfounded, as I'm now face to face with Paul Winther, who is waiting to get on the elevator.

"Why, it's John Cannon," he says. "How have you been, John?"

I'm speechless since I assumed Winther was in federal custody for planning the strike against the Annapolis midshipmen. He kind of forces me to step back a little to let him get on.

"I must say, John, you certainly look no less for the wear and tear."

I finally find my voice, "Fuck you, Winther."

He throws his head back and laughs out loud as he reaches across me to push the button for a continuation of the ride down. "I guess you're surprised to see me. I shouldn't wonder, given the fact I was under lock and key courtesy of the FBI and Homeland Security. Shows you how important it is to have friends in high places."

"I can't believe Jacobs got you out of jail."

"Oh, my dear boy. There's a lot you need to learn about how things work in the world."

"Don't *dear boy* me. You're a terrorist, and a murderer, and that's that."

"Well, from my point of view, you're not in a real good position right now, so you'd better put on your sweet face."

"Yeah, so what are you and Jacobs going to do, kill me? You already tried more than once."

"Well, we're in a great position to do whatever we desire when it comes to you."

I say, in my best Clint Eastwood impression, "Go ahead, make my day." Just then, the elevator comes to a stop. The doors open to a grand lobby of what looks to be a hotel. Winther steps out and motions for the big guy and me to follow him. We walk across the lobby to an area reserved for conference rooms. A sign on the wall reads: Conference Center, and has an arrow that points in the direction we're headed. We keep going until we come to the end of the hallway. The door in front of us, unlike the rest of the rooms, has no windows.

Chapter Fourteen

The door opens, and Winther goes in. The big guy gives me a little push, and I go through the doorway as well. The room is much bigger than I had thought it would be. Comfortable looking chairs surround a conference table. The leather-covered chairs look large and designed for long hours of sitting. However, the table and chairs look rather small given the expanse of the room. At the far end opposite the door is a buffet table covered with fruit, sandwiches, and drinks of all kinds. A couple of urns of coffee sit on the table as well.

"Please, help yourself to coffee and something to eat." Winther sounds as if he is the maître d hôtel.

"I could use some coffee. By the way, what happened to the rest of the crew on the plane?"

"We will have a complete discussion when the others arrive." Winther goes to the table, takes a dish, and uses the tongs to select some of the items there.

I go to the coffee, put a cup in place and cannot help but feel the need for caffeine, as the hot liquid fills the cup and gives off a delightful aroma. Next, I pour some cream into the coffee and take a saucer and two packets of Equal. "Sit anywhere?"

"Why don't you take the place of honor at this end of the table?" Winther pats the chair back of the one furthest from the door. Jacobs will probably take the chair at the other end.

After I set the coffee on the table, I pull out the chair. Winther asks, "Are you going to eat anything?"

I lie and say, "My stomach's upset. I don't feel well enough to eat." Don't know why, but I just don't want to accept anything from these pirates. Of course, coffee is as special as breathing the air as far as I'm concerned. I take a sip and recognize Jacobs' custom coffee. Its taste takes me back to the ship when he first offered it. He may be a cold-blooded killer, but he sure has good coffee.

As if thinking of him caused the action, Jacobs comes rushing through the door. Ten or so people accompany him.

"Don't get up, Mr. Cannon," he says. He then brushes by and heads for the food table. A guy stands there and waits, and Jacobs points to a few things. It is obvious the guy will fetch them for him. He comes back and stands at my end of the table. I think he's going to say something smart, but he just looks at me and then sits next to me. The last time I saw Jacobs, he wanted to kill me. Has he had any change of heart since I cost him millions on his last caper? Probably not.

He drums his fingers on the white tablecloth. I swear I can feel the vibrations through my chair. The goon brings him his selection. I assume this is lunch, but I have no idea what time it is. "Excuse me, but do either of you gentlemen have the time?"

"Shut up, Cannon," Jacobs says. He thanks the goon and proceeds with his meal.

Winther comes to the table with a plate and a Coke on ice. He sits next to me, across from Jacobs. No one else who came in with Jacobs sits at the table and they stay out of earshot of the three of us. My stomach makes me question my decision not to eat, so I get up and get a plate for myself. When I push back, Jacobs asks me in a low voice, "Where are you going?"

I give my excuse in a whisper, "Thought I would get some food."

"Stay where you are. Didn't anyone ask if you would care for something when you got here?"

"Yes, but—"

"In case you don't realize it, Mr. Cannon, you're not my favorite person."

"I know—"

"Can you please let me finish, or do I need to have one of these men tape your mouth shut? Or, better yet, relieve you of your tongue?"

For fear he will do it, I decline to answer. Instead, I nod and sit back in the chair. I look around, and no one seems to notice us talking.

"Mr. Cannon, your little stunt of saving the midshipmen cost me north of one hundred million dollars. I can't believe you can sit there and act as if this kind of loss won't have any effect on you. The fact you think you can casually get up and help yourself to food shows how totally delusional you are."

Jacobs is working himself up to perhaps letting me know what he intends to do with me, and I sit here without saying a word. He looks down at his plate and, after what looks to be the contemplation of the food, he raises his gaze to me. Without looking at it again, he pushes his plate away.

Still watching me, he says, "You know you're a laughable character. Somehow you managed to escape from being blown up in your boat. You also had enough guards to avoid being killed on the way to Washington. Now you sit there wondering what the outcome is going to be."

"I think I have a good idea."

"I don't think you have any idea of what I have planned for you. I'll give you a hint, though."

"Is this a guessing game?"

"Again, John, shut up. Here is your hint. You will understand more on how you screwed up as time goes by."

"Why do you hate me and my country so much?"

"You know John, you have the balls of an elephant. Hating you is a matter of course given how you made me look like a fool in court—"

"But you were guilty."

"Don't interrupt me, John. Guilt is beside the point. You could have proven your case without exposing me as a foreigner. The way you did it was humiliating. Dragging out those poorly written letters for all to see was unforgivable and proved nothing as far as the case was concerned. You knew you were making me look like a fool and you enjoyed it."

It doesn't sound good. I want to ask further questions, but think I'll wait out whatever Jacobs has to say.

"What's the matter? Cat got your tongue, as they say."

"May I speak?"

"Knock yourself out. What do you have to say?"

"I needed to win the case and you were violating my client's patent rights."

"Yet you continue to defend your actions. What was your other question?"

I'm now reluctant to ask but go ahead anyway. "Why so much hatred toward the West. Is it because of your parents being killed?"

"You are not married so you can't possibly understand what it is like to watch your wife and two little children torn apart by some bomb planted by an army which had no right to be in your country. The West slaughtered my family. How should I feel John? You are a representative of the great Christian faith. Should I turn the other cheek and forgive that brutal act. No, I think an eye for an eye is more relevant in this case."

"I can't answer the question. I'm sure you'll do whatever you think is justified in your desire to have revenge on those you feel have been unjust to you and your people. You must understand, most in the world believe you to be a criminal and a terrorist."

"It's true that some of the world may think like a capitalist and call me a criminal. My countrymen consider me a hero."

"Well, a matter of opinion, of course. Do you think the legal system won't catch up with you?"

"Ha. You're so naïve. Look at Winther and tell me the legal system is something I should fear."

Winther smiles, and I must ask the next question, "How did you get him out? I thought he would have been on the nasty end of a water board at Guantanamo right now."

"Oh, that should have been what happened all right, if the US government had its way. Seems a little principle of sleight-of-hand got in the way."

"What do you mean?"

"It's like this: You can have a bunch of guns, and guys dressed in black jump on your container ship shouting things about the Terrorist Act, but—when push comes to shove—there's no evidence of wrongdoing. And no eyewitnesses to any terrorist activity."

"What of all the soldiers on board?"

"Pirate protection."

"And the system bought it?"

"Not exactly, but I caused a case of watery bowels when my lawyers and several Senators descended on the federal District Attorney in charge of New York. It's amazing how much due process gives way to a ton of influence and the threat of a massive lawsuit. So the system was warned not to tread too heavily on my boy Winther, here. Consequently, his double was an easy placement with no undue scrutiny by the authorities."

"What do you mean, double?"

"I'll let Winther explain that to you at a more convenient time."

"You spring Sarah as well?"

"You mean your girlfriend?"

"I mean the person who works for you."

"Yeah, of course. She amuses me, so why not. Would you care to say hello to her?"

Jacobs has to be the most dangerous person on the Earth. If he could get Sarah and Winther off the hook, there's no telling what he could accomplish. Just looking in his eyes gives me the impression Satan has already claimed his soul. "So you're saying she's here?"

"No, not, but she will be where you and I are going after this meeting is over."

I couldn't help falling for the trap. "Where are we going?"

"Oh, don't you worry. You don't need to know any more. Are you finished with your coffee?"

"Yes, and it was as good as the last cup you offered on the container ship."

"My dear Mr. Cannon, you must be mistaken. I have no idea what you're talking about."

"So you're saying you and I never met on the ship."

"It doesn't matter what I say or do. I simply want to keep you more or less on the side of truth."

I'm confused now. Jacobs has all the cards, and he sounds as if he's someone who thinks the conversation is being recorded or something. We're in his place, and there doesn't seem to be any need for his reticence. "You sound as if you're thinking you're being recorded."

Jacobs laughs out loud. "Is this what you really think?"

"Yes."

"Well, as usual, you don't know everything. Let's finish our meeting so that we can be on our way."

With those words and a wave from Jacobs, everyone in the room descends on the table and opens a laptop. Jacobs nods to Winther, who begins talking revenues. He obviously has some charts he is going over. The rest of the people at the table stare at their laptops, and I have to assume they see the same information. Jacobs sits passively, nodding slightly every so often. Winther describes the fact that the company is doing well. He has a smile in his voice as he covers some of the figures showing how Taft stands as compared to last year.

Jacobs seems pleased with the report. Winther calls on another guy, who talks assets and capital expenses. He is obviously from the finance group, and again his report seems positive. While the finance guy speaks, it occurs to me that these people have no idea their CEO is a bloodthirsty killer. Trying to hide his real personality is why he is so strange and secretive. He doesn't want them to think he's capable of doing anything wrong. I can't imagine what he told them regarding my being there. Surely some of them know I was to be given an award by the President. My picture was all over the papers.

"Thank you, people. The business is in great shape. I appreciate the way you're handling things. As you know, the heart of this company is the people who work here. I'll look forward to next month." Jacobs gets up, and everyone else does the same. He nods to Winther.

Winther pulls his cell phone out and makes a call. He says just one word, "Ready."

The door to the room opens, and a couple of guys who look as if they were hired to collect a loan come in. They cross the room to where I sit. The one nearest me gives a little motion with his fingers that's a clear message to get up. I slide my chair back and rise slowly. Jacob smiles at me as if I'm a dog who just obeyed a command. I could scream out that I'm being held against my will, but I bet I wouldn't get the words out of my mouth before these two thugs would shut me up. And that would likely just put the workers in jeopardy along with me. We all know what happens to witnesses.

They each take a position on either side of me, and it's clear we'll all be close until we get out of this place. "Let's go," Jacobs says.

We all walk forward at once, and I find myself wondering if we'd be able to go through the door side by side configured this way. My thoughts are for naught, as the door is plenty wide enough for us to go through. Once in the lobby, Jacobs and Winther take the lead. A noise sounds behind me, and I turn to see two more Blues Brothers imitations take up the rear position. We cross the lobby to the front door. The doorman tips his cap while we go out into the cool air. August is the coldest month in San Francisco, but this is June and still feels as if it's August. I take a deep breath and can smell the sea mixed with the smell of the city. A big SUV waits outside the building. The rear door opens, and I'm told to get in. I don't think an argument is something I have the inclination to start, so I get in, offering no trouble. Jacobs grabs the front passenger door and climbs into the vehicle. Winther goes around and slides in. Jacobs says something I can't hear to the driver, and we pull away. I assume the others have jumped into another car. What did my appearance at that meeting mean? Knowing Jacobs as I do, he'll have a definite reason. I have a feeling there's more to wonder about, and try and be patient.

Chapter Fifteen

"Is it a secret, or can you tell me where we're going?" To be heard by Jacobs, I have to speak up, since he seems occupied with his smartphone. I've put patience on the shelf.

He turns toward me and smiles. "It's no secret, Cannon. We're taking you to one of our safe houses. We'll be entertaining some important clients, and we think you'll enjoy being part of the evening's activities. Any more questions?"

Winther raises an eyebrow and wears a smirk on his face, which signals to me I'm a dead duck. I look down at the door on my side to assess the possibility of simply opening it and jumping out of the SUV. To my disappointment, where I'd normally find a handle to pull, is a plate that doesn't look as if it's a factory install. Besides, the driver would probably have had the kid-proof feature engaged even if there had been a handle.

Escape seems out of the question just now. "So, how am I involved in the evening's activities?"

"I didn't say you're part of the evening activities, I just said you would enjoy them."

It might have been my imagination, but Jacobs' tone leads me to believe I'll somehow be a part. Not wanting to push any further, I sit back and watch the scenery roll by in slow motion. We head toward the Golden Gate Bridge on Highway 101, and it looks like we're going to Marin County. The destination doesn't surprise me. Marin holds a number of conference centers. Also, the spaciousness of the county will allow these guys to move around without being noticed. This thought brings a little nervous flip to my stomach. I sigh and see we've entered the San Francisco side of the bridge.

"We will be there in ten minutes," Jacobs says.

The timeframe means the location is in one of the close cities; Sausalito, Larkspur, or Corte Madera. Just when I'm satisfied I know where we're going, the driver puts on a right turn signal just as we leave the bridge on the Marin County side. I now need to pay attention since it looks as if we are going into the Marin headlands. I have to wonder why we are going here since this part of Marin County is mostly government owned.

We go under the roadway and are now on Conzelman Road. I recognize this route since I have taken it a few times on my bike. Conzelman Road ends at Field Road near the old Bicentennial Campground where all the old hippie types camped out for the millennium change. If we take Field Road, it will wind back up to the old Nike base. I cannot imagine these guys having any so-called safe house right under the nose of the US Park Service. We reach the Field Road junction and take a hard right turn and another hard right. This route will take us to the Marin Headlands Visitor Center. We begin to slow, and the driver turns right into a parking lot. We have pulled up to an old military warehouse built in the civil war era. Field Road passes between the two buildings making up the whole facility. We come to a stop, and Jacobs announces we have arrived.

Winther opens his door, comes around, and opens mine. Jacobs is slow to get out and is giving some instructions to the driver. He does get out, and the SUV pulls away. The other follows, and the rest of Jacobs' party join up with us. Winther has a key to the building. It is available for rent for functions since there is a small sign to that effect beside the door. Winther unlocks the door, and we go inside.

It is quite surprising, as the inside of the warehouse looks to be a nightclub. There is even a mirrored ball in the center of the room. Across the far side is a long bar and nearer are tables sort of hugging the other walls. I suppose when a function is going on, the people sit at the tables and the center of the room is for dancing. During the day, the place looks quite shabby. It also has a smell I describe as the essence of smoky-brewery. It makes you wonder why a guy with billions would want to hang out here. There must be a very good reason since not only are the surroundings pretty dreary, but also this is a very public place. It would be easy for anyone to remember two black SUVs traveling down the road and then stopping here.

"Who would care for a drink?" Jacobs asks.

One of the goons immediately goes behind the bar and looks prepared to take orders.

"I'll have a Tanqueray on the rocks if you have some." I decide it's silly to be bashful with these guys. Besides, I could use something to calm my nerves, and as I'm not driving, I don't see much point in holding back. I'm not sure how this whole thing with Jacobs is going to work out. The last time we met, he wanted to kill me with his bare hands, and now he seems somewhat reserved, but I think he still wants revenge, given the fact his guys have already tried to kill me twice. The goon says, "Yeah, we have Tanqueray gin."

I ask for two olives. Jacobs rolls his eyes.

"We have an important client arriving in a few minutes, and I don't want any trouble from you. You understand, Cannon?"

The goon places my drink on the bar, and I walk over. "I don't see how I can be any trouble under these circumstances." I pick up the drink and take a sip. The juniper aroma and spicy flavor is delicious. "Nice drink, thank you."

"You gave me a lot of trouble the last time, but today will be different. I won't need any restraints, and you'll do whatever I say exactly as I tell you."

"What makes you think I'll be so cooperative?"

"We know where your girlfriend is being treated, and if you want her to get well soon, you'll do as I say."

"What do you mean, my girlfriend?" I want to throw Jacobs a curve, as I believe he's referring to Stephanie, and maybe I can throw him off the trail.

"Stephanie Savard. Wasn't she the one you were shacked up with the night before last?"

My gut gets real tight, and I rehearse in my head what I'm going to say next, so there'll be no mistake. I also don't want my voice to crack so Jacobs can confirm he has me. He does, but I don't want him to know it. "What makes you think Ms. Savard and I 'shacked up' as you call it?"

"Oh, grow up. I have people placed everywhere. I know all there is to know about you and Stephanie, so believe me, if you give me any trouble, her head wound will get a lot worse."

"She has a head wound?"

"Yeah, my guy is good, but he sneezed or something and what should have gone between her eyes went a little to the left. I understand her wound was slight. As it turns out, I should thank him because we can finish Stephanie off anytime, but in the meantime, if you play ball, she will be okay. I really wanted to kill her so that I could hurt you, but it has turned out better since if you do as I say she lives."

I can't help but feel relief that Stephanie was only wounded. I take another sip of the gin and let my breath out slowly, hoping Jacobs can't see how much the news of Stephanie has affected me. I'm relieved, but don't want to show it. "So, as long as I behave, Stephanie lives. Do I have it right?"

"Now you're beginning to understand the deal."

"What if you decide to kill me? What happens to Stephanie?"

Jacobs looks as if he had never thought of the situation. He doesn't speak for a few seconds. "Tell you what, Cannon. If you behave yourself, no matter what happens to you, Stephanie will be okay."

"How do I know you'll keep your word?"

"You don't. Also, I'm not here to bargain with someone who has no chips to play. You will simply have to have faith I'm a man of my word. I don't think I've ever lied to you. Right?"

Jacobs still sounds as if he needs approval for his actions. I'm way beyond trying to understand what makes him tick. I decide to end the conversation about Stephanie. "No, you've never lied to me."

Jacobs smiles broadly and accepts a soft drink from the goon. He lifts his glass in a gesture of understanding. I lift mine as well, even though I want to hit him with it. I figure going along with this madman will keep Stephanie and me alive a little longer. As I thought before, Jacobs doesn't seem to be the same person he was when I first met him. Pure speculation, but maybe he isn't going to kill me, after all. It could be I can figure a way out of this mess.

While I'm deep in thought, a few more people arrive. They come in, but I don't turn around. I'm in no mood to meet more of the cutthroats Jacobs calls associates. Jacobs walks around me and greets the new arrivals. A lot of chatter ensues, and I turn around slowly to see who's arrived. I feel a little disgusted but can't help myself. As I turn, a familiar voice cuts through the crowd. "Well, I'll be damned! It's John Cannon." The voice belongs to the creep Randy Stovall; the guy from Port Aransas who rented his warehouse to people he thought were film producers but turned out to be on Jacobs' payroll. He pushes his way toward me, and my first instinct was right—he's working for Jacobs as well.

"Hey, John," Stovall says. "I didn't know you worked for Jacobs."

"I don't." I'll keep my information close to the vest.

"So what are you doing here?"

"I don't know. What are you doing here?"

"Oh, man. I can't tell you how much money I'm getting for my buildings. Jacobs wants to buy them."

"Do you know what he does for a living?"

"Yeah, he's a businessman. The head of a major corporation."

I stay quiet. Either Randy is out of the loop, or playing a part. For my purpose, it doesn't matter. As far as I'm concerned, I don't need to give him any information. We look at each other for a minute, and he says something about how good my drink looks, and he is going to get one. He gives me a smile that I don't return and walks over to the bar.

"So, do you remember Randy?" Winther takes me by surprise. I turn to look at him.

"Yeah, I remember him. I guess he's on the payroll."

"He's a nobody," Winther says. "Jacobs is using him for some of his real estates. Port Aransas is the perfect place to carry on some of our operations. We can move around without a lot of federal agents breathing down our neck."

"So Randy is just a pawn?"

"Oh, John, I wouldn't say 'pawn.' He favors the money we pay."

"I'm sure whatever you thugs are up to is illegal, so what happens if the police catch on?"

"Well, then Randy takes the fall."

"You say he isn't a pawn?"

"Hey, who cares? Sure, but look at him. He's as dumb as they come. I'd say he's fat and happy taking the money with no questions asked."

"What *is* the purpose?"

Winther throws back his head and laughs with his usual gusto. "You'll learn what's in store for the buildings in due course. Now, I have some people I need to talk to, so if you'll excuse me."

I nod, and Winther moves across the room and joins Jacobs at the bar, and I slide into a chair at one of the tables. I watch the various characters come into the room. They don't look to be your typical business people. More like actors and actresses than folks who need to work for a living. I don't know why I have this opinion, except for the fact their gestures and mannerisms are exaggerated, almost as if they're on a stage.

All of them talk in an animated way while having drinks and smoking cigarettes. Jacobs seems to know each one, and they obviously appreciate being in his company. Jacobs talks loudly and laughs often. Slowly, I reach the conclusion that these people have been hired to play the part of a partygoer. No other reason for this similar behavior of everyone in the room makes any sense. In a normal situation, some of the participants would break away from the main group and engage in separate discussions.

So far, they're all hanging together as if attached. The conversation doesn't seem to make any sense either. I can't pick out a single discussion stream. It's as if these people were told to come through the door and pretend to be at a party. All they have to do is look to be having a good time, and they seem to be accomplishing their goal. The door opens again and in steps a female form. The sun is so bright outside I can't make out any more than that she is female. The door closes, and I get a better look. I rise from my chair and can't believe I'm looking at Sarah Barsonne. She goes over to Jacobs, and they both glance at me.

I sit back down, and Jacobs and Sarah head my way. I get up again when they reach the table. Jacobs says, "I suppose you remember Sarah."

"Sure do." I give her a hard look. "How's the terrorism business going?"

"Now, John," Jacobs says. "No need to be bitter."

"Yeah, I don't think the term bitter quite describes how I feel regarding her."

Sarah attempts to look away, but Jacobs turns her to face me. "Tell John you've missed him." Jacobs puts pressure on Sarah's arm.

"I missed you, John," Sarah says.

"I'll bet. When did you miss me? Right, after you called Jacobs' hired killers to shoot me while I drove to the police station? Or was it when you realized Jacobs was going to kill me like he killed your best friend? I'll just bet you missed me."

A small tear forms in the corner of Sarah's eye. Maybe Jacobs had her under some threat, as he now has me. She opens her mouth to say something, but Jacobs interrupts and lets us both know the conversation is over, "We need to get some business done," Jacobs says. "Please, excuse us."

He pulls Sarah over to the bar where he begins a hushed discussion. He looks up frequently to make certain no one else gets near. I try to read his lips, but he covers his mouth or takes drinks from his glass. In any case, I can't make out a thing he says.

Occasionally, Sarah and Jacobs look up from their conversation and toward me. Them looking at me leads me to believe they're discussing some plan I'll be part of sooner or later. I'm not sure how I feel on the two of them conspiring. It's clear that Jacobs has some plan that doesn't include killing me right away. I'm interested in how Sarah fits into this.

While they talk, I watch Sarah intently. She's still as beautiful as always. I can't get past the fact that she sold me out, but am still very much attracted to her. How did she manage to get away from the FBI? Do they have her on the Most Wanted list? A booking photo would probably look good—I don't believe there would be a way for any camera to mess up Sarah's appearance.

Busy watching Sarah and Jacobs, I don't notice Randy until he sits down next to me. "She sure is good looking," he says.

"Excuse me?"

"Sarah is very good looking. I understand Jacobs has some strong feelings for her."

"What do you mean, strong feelings?"

"As I hear it, she got into some trouble over the mess with the people who wanted to blow up the Annapolis midshipmen and Jacobs got her off."

Chapter Sixteen

"How can it be?" What's going on? And what does this goof, Randy, know? He must know about the kidnapping, and I was the one—along with Jason—who stopped the attack. My picture has been in every newspaper and magazine for the last two weeks. He must also know that Jacobs is more than just a businessman. Randy is still talking to me, so I turn my attention to what he's saying. "So, Sarah was accused of helping the terrorists. She did it by diverting the attention of the security guards when they tricked you into believing the FBI wanted you to sell your boat."

I blush at the thought. "Yeah, and how was it swept aside?"

"Easy. The only thing the cops had on her was that she brought some security guards coffee and cake. No law against buying cake, and apparently an expensive lawyer made a mockery of the case."

"But she did aid a terrorist plot."

"Well, legally they had no plot proven. In fact, Winther is suing the government for storming his ship and killing some of his security guards. He maintains he was heading to New York to pick up a load of containers being shipped to Europe. The paperwork on board the ship confirmed that to be the case. Winther works for Jacobs, of course, so in essence Jacobs is suing the government."

I'm totally in shock. I can't believe this turn of events has taken place. Why was there going to be an award ceremony if the terrorist plot wasn't an accepted fact? I push Randy for more information, "You're saying the government has no case? Then why was the President going to give an award?"

"Good question. The award ceremony was called off at the last minute. It seems that when the sniper hit Stephanie, they felt that having the ceremony would be too dangerous. Also, the Attorney General was informed that the substance of the case relative to terrorist activity was beginning to unravel. Other than you and the Port Aransas Police Chief, they have no witnesses, so the case all but dissolved into thin air."

"What about the attempts to kill me?"

"Well, I guess that remains a mystery. I haven't thought too much on that."

"How are you connected to this whole thing?"

"I'm just selling some buildings is all."

"Why do you know so much about Winther, Jacobs, and Sarah?"

"I just keep my ears open and my mouth shut."

"Do you know Jacobs is going to kill me?"

"Yeah, he did mention it a couple of times, but I don't think he's serious."

"How do you know?"

"I don't, but it looks like he went to a lot of trouble to get you here and, given all the trouble, why would he simply kill you?"

"How did I get here?"

"You'll have to ask Jacobs."

"Do you know why he's meeting in this place? It seems so open and possibly dangerous for him."

"I heard Winther say that Jacobs believes having a meeting isn't against the law, and that no one at this meeting is of interest to the government."

"Except Jacobs himself."

"I wouldn't know."

"Come on, Randy. You know damn well I shouldn't be here, and something is up since Sarah and Winther are here as well."

Randy gets up from his chair. "Real nice talking to you. We should do this again sometime." He walks toward the bar.

Son of a bitch. These bastards are sitting here in Marin County, totally out in the open, plotting some mayhem, and I'm powerless to stop them. I could make a break for the door and try and run to the marine sanctuary and call for help. Of course, if I do, I have no doubts Jacobs will make good on his threat to harm Stephanie. Also, there's no guarantee I would make it. How many of these partygoers are killers for hire? I look from one to the next and, for the life of me, can't tell.

I take a sip of my drink. The ice has melted, and it's no longer enjoyable. I get up, walk to the bar, and put the glass down. The bartender asks if I'd care for another, and I decline. Winther moves down the bar and stands next to me.

"How did you get the Air Force guys to help kidnap me?"

"John, for a man with no options, you're always curious. Let's just say, you will find answers to your questions in due time."

"How long are we going to stay here?"

"I believe we're getting ready to depart shortly."

Again, it's as if the act of asking the question causes the action to begin. Jacobs announces that we're all leaving, and everyone should drink up and prepare to depart. I ask

Winther the destination, and he gives me a rolling eye look that tells me he isn't going to give me any information. Everyone gets up and moves toward the door. Jacobs gives me a sign to wait, and then he, Winther, and Sarah turn and walk around to the rear of the bar, where Jacobs signals me to join. While the rest of the mob goes out the main door, we slip out a door leading to the large black SUV. The doors stand open, and we all get in and the driver pulls away before we even have our seatbelts fastened. Jacobs sits in the front. Sarah, Winther, and I sit three across in the back. I'm next to Sarah, and her warmth radiates from her arm, which touches mine ever so slightly. I can also smell her perfume, which has to be some exotic custom concoction—I've never smelled this scent before. I know perfume smells differently on different women, but this is clearly one of a kind. "Nice perfume," I say.

Sarah looks at me as if I'd complimented the lift in her bra. Jacobs tells me to be quiet since he's on the phone. I think he suspects Sarah and I'll get into a good row sooner or later. I didn't mean anything by the perfume comment but decide to let these two think I did.

I don't say anything more. The SUV pulls out of the Marin headlands and heads south on Route US 101. After five minutes, the car exits on California 37, and we pass the Vallejo twenty miles sign. Why are we heading for Vallejo? I close my eyes for a minute, and the lurch of the car turning causes me to come fully awake. Now on California 29, we head toward Napa. Just past American Canyon, it hits me: We could be going to the Napa County Airport, which—according to my estimate—is five miles to the north.

It doesn't take long to confirm my guess, as we turn left at the airport entrance and speed toward the general aviation terminal. When we pull onto the tarmac, I catch a glimpse of a Gulfstream ahead of us. The driver stops just short of the bottom of the stairs, and Jacobs opens his door and steps out. Winther opens his, and the driver gets mine. All out of the vehicle, Winther motions to Sarah and me to go up the stairs. "What if I refuse?" I say.

Winther reaches under his jacket and pulls out a chrome-plated magnum .44. "Please don't make me shoot you in the knee. There will be a mess to clean up, and it will only delay us all."

I scamper up the stairs. No prodding is necessary for Sarah, and it's obvious she works for these guys. She follows me up and enters the cabin. I take the first seat, which faces rearward in the first row, and she sits in the seat across the aisle next to me. Why is she staying so close? Despite everything she's done, I can't help liking it this way. I buckle my seatbelt and look out the window. Rainclouds are forming off to the west. Will we be heading in that direction—out over the ocean, or east? Sooner or later I'll find out. Winther and Jacobs enter the cabin, move further to the rear of the plane, and talk in low voices. I turn to Sarah, "How've you been?"

Without a response, she looks out of the window. Although little more than a foot away, she might as well be on another airplane.

One of the pilots goes to the doorway and pushes the button to retract the stairs. He then closes the door, and the whine of the first engine starting thrums through the cabin. The pilot goes into the cockpit, closes the door, and turns on the "fasten seatbelt" sign. I think back on the Major and wonder where he is right now. Did he work out a plan to explain losing me? Of course, if he's no longer in the US, he doesn't have to worry. On the other hand, the way Jacobs treats his friends, the Major may be dead.

The second engine starts, and we begin to roll. I look in the seat pocket by the armrest and see we are in a Gulfstream G650. I remember reading on this model. It's capable of seven thousand miles nonstop. We could make it to Hawaii if we were heading west, but my money is on an eastern destination and somewhere in the US. The long taxi takes us to the end of the taxiway, and the pilot stops the plane after we turn onto the active runway. He applies a power run up slowly, and the plane strains against the brakes that hold it in check. Then he releases the brakes, and the force of the acceleration presses me into the seat, and I can feel a furious race to pick up enough speed to lift off.

In seconds, the nose makes its rotation and is followed by a sense of quiet, as the wheels no longer engage with the runway. The powerful engines boost the craft into the air as we make the take-off climb to the assigned altitude. Through the window, I can see the tree line and realize that we didn't have a lot of runway room to spare. That's why the pilot revved up before starting his takeoff roll.

The airplane banks to the left and continues to climb smoothly. The sun shines on my left, and the airplane comes around to face it directly. A few minutes of turn brings the plane to a position where the sun sits directly on my right. Since, at this time of day, the sun is more to the west, we must be heading south. If we were heading north, then the sun would have remained on my left. We've made a half circle on the compass, and as I'm trying to keep up with the direction, the airplane wings level, and we continue to climb. Below, all I can see is ocean. The other side must have a view of the city of San Francisco. I want to ask Sarah if this is true but decide against it. She probably wouldn't answer me. Instead, I sit back and relax, as I don't have much else to do. Eyes closed, I drift into a semi-sleep.

"John. You awake?" Winther says. I open my eyes and find Winther has taken the seat opposite me.

"Yes, I'm awake."

"Good, because I need to fill you in on a few things. Mr. Jacobs wants me to brief you on what is to happen."

"Oh, this should be good. I'm happy Mr. Jacobs is so kind as to bring me in on his little plan."

Winther smiles. "Yes, well, the first thing you should know is that Sarah and I are not technically out of custody. We are playing a little game with the US authorities. In exchange for getting some information on Mr. Jacobs, the feds let her out on bail with the understanding that she would turn state's evidence against Mr. Jacobs. Sarah agreed to do so, and here she is."

"She's turning against Jacobs? Randy told me there wasn't enough evidence to hold the two of you. He said you were suing the government." I cannot believe what I just heard.

"The feds *think* she's turning against Mr. Jacobs, but surely you don't believe her loyalty is so tenuous? Also, you can forget anything Randy told you. He has no credible information."

"Randy sure fooled me. As for Sarah turning on Matt, yeah, you're right, I don't believe it, but how did she convince the feds she was serious?"

"It was relatively easy. They wanted to believe she was loyal to America, so all she did was agree to wear a listening device and be confined to her house unless it was necessary to contact Mr. Jacobs. They bugged her phones and Sarah had a monitoring device attached in addition to the microphone. It was risk-free for the government."

"So how did you both get away?"

"As far as the government knows, she's in her home right now. I think Sarah is listening to music, and I'm still in a cell at Guantanamo, probably resisting talking through torture right now."

"Okay, now you've lost me completely. You mean to tell me you got away from Guantanamo?"

"No, not really. I never went there. You see, when government forces arrested me on the container ship, they arrested my stand-in, not me. I left with Mr. Jacobs on his helicopter. You didn't even spot the phony Paul Winther. It's simple. There are two people who are stand-ins for Sarah and me. They're under the close control of their handlers."

I look at Sarah, but she continues to look out the window and is deep in thought. "But there were all those people at the office and at the warehouse in Marin who saw you there."

"They're paid employees who have seen nothing."

"Why did we go warehouse?"

"We had to get close enough to the airport and wait for Sarah to get away. Mr. Jacobs felt a big party at the Marin headlands wouldn't attract any attention. With the number of people there, if any law enforcement types came around, a big diversion could be launched. It worked quite well."

"Randy Stovall got a good look at Sarah."

"Randy is, as they say, 'sleeping with the fishes.' We don't need him anymore. We've finished with Port Aransas and his buildings."

"So Randy's done?" I have no doubt Randy is where Winther says he is, and it doesn't surprise me. Randy was too dumb to play with these guys, so I don't feel sorry for him. I need to think about what I'm going to do.

"Yup, Randy is done," Winther says. He then sits back and gives me a smile. "You don't want to end up with Randy, do you?"

I look at Sarah again, who now leans back in her seat with her eyes closed. "I have a choice?"

"You know we all have choices. In fact, I have a proposal for you that I think you may find interesting."

"When you propose something interesting, it proves downright dangerous."

Winther gives me a big bad-boy kind of smile. "Yeah, I guess I deserve the accusation."

"What kind of proposal do you have?"

Winther glances at Sarah as if he wants her to say something. Since she seems to be avoiding any interaction, he clears his throat. "We think you would make an excellent agent for our cause."

"Excuse me? Are you serious? Why in God's name would I be an agent for a murderous bunch of thugs like you and Jacobs?"

"Well, I can think of two reasons right off the bat."

"What two reasons?"

"Reason number one. If you don't help us, we will kill you."

"You're going to need to do better. There's no way I'd try and spare my life just to help you people with whatever you're in the process of conjuring up."

"Yeah, we thought you'd have such a position. At least, you would have until it came right down to having a cold gun placed against your head moments before you're no longer viable."

"Well, why not try and see?"

"We have plenty of time to see, but in the meantime, do you want to hear reason two?"

"Well, this ought to be good. Sure, tell me reason number two."

"You remember Jason's sister Stephanie, don't you?"

"Yeah, of course, I remember her."

"Right now, she's in the hospital in Washington, and it looks as if she's going to be okay."

"So, tell me you're going to kidnap her and then threaten to kill her if I don't cooperate?"

"Aw, come on, John. You know as well as I, the threat of killing her isn't enough to motivate you any further than we already have. When I tell you the assignment we have in mind, you're going to give me the same crap on Stephanie you gave on yourself."

"Okay, and how are you going to prevent my crap?"

"Well. Consider this. You know Stephanie is in the hospital and will be there for a week more —"

"I didn't know."

"It's true. She won't go home until after we finish our little assignment."

"What changes the fact that you won't get me to do what you want, no matter what you do to Stephanie or me?"

"Do you know how many people are currently in the hospital as workers and patients?"

A cold feeling forms in the pit of my stomach. This is not going to go well. I try to sound brave, "I have no idea."

"Two thousand, give or take a few hundred."

"So what?"

"Think, explosion. Think, big explosion."

"You son of a bitch. You can't kill those innocent people."

"Well, now, you know we can. Of course, you can prevent it."

"How are you going to blow up a hospital? Don't you think they have security around there, and might notice a bunch of lowlifes trying to sneak in with explosives?"

Winther laughs. "I enjoy the term 'lowlifes.' So judgmental of you to believe only the scum of the earth would have the capability of taking innocent lives."

"It's true."

Chapter Seventeen

"John, did I not teach you anything regarding passion for justice? The explosives have been in place for weeks. When we began our campaign to embarrass the United States and bring attention to our cause, we had some contingency plans put in place in case our major effort didn't work out. One of the plans was to blow up Bethesda Naval Hospital, and all souls caught inside. The choice to blow up Bethesda had been intended as only a minor engagement, but now it's turned out to support our major campaign quite well. Just so happens, your girlfriend is there as well."

"How in the world do you sleep at night?"

"Gee, John, your question is apropos of nothing. I sleep very well knowing I'm doing my part to wreak havoc on the Western devil. The question is, do you want to prevent the loss of lives, not to mention the hospital itself?"

"How can I prevent the loss of life?"

"If you do as we say, we will spare the hospital."

Winther already knows I'll want to stop them somehow. I must figure out a way. Maybe it would be good to play along and perhaps buy some time. I ask, "What is it you want me to do?"

"Not much, really. We're on a heading to a location in South America. We have a television studio there, and we want you to make a broadcast."

"A broadcast? What kind of broadcast?"

"Nothing difficult. Since you're now a well-known hero, we think it's time for you to help us disrupt the poor citizens of your country with a few truths regarding their government."

"Now you've lost me. What *truths*?"

"The first truth we think you should explain is your mistaken idea that there was going to be some attack on the Annapolis midshipmen."

"I was not mistake—" I pause to gather my thoughts when I get it. These guys want me to be part of their propaganda machine and, if I say no, they'll blow up the hospital. I can't imagine what the other truths are, but I need to be real careful here and not cause them to believe they need to pull the trigger. How will I prevent a disaster? I need to figure out a plan.

"You were saying," Winther says.

"Yeah, I get it now. You want me to say I made a mistake in what I thought was the potential attack. To say that I made a mistake, will lead people to believe the government has somehow lied to them. Since what I'll be telling is a lie, the government will have a tough time proving they were telling the truth, and people will no doubt believe me first. What are the other truths you mentioned?"

"The second truth we want you to explain to your countrymen is that the Arab world wants to sell more oil at a cheaper price and thus reduce prices of gasoline and other commodities. The US government, in collusion with American oil companies, refuses to buy more oil and, therefore, the price stays high. We will write your script, but can you imagine the impact of this information. Since it will be coming from such a credible source as you, the stability of your country will be questionable after the statement and this will have a negative result on the rest of the world as well."

"Again, I have to believe you're all mad."

"And I have to believe you underestimate us and the cause we are willing to die for."

"You can't believe that just on my word there will be any reaction to my claim that the government refused to allow the price of oil to go down?"

"Not on your word John. On the word of a hero who will have evidence, the government is keeping the price of oil artificially high. I think this information will be interesting to the oil producing countries and may even cause them to take some unilateral action. We think after all the denials and the arguments are over the oil producers will be pissed off enough to do some real damage. The idea contained in our little subterfuge that they would have to ask the US to buy more oil to reduce the price is enough to send them over the edge. Also, the American public would not react well to the President knowing he is costing them more money than need be for gasoline.

I look at Sarah, and she seems to be still asleep. "Is there anything else I should know about this scheme?"

"Not too much more. The television studio has a complete broadcast facility, so your message will be delivered throughout the world. In fact, we plan to make the message available to the networks and all suppliers of television programming."

"After I deliver the message, then what?"

"I don't know. I guess we'll drop you off wherever you want to go."

"I don't suppose you have a flight to Mars, do you, since that will be the only place left for me to go."

"Oh, get serious. No one will give a crap about you. In fact, your fifteen minutes will be over, and you'll be old news." Winther leans back in his seat, clearly finished with his update.

I lean back as well. There doesn't seem to be any point in going on with Winther any longer. I now have a pretty crucial decision to make. If I refuse to do the broadcasts, then thousands of innocent people will die. If I do the broadcasts, there's no telling how many people will be affected. Also, by doing the broadcasts, I'll be confirming the aims of these maniacs and helping their cause. Is there some way I could pretend to go along with the scheme? Then, at the last minute, get a warning out to the people in the hospital. Also, I'd need to let the world know I'm being held under duress and not telling the truth. If I can pull it off, it will most certainly mean my demise, as I can't imagine being let go after the kind of treachery my action will entail. Not that I believe they'll let me go regardless.

I close my eyes and think of alternatives. If they pre-record the broadcast, then all bets will be off. There'll be no way to spring any surprises at all. They'd simply stop the recording, probably beat me senseless, and then resume when I'm able. I guess I'll need to understand how the broadcast is put together before I can plan some alternate method.

"Would you care for anything?" The voice of a stranger makes me open my eyes quickly. I must have fallen asleep. It is an attendant speaking to Winther. He asks for water, and the attendant looks my way, and I also ask for water. "How long before we land?"

"I think another two hours or so. We have been in the air five hours, and it is seven hours to Ecuador. We will be landing in Guayaquil at the José Joaquín de Olmedo International Airport."

"Only seven hours? How many miles?"

"I'm not sure, I think around four thousand."

"Wow, I would have thought it would take longer."

"It does by commercial airline. The increased speed is the beauty of private air travel."

The water arrives, and I see Sarah is awake and reading a magazine. I want to say something, but I feel she'll try to ignore me again, so I decide not to waste my time. Instead, I take a long drink, and the attendant asks if I'm ready to eat something. At the mention of eating, I realize I haven't had anything for quite a while. I can't count the olive in my martini back in California. When I tell him I want something, he gives me a choice of salad with or without grilled chicken, filet mignon, or fish. If we were on a boat somewhere, I'd order fish, but go for safe with the salad. Winther orders the steak and Sarah the salad as well. The attendant leaves. Sarah stares at me.

"So, John," she says. "Tell me how you managed to escape being blown to bits by Winther's team."

I'm totally taken by surprise and can't seem to find the words. "Well …" I stop, and then begin again, "I guess I just got lucky."

"I would say you were a little more than lucky. I would say you're blessed."

Winther looks at Sarah and frowns. He probably never thought of the possibility of divine intervention being part of the equation.

Sarah says, "I hope you know I didn't have anything to do with the whole episode. I merely helped Winther disable the cameras by distracting the guards at the towers."

"I want to believe, but I also know you were the only one who knew where I was going the morning the thugs ambushed me on the way to Ned's office."

"Oh, I can explain," Winther says. "We had Sarah's phone bugged. She never told us anything regarding you. We knew your movements because you made a phone call to Sarah and told her."

I don't know why, but I'm glad Winther spoke up and cleared Sarah of at least being part of my kidnapping. I ask her, "Why did you even agree to help these guys with the camera?"

"I had good reasons. I don't think it'll help to go into them now."

"Again, I can be of some assistance," Winther says. "Maybe it would help to know that we are holding Sarah hostage. She's not a hostage in the usual way, but she is a hostage nonetheless."

Sarah frowns but stays quiet. I say, "I can't imagine you allowing these thugs to have control over you to the extent that you've violated trust, not to mention being accused of terrorist activity."

"Yeah, well, these guys can be convincing."

"What could they possibly have had on you?"

"I have a younger sister whom Winther assures me will be fine as long as I cooperate."

"Couldn't you have gone to the police—?"

Winther interrupts, "John, you're so naïve about how we operate that it sometimes hurts. Don't you think if Sarah had gone to the police, we would have known and then be forced to harm her sister?"

"What kind of harm?"

"The usual: rape, torture, and murder."

"You're disgusting."

"Yeah, well, we try and do a complete job. Can you imagine telling Sarah that she needs to do what we say, or we will kill her? She'd tell us to go ahead. Bring in the sister and it's a whole new ballgame. Also, it wouldn't work if we said we were going to scare or beat up the sister. The results of non-compliance had to be more severe than the results of doing what we say."

"So Sarah is living under the same threat?"

"You betcha. You and she have a lot to lose by not being cooperative. Not for yourself, you understand, but for the pain and suffering you'll bring upon others."

"You're one sick fuck."

"Well, aren't we the adult one?"

"Winther, I can't tell you how much you piss me off. You were the cause of a very good man's death—Jason, and now you're holding Sarah and me hostage for your twisted sense of revenge on the western world." I glance at Sarah, and her dulled expression has changed. She is pissed off as well. Her eyes have a shine that hasn't been there since we left San Francisco. Can she hate enough to help me get free of these insane people?

Winther isn't one to be put down, "You say I'm responsible for a good man dying? All the Muslims that your people have killed through the ages makes me want to laugh when I hear of the one good man."

Sarah bolts from her seat and grabs Winther by the throat. I jump up and turn to meet the biggest fist on earth right between the eyes. Momentarily stunned by the blow, I drop back into the seat. After taking care of me, the attendant grabs Sarah and throws her hard into the aisle. She gives a little shriek as she hits the floor. Winther jumps up, coughing. It looks as if Sarah may have cut his air off during the few seconds she had him by the throat. The attendant picks up Sarah and throws her roughly into her seat. He buckles her in and, as I start to come around, I see Sarah is pale. I guess she broke a rib when she hit. The attendant moves toward the galley where Jacobs sits reading his newspaper. I don't think he even looked up during the episode.

"You oka—"

Winther says, "Shut up, Cannon. You two are lucky you didn't get away with your trick. Why the hell did you think you could get away with trying to overpower me? What were you going to do?—Jump out the window at forty-five thousand feet?" He sits in his seat and rubs his neck, then turns to Sarah and asks if she's okay. She nods, but I can tell there's something wrong.

"I think your stooge broke a rib," I say.

"Well, if he did, Sarah deserved it." He turns to Sarah again. "Did something break?"

Sarah gives a weak smile. "It's nothing. I think I just bruised something."

Winther looks at me and frowns. "You better behave yourselves. Another stunt and we might as well part company along with a couple of thousand innocents, plus Sarah's then-to-be-highly-tortured-and-killed sister."

"Yeah, I'm sure," I say. Sarah closes her eyes and sighs.

"Oh good, here comes the food," Winther says.

With care, the attendant pulls Sarah's table out of the armrest and unfolds it across her lap. He places a tray with her meal on the table and asks if she would like something to drink. She asks for water in a strong voice, and I'm glad to hear it. He places Winther's tray, takes his drink order, and then goes back to the galley. I ask, "You feel better?"

"Yes," she says.

Winther doesn't look up from his tray. The attendant returns and lays the tray on the table I've pulled out of my armrest. "I'll have another water, please." He delivers Sarah and Winther's drinks, and then gets mine.

We finish eating without any conversation. I needed to eat something. The salad goes down a little too fast, and Winther notices me wolfing my food. He doesn't say anything, but I can see a little reproach in his expression. He takes his time and finishes like a gentleman. Obviously, he hasn't missed any meals recently.

After the attendant clears away the trays, I close my eyes again. I'm ready to drop off when I sense someone standing next to me. I figure it's the attendant, so I tell him without looking that I don't need anything more. Jacobs says,

"Well, I'm so happy we've taken care of all your needs. Mind if I join you?" He waves Winther away and takes his seat. I'm now fully upright and alert. I glance at Sarah, and she looks a little nervous.

"By all means," I say. Even though Jacobs is already sitting in Winther's seat, I decide to answer him politely.

"Thank you. Now, what was all this unpleasantness a while ago?"

"I guess Sarah and I wanted to try and do something to help our situation."

Jacobs sits and looks at me. By the surprised look on his face, he'd expected some cock and bull story but got the truth instead. The truth impresses him, no matter who tells it. The truth surprises leaders of companies, as they hear so much crap from subordinates that they fully respect the truth even if it comes from an enemy.

Chapter Eighteen

"I hope you understand that we won't tolerate any more outbursts." He delivers his message in a carefully controlled way that leaves no doubt to the severe consequences if disobeyed. "Now, since the unpleasantness is over, I wonder if Winther gave you a briefing on what we want you to do?"

"Yes, he did. You want me to lie to the American people about your attempt to kill Annapolis midshipmen. You also want me to lie and say the oil-producing countries are being prevented from producing more oil by the United States."

"Correct. I'm pleased with Winther. He seems to have covered the subjects well." He raises his voice and congratulates Winther, who now sits in the rear.

"You've placed me in a difficult position."

He raises his eyebrows. "How so?"

"If I tell those lies, number one: You and Winther will have gotten away with a terrorist mission. Number two: There will be political mayhem and turmoil while the markets and the politicians try to make some sense of the idea that there's enough oil available to be able to lower prices. The President will be in a bad position since it will look as if he has been lying to the people. OPEC will be pissed off that the world now thinks it has no power to control prices I'll bet they will raise prices just to show who's in charge. I can see some negative effect on oil stock in the confusion. All in all a very difficult time for everyone in government and in oil."

"I have to agree with you. The pain delivered to the western world is why we thought up this little plan. You caused us to fail in our previous attempt to blow up the Annapolis midshipmen to score a spectacular event. In retrospect, you're the inspiration for this plan. You got your face on every major magazine and in front of every TV camera. 'John Cannon, the American hero' was broadcast everywhere. You were something. The President is furious right now. The cancelation of the medal ceremony denied him a perfect occasion to spout more anti-Muslim propaganda. I guess the little shot at Stephanie took it off the table."

"You'll be awfully pleased with yourself then."

"Oh, my dear man. I'm so pleased with myself that I might even find a way to reward you for your help."

"I should feel grateful?"

"It doesn't matter what you feel. The point is, we have a job to do, and you're going to help. If you decide you don't want to help, well, I'm sure Winther described what would happen."

"He did, but I want to hear it from you."

"There isn't a whole lot to say. If you don't help us, your girlfriend and a bunch of other folks are going to be martyred for the cause."

"This doesn't bother you?"

"Well, if you mean by blowing up those people because you wouldn't allow us to complete our plan, then yes, it would bother me."

"No, I mean killing innocent people."

"They are the same as you and are not innocent. They've been born on the wrong side of perpetual combatants who will only stop fighting when my people are given their rightful homeland back. It's not their fault, but it's their fate."

I grit my teeth. "There's no talking with you."

"There is no talking 'innocent' because there are none on your side of the conflict."

"And on your side?"

"I believe we are all innocent, and it wasn't our people who took the heritage lands away. It was your culture that decided we were no longer the rightful overseers of Palestine. Think for a moment how you would feel if a bunch of soldiers moved into your neighborhood and then told you to find a different place to live if you didn't care for what was going on. If you decide to stay, then think of being under military law with no rights whatsoever."

"This is still your viewpoint. There are two sides to every issue. Didn't the Jewish settlers have a right to live as well?"

"Okay, let's go back to my example concerning your neighborhood. What if a bunch of people moved into your area and simply squatted on the unoccupied land? Because of their political power, the world politic gave them the land, and you found yourself having to make the choice to stay or go."

"Yeah, well, I can say I wouldn't care for it, but I can also tell you I wouldn't be killing people over it."

"You only think you wouldn't." Jacobs rises. "I believe you would be capable of killing those who were taking away what belonged to you. You smugly say you wouldn't because you have never been in our position. Also, if you, like me, lost some people very dear to your heart at the hands of your enemy, you wouldn't think twice about who is innocent and who is guilty. Thank you for the chat." He walks back to the rear of the airplane and he and Winther discuss something that seems important, as Winther frowns deeply.

I lean over to Sarah, "You okay?"

"I am. I think," she says.

"I don't know how we're going to get out of this mess. Speaking of mess, have you given any thought to what'll happen if the government discovers you're missing?"

"I try not to think," she says. "I know I'll be in a lot of trouble, but I figure as long as I'm alive, everything else is secondary."

I nod, and can only agree.

She looks out through the window, leans her head back against the seat, and is out of the conversation. I lean back and close my eyes again. I wish I could take her attitude and be in the moment and not worry. It'll never happen, though.

I must've fallen asleep again since the sound of the pilot's voice causes me to twitch like a dog on a couch. He speaks directly to Jacobs over the public address system, "We are beginning our final approach to the Guayaquil airport. Please, check to make sure you are buckled in."

I look over at Sarah, and she must have been asleep as well, as she has the soft look of someone just waking up. She gives me a weak smile and checks her seatbelt.

Winther isn't back in his seat opposite me yet, and I guess he spent the rest of the trip with Jacobs. "I wonder what those two had to discuss." With a nod of my head, I indicate Jacobs and Winther in the back.

"I'm sure it will involve us, whatever it is."

I smile at Sarah's humorous response. I then think how glad I am that she didn't help these guys of her free will. Surely the government can find a way to declare somebody innocent if they're being forced to commit acts that are illegal. I try to think of a legal precedence that might apply. Unfortunately, I keep coming back to the letter of the law. You do the crime; you do the time. I make up my mind to research extenuating circumstances to try and figure out a way to launch a reasonable defense once we are out of this situation. Of course, she hasn't appointed me her lawyer yet, but worse case, I could be of assistance to whomever she does appoint.

The airplane makes a banking turn, and I can see the city out the window. This is my first visit to Ecuador, so this scene looks new. Being green, it's a complete contrast to the sandy look of Mustang Island. It hits me all of a sudden that I don't have my passport with me. I had no reason to carry it to Washington, as I didn't think I'd be leaving the country. Of course, this could be a nice opportunity to get away—I could simply tell the customs officials I don't have one, and they would throw me in a holding cell and send me on the next airplane back to the US.

"Psst, Sarah." She turns with a surprised look on her face. "Do you have your passport?"

"Why, no," she says.

"Great. I think this may be our way out."

"What do you mean?"

"When the customs officers want to see our passports, we won't be able to produce them, so they'll deny us entry to Ecuador."

"Yeah, but then what?"

"They'll take us away and put us on a plane to the US."

"You think Jacobs hasn't thought of this eventuality?"

Sarah's question causes me to stop and think. Jacobs will have thought the passport situation through. For us to get into the country, he'll have to produce phony passports. When he does, then Sarah and I just need to speak up, and it will be over.

Sarah looks at me seriously. "You know how he keeps me under control?"

"Yes. I mean, I'm just saying."

"If you value the life of Jason's sister and all those hospital folks, you know you'll say nothing."

Unfortunately, Sarah's right. No way will Jacobs let us simply walk away. Ready to land, the pilot deploys landing gear and the flaps. The moment passes, and the soft bump and slight screech of the tires tell me we're on the ground. The hangars and buildings are a blur as the nose settles into a parallel position to the ground. The reverse thrusters bring the speed down, so the scenery outside seems to pass by at a more leisurely pace.

Winther walks to our position. "I don't have to tell you to keep your mouths shut, do I?"

Sarah and I both shake our heads.

"Good. Here's how it's going to work. We'll taxi over to the executive aviation hangar. We will all stay on board, and a representative of the customs department of Ecuador will come aboard. The pilot will give him our passports. He will check to see if you two look like your pictures. He won't ask you anything, but if he does, just answer the question. Your passports are in the names of John J. Dannon and Sarah Dannon. You're married. The rest of the information on the place of birth and so on is exactly the same as your real passports. So, if they ask, just tell the truth. We chose Dannon because it's close to Cannon, and you won't get too confused. So that's it. Any questions?"

"Yes, I have a couple," I say.

Winther sighs. "I'm not surprised."

"What if the guy recognizes me?"

"He won't."

"What if he asks me a question I can't answer?"

"He won't."

"How do you know?"

"I thought you said a couple of questions?"

190

"Well, I don't want something to come up that might jeopardize Stephanie. That's all."

"Believe me, there won't be anything asked that you can't answer."

The airplane takes a hard right turn, which causes Winther to lose his balance. He grabs the back of my seat to steady himself. The airplane taxis to the front of the executive aviation hangar. The engines groan to a stop, and the attendant pulls the door release and hits the button to power the stairs into the down position. The warm, moist air of South America rushes into the cabin and seems wetter and hotter due to the dramatic shift from the cool cabin air. My first feeling is that I'm going to sneeze, which I stop with a deep breath.

Jacobs moves from his seat in the rear to a jump-seat opposite the door up front. He looks in the direction of the cockpit door as it opens. The pilot comes out and smiles at all of us in turn. Jacobs hands him a bunch of passports and the pilot goes through the airplane door and down the stairs. I can see the top of his head through the window, and the uniform cap of the person he is addressing. It looks to me as if the customs officers have arrived.

A few more minutes pass while the people outside continue speaking. The pilot talks in Spanish, and I think he's truly a valuable member of Jacobs' team. The cabin becomes uncomfortable, and sweat forms on my upper lip. Not a good sign. My psychosocial trial training taught me that a sweaty upper lip is a sign of someone nervous, or worse, lying. I wipe my lip with my hand, and the movement causes Winther to look over at me. He raises an eyebrow and seems to be telling me to stay calm. I glance at Sarah, and she looks as if she might want to be sick. I give her a little smile, but she doesn't respond. She dabs at her face with a paper napkin she saved from the meal.

As the tension rises, the pilot comes through the door, followed by a uniformed official. The pilot steps aside and the official stops in front of Jacobs. He looks at one of the passports and asks Jacobs his birth city. "Detroit," Jacobs says with a smile, and the official hands him the passport after making a note in it. A car pulls up beside the airplane. I'm afraid to take my eyes off the official, who heads toward me. He stops at my position and looks at another passport.

"Excuse me, Mr. Dannon, I need to know your city of birth."

"Nashville, Indiana," I say. I don't hesitate, and hope the passport says the same thing.

"One more question if I may. Are you any relation to the Dannon yogurt company?"

The question takes me totally off guard. I break out laughing at the ridiculous nature of the question. The official joins me, and I guess it's his idea of a joke. "I wish I were."

"Thank you, sir." He hands me my passport. "I think all is in order."

He then gives Sarah her passport. He touches his cap with his fingers and wishes us a pleasant stay in Ecuador. I look at Winther, and he gives me a "told you so" look. The official turns and exits the airplane.

Winther gets up and directs us to deplane and get into the waiting car. Jacobs has already gone down the stairs and is probably sitting in the car. Sarah and I move to the door, and a person waves us to the waiting SUV. A guy in black holds the door, so we descend the stairs and get into the vehicle.

Jacobs is, indeed, already in and sitting up front. Winther arrives last and asks Sarah to move to the middle of the seat. I assume he'll sit next to the window, but he surprises me by pulling the seat forward and climbing into the third row. The guy in black shuts the door, and Sarah moves over closer to the door. With Winther in the third row, Sarah won't want to sit too close to me. I miss the warmth of her arm, and it would have been nice to have her there for the trip, no matter how short. I don't understand my protective feelings for her, but they are there.

The SUV pulls away from the airplane and rolls up to an automatic gate next to the hangar. The gate inches open, and the SUV pulls through and makes a hard right onto an access road. The tarmac leads to a larger road, and we make a left turn and head away from the airport. None of us has said anything since we left the airplane. I'm not going to be the first to speak up, so I sit back and watch the scenery.

"You're pretty quiet for once, John," Winther says.

"I don't have a lot to say."

"You worried about the customs officer for nothing."

"Yeah, I guess I did." I'm not going to engage Winther in a childish game to satisfy his ego. He wants me to ask why it was so easy, and I'm not going to jump to the bait.

"Don't you want to know why there was no hassle?"

"Not really."

"Oh, come on, you know you're dying to hear how we did it."

"Paul, I couldn't care less. Why don't you impress Sarah with your tale?"

"Hey, leave me out of this. I don't care either."

"Boy, you two are a couple of whiners, aren't you?"

"We don't want to break the law, unlike the rest of you. We have no interest in learning how you persuaded those officers to let a couple of people into their country with phony passports."

"Okay, I get it. I just thought you'd enjoy knowing that those guys work for Mr. Jacobs. That's all."

"No, I don't enjoy knowing this information. In fact, it makes me want to heave."

"All of you. That's enough," Jacob says.

Chapter Nineteen

Winther sits back in his seat and keeps to himself. As we head into the city, I get a chance to look at the countryside. We pass a number of areas that look like industrial parks. The scenery doesn't look inviting, so I lean back and try not to think about what's ahead.

Eventually, we run out of industrial views and travel through the midst of a relatively sizable city. It doesn't take long before the SUV pulls into the driveway of a large building. A garage door inches upward when we approach. The garage sits under the building, and we make a descent down a long driveway into a huge, dimly lit parking garage. The driver pulls the SUV to a stop in front of a lobby area that stands out because it is well lit. Through the glass door, I can see two elevators.

Jacobs gets out of the front seat, and a guy opens the rear door and gestures for Sarah to follow Jacobs, who's already gone through the glass door. The driver opens my side and points toward the glass door. I get out and nod, understanding his direction. The driver smiles when I make my way around the rear of the vehicle and go through the door as well.

"We'll wait for Winther, and then go," Jacobs says.

I look back at the SUV and catch Winther having some trouble getting out of the rear seat. He likely hasn't had much experience sitting in the back. I smile. I'm sure when Jacobs isn't around, Winther is the one who rides up front.

Winther finally makes it to the door, and Jacobs punches a button on the little panel next to the elevator. The doors open and we all get in except for the driver, who climbs back into the SUV and pulls away. Jacobs calls out to Winther for the fourth floor. Winther hops to it and punches the button. The doors close, and I get the feeling we're going down not up. When we reach the fourth level, the slight force of stopping gives our downward direction away.

"Going down, huh?" I say. Neither Winther nor Jacobs answers. I look at Sarah, and she just shrugs as if she knew all along the direction would be down. I sigh, as I can't seem to catch a break on getting any acknowledgment from Sarah to confirm we should be conspiring to stop these guys. She's just going to go with the flow and not cause any trouble. I can't say I blame her, though, because right now it looks desperate for us both.

The doors open and Jacobs takes the lead. We file off the elevator, make a right turn, and walk down a long hall. Winther takes up the rearmost position. Not sure what that means, but it's different. We walk past a few doors then come to a double set of glass doors. Jacobs pushes one door open and holds it for the rest of us to pass through. When Winther gets past, Jacobs lets the door swing shut.

We stand in a business reception room. A counter sits at the far end, where you would expect to see a receptionist. Instead, a grumpy-looking guy sits there with some serious weaponry. He wears a Kevlar vest and has at least two automatic rifles lying on the counter. He bids Jacobs a good day and nods when Jacobs runs a security keycard through a reader next to a door. The door looks solid, and there's no telling what's behind it.

A buzz sounds, and Jacobs leans against the door, which opens slowly. The door seems to be of a heavy material, and I'd guess it takes some effort to move it open. Once the door is fully open, Jacobs waves us in and, as he did with the glass door, he lets this one move into the closed position. He waits until he hears a loud click engaging the lock.

We stand in a large warehouse room with several sound studios inside it. Jacobs hits a switch and the room floods with an intense light. Three studios take up the space in front of me.

"Welcome to our equivalent of Al Jazeera. We have a number of TV studios capable of broadcasting live or recorded messages to any place in the world. You will be giving your outstanding performance from studio three."

"Yeah? So when is this going to happen?" I want to find out as much as I can.

"We think the time will be right in two days."

"Why the delay?"

"We need to make certain you deliver the message when the President is out of the country. We want him to have the most trouble possible trying to head off what's sure to be a political disaster. We're trying to estimate when he'll be flying in Air Force One. We know he has communication capability, but think it will still cause some problems in setting up a broadcast from an airplane. Of course, after your little show, he'll want to get on the air as soon as possible."

"Tell me again what happens if I refuse?"

"Please, John. I wouldn't go there if I were you." Jacobs walks away and gives me a sign to follow him. When we get out of earshot of Sarah, he lowers his voice. "You refuse, and a bunch of people gets killed. It's simple. In fact, let me add a kicker. You refuse, and I'll see Sarah and her sister suffer more than you could imagine before they die as well." Jacobs looks to be an enraged bully. I want to punch his look into the next room, but figure I'll have accomplished nothing. I give my response a cool treatment instead, "Okay, Matt," I say. "You don't mind if I call you Matt, do you?"

"Why should I? It's my name." Jacobs is back to normal

"I just don't want to seem too presumptuous. After all, you have all the cards, and I don't need to give you any excuse to harm innocent people just because I've made you angry."

"Don't be silly. My anger at, or thoughts on you, have nothing whatever to do with this mission. You just need to do as I say, and everyone will be fine."

"What happens after the broadcast? Do Sarah and I go free?"

"After the broadcast, I'll make certain you both return to the US. I don't know why you would want to go there, as you'll be a pariah in your land. You'll be lucky to last a day. If some deranged commodity broker who bets the wrong way on the oil market doesn't take you out, I'm sure the FBI or some other agency will."

"Why do you say so?"

"You think the government is going to put up with the fact you accused them of manipulating the oil market? They'll think your whole broadcast is a terrorist act, and you'll never survive."

"I hope to be able to explain—"

"Yeah, sure, you can explain, while you're lying on a water-board choking and gasping for air, courtesy of Uncle Sam." Jacobs laughs at his joke. I don't think it's particularly funny, so I don't join him. I give him one of my bored looks, and he finally stops and resumes a serious composure.

"I think it's time to show you to your accommodations. Winther will take you to your rooms. I have some important matters, so please excuse me." Jacobs waves at Winther and motions him to come over. Winther walks over slowly and, when he gets close, Jacobs tells him to take Sarah and me to the overnight accommodations. Winther asks us to follow him, which Sarah and I gladly do.

Winther leads us out of the huge room and down a hall. He stops at a door with a security pad and punches in some numbers. I try to see what the numbers are, but he turns his back to Sarah and me. "Wouldn't do to let you see the code," he says. It is as if he can read my mind.

We go through the door and into another hallway with doors. "Come with me, and I'll get you settled," Winther says. He then pulls open the closest door and bids us enter. When we go in, I'm amazed to see a large room that looks like a lounge in a major hotel. It has the feeling of a concierge space, including comfortable-looking chairs, and some magazines on a low table in the center. A television sits off to the left side, and a self-serve bar runs along the right wall.

"I'll need to go and check into your rooms, so if you would make yourselves comfortable, I'll be back shortly. There's coffee and tea in the bar and if you would rather, all manner of cocktails. The ice is in the refrigerator under the bar." Winther turns and leaves the room, and the door closes soundlessly behind him. I quickly go to the door and try to open it, but to no avail. "We're locked in," I say. I try to sound casual but feel trapped. The only thing to do is see if Sarah wants something to drink. I walk back to her and sit in one of the chairs across from where she sits. "Would you care for something?"

She looks up and gives me a slight smile. "No, thank you. I don't feel I want anything right now. I'd like to ask you a question, though."

I'm surprised, as Sarah hasn't said many words since we met up again. I try to hide my surprise, but don't think I succeed. "Sure, go ahead," I say. It comes out a little too hurried for my liking.

"Is the girl, uh, Stephanie, your girlfriend?"

Where's this going? With a shrug, I give a straight answer, "No. She and I met as a result of her brother's death. She's Jason's sister. Jason was the one who—"

"I know the story. It's been in every newspaper for weeks. So, you and she aren't going together?"

"No, we only met briefly." I want to try and figure out what's on Sarah's mind before I make any statements on my affair with Stephanie.

"You're only acquaintances, then?"

"Yes, that's a good way to put it."

"Then why did Jacob's team decide to pick her as a method to get you to do what they want?"

Sarah surprises me with her logic. My response is the first thing that pops into my head, "I can only imagine they thought that killing all those people and, on top of it, someone I knew, would be a powerful persuader."

"I guess it worked."

"Well, I have to say, I'm not sure if I can go through with what they want me to do. I hope I can figure something out before the broadcast. Right now, I don't have a clue."

"I hope you know I was sorry to have helped them, but I had no choice."

"Yeah, I know."

"I wish we could have spent more time together and gotten to know each other better, as you once put it."

"Yeah, me too."

"Is it too late?"

I look at Sarah, and a feeling of wanting to protect her comes over me. Although she was the one to finger me for those assassins even though she didn't know it, I still have some feelings for her. After all, they held her hostage as well. I think a little more before I respond, "It seems it is too late for both of us. We may die here."

My fear the words would upset her proves to be well founded. Sarah looks down, and a huge tear falls from her eye into her lap. She doesn't seem to notice and sits crying softly. I can't stand it anymore and move over to her chair and pull her into my arms. We both slide down, ending up sitting on the floor, and she cries with big sobs as if ready for a complete breakdown. I try to comfort her, but she only cries harder. She wraps around my neck and squeezes me 'til I have difficulty breathing. I pull away slightly and look into her eyes. She resembles a wild animal caught in a snare—her look not one of terror but resignation. Her warm lips reach mine, and she pulls me into her with a passion reserved for lovers. I can't resist her sweet, salty taste and the magical way her tongue slips under mine. My heart responds to the desire, which has lain dormant since this situation started. I give in to her mouth and her embrace and respond in kind.

We don't hear the door open, and Winther clearing his throat causes us to jump like teenagers caught on the couch. "You two ready to go to your rooms, or do you need another minute here?"

"No, we're ready," I say. I look at Sarah, who nods and gets to her feet. She pulls me to mine, and we both smile. She asks Winther, "Is there a restroom near?"

He points to the door. "There's one in your room," he says. He starts for the door, and we follow. Sarah continues to sniffle, and I grab one of the cocktail napkins as we leave. She seems grateful as we follow Winther out of the room, and again we start down the hall.

After passing a few doors, Winther stops and tells Sarah this will be her room. Number three is on the door. The other doors we've passed didn't have numbers. Winther opens the door and signals Sarah should go inside. She turns and asks Winther, "Is there a key?"

"My goodness, no. We don't have keys for any of the rooms. You'll see a latch on the inside of the door if you feel the need to lock it."

"What happens if I leave the room?"

"You won't be going anywhere much. You'll join Mr. Jacobs, John, and me for dinner, but that's it. If you have anything of value, you can put it in the safe in the room. It's in the closet, and you can set the combination."

"What are the arrangements for breakfast?"

"Room service has a card on the desk. Just fill it out and put it on the door by midnight. The service will bring your breakfast to you. We'll rehearse John's broadcast tomorrow, and you're welcome to join us. Lunch will be in the studio, so if you don't want to watch the rehearsal, you should at least plan to be there by twelve thirty. Do you think you can find your way back there?"

"Oh, I think I'll be just fine. Thank you."

"Good. John and I'll come to get you for dinner at seven. The time between now and then will give you a couple of hours to rest and freshen up. You'll find your things in the room. Your suitcase is in there too."

Sarah has an expression on her face as if she wants to ask more, but she apparently decides not to. She thanks Winther and closes the door.

"Okay, John, follow me."

We pass a number of doors again and come to one with the number five on it. Winther opens the door, and I go inside. The room looks spacious and like the kind of well-appointed room you'd get at a five-star hotel. Two queen beds take center position, and a nice lounge area lies beyond.

"I'll swing by a few minutes to seven. You'll find everything you need. We're doing business casual tonight. No tie."

"Well, what a relief. I'm tired of wearing ties."

"You kill me." Winther lets the door swing closed, and I hear him still laughing as he goes down the hall.

I go to the closet and pull open one of the two doors. A couple of suits, some shirts, and a sports jacket hang from the rail. Some shoes sit on the floor. I go over to the chest of drawers and pull one open. Sure enough, underwear, socks, and pajamas line the drawer. All are neat and look to be new. Jacobs is like the government and seems to be the master clothier given the number of outfits he's provided. How does everyone manage to get me changes of clothing without measuring me? I shrug and check the waist size on the boxer shorts—thirty-fours. How would they know my size? The t-shirts are large, which is also my size. My curiosity gets to me, so I go to the closet and check the suit sizes as well. The suits are a forty-three regular and the shirts a perfect fifteen-and-a-half neck and thirty-floor sleeves. Two ties on a hook surprise me—I'd assumed Winther was kidding about the tie. A pair of slacks dangles from the same hanger as the navy sports coat. The khaki color goes well with the coat. The size is as perfect as all the others.

The only thing I'm missing is a belt. There's never a belt. Maybe they think I'll hang myself if they give me one. I go into the bathroom and check out the stock of shower and hair supplies. The bathroom's huge. Two pedestal sinks each have a mirror above. The backsplash is white beadboard topped with a shelf made of tile. The rest of the room contains a large soaking tub and a walk-in shower with two showerheads. A commode sits in a separate little room. The paneling of the entire room is white beadboard with white subway tile over the bathtub and in the shower. The overall effect is of a summer cottage somewhere by the ocean. The bath and hand towels have a design of white coral on a red background, which enhances this effect.

On the shelf, I find an assortment of shampoo and conditioner much the same as at a hotel. Also, a hair dryer hangs from a hook on the wall, and numerous French milled soaps lie in several places. The bathtub has a few loofa sponges in an attractive basket on one edge. It would be nice to soak a while. I go back to the bedroom to take off my clothes and, on the way, see a terry cloth robe on the back of the door. The hotel-like atmosphere is ridiculous, I think, but grab the robe.

While I undress, it occurs to me that the last change of clothes was at Jacobs' office this morning. No wonder they've gotten a little uncomfortable—what with the seven-hour flight, the heat, and all. I look for a place to stash them but have to be satisfied with the cleaning bag I find in the closet. I push everything in and seal the bag. I'm not certain I'll hang it on the doorknob of my room, but for now, it's out of sight.

With the robe on, I head to the tub. It's one of those with jets for creating a whirlpool effect, and big and deep. I turn on the hot and cold water and adjust the jets, so the water is slightly hot but not scalding. A small card describes how to operate the tub. The instructions ask that bath salts and bubble liquid not be used. I imagine that someone turning on the jets and creating a mountain of suds was the reason for this suggestion.

The water is finally deep enough to cover the jets, so I drop the robe and, cautious, put one foot in the tub. The water is hotter than I thought it would be, but I go ahead. I pull in the other foot and then sit down. The tsunami created by my body mass displacing the water nearly goes over the lip of the tub. I turn off the water and pull the stopper to let some of it run out. At last, I can relax and push the button that starts the air flowing through the water. It feels so good to relax, and I lean back, shut my eyes, and feel myself drifting into a light sleep.

"Hello, John," Sarah says. I sit up with a rush and splash water on Sarah, who sits on the floor next to the tub. She wears a terry cloth robe, and her hair is tied in a twist and up high on her head.

"How did you get in?"

"Your door is without a lock, so I just walked in."

"How long have you been sitting there?"

"Long enough to see you totally relaxed. Do you mind if I join you?"

I don't know what to say. Sarah is a beautiful woman, but I have mixed feelings on whether or not I can trust her.

"I'll take your silence as a yes," she says, and then stands and unties the sash on her robe. With a shrug of her wide and beautiful shoulders, the robe slips soundlessly to the floor. Stunned, I sit in the swirling water and can feel myself reacting to the sensuous curve of her waist and the sight of her full, slightly upturned breasts and the dark smudge of pubic hair. She smiles and lifts one long, well-toned leg over the edge of the tub. She doesn't have any tan lines, but her skin has the hue of someone who sunbathes in the nude. She brings her other leg over the lip of the tub and turns around with her back to me. Her back is every bit as beautiful as the front. Visible muscle tone defines her legs, back, and buttocks. Slowly, she sits down in the water, and the tide rises once more. My voice cracks when I ask her to hit the drain handle to let out a little more water. She giggles, and I can't tell if it's from my nervousness or the fact the water is rising as a result of both of us being in the tub.

She releases some of the water and then leans back, so she sits more or less between my legs with her back resting on my chest. She takes both of my hands and places my arms around her. "Now, isn't this nice," she says. I sigh and have to agree that it's heaven. The only problem I can see right now is that I'm reacting to the silky presence of her skin against me.

"You'll have to excuse him; he has no manners."

"Oh, I think he has enough manners to compliment a lady who's near."

Her words are all it takes for me to give in completely and stop worrying on the trustworthiness of Sarah or the present situation. All I can focus on are Sarah's hands on my arms and her soft hair against my cheek. To seal the deal, she takes my hand and places it on her firm breast. Her nipple stiffens in response to my touch. Gently, I squeeze her breast, and she sucks in a little air, letting me know this feels good to her. I move my hand down her side to her stomach. Her body arches as if to meet my hand. My temples pound, and I lose track of anything but Sarah. I'll not be able to survive if I don't consummate this passion. My heart thumps while I feel her slippery skin and trace my fingers down the crease formed by her raised leg. My hand comes to rest on the soft, tender spot on her inner thigh.

I haven't noticed until now, but Sarah has been moving slowly against me, so I can feel my arousal, but caught under her. I now realize she is rising up and spreading her legs to let me be positioned to touch her. She makes a back and forward motion that causes my member to rub against her in a provocative way. "Should we go to the bed?" I whisper.

"Not yet. This water, and you close feel so good. Don't you feel it?"

"I sure do, but I'm not sure I'll be able to do my best while lying in the water this way."

"Let me do the work. You just enjoy."

Sarah gets up on one knee, and then sits back down on top of me while guiding me into her. I feel as if I'm being swallowed up as she makes an up and down movement against me, and I can't possibly last too long. She makes a whimpering sound that I take to be enjoyment. With a firm grasp of her sides, I direct some of the movement, which causes her to moan "yes" a number of times. She reaches a climax two seconds before me.

We lay in the tub catching our breath. Neither of us has said anything for the last two minutes, so I break the silence, "That was something. Thank you."

"No need to thank me, John. I enjoyed it too."

"I know, call me old-fashioned, but I did appreciate getting together with you, after all this time."

"This won't be the last. Why don't we take a shower and you can demonstrate your winning techniques in the bed? How does that sound?"

"As if I should be trying to wake myself up since this dream is getting out of hand."

Sarah laughs, as I hoped she would, stands up, steps out of the tub, and goes into the shower. I follow her and, after a nice shower, we start again, but this time it's my turn to lead.

Chapter Twenty

When I hear a tapping at my door, I assume it's Winther since it's close to seven. So I'm not surprised when I open it to see that he has Sarah with him. She and I more or less avoid looking at each other. It's not from embarrassment or some other kind of awkwardness, but that we'd rather keep our personal lives to ourselves.

"You two enjoy the afternoon?" Winther asks while we walk down the hallway. Sarah and I exchange a quick glance. How much does Winther know? I make the assumption he knows nothing and speak for both of us, "It was very restful. Thank you."

Sarah stifles a smile, and it's a good thing we're following Winther because we now have the demeanor of two school kids. Winter says something that sounds close to "that's good." He doesn't say any more, so I assume he didn't know anything after all, and I congratulate myself for making the decision to stonewall on my response.

We stop before a set of double doors, and Winther knocks with the same tapping noise he used at my room. The door opens and a guy who looks like a butler bids Winther enter. Winther motions us in before him, and so we go through the door. The foyer looks huge, with a big staircase off to the right that leads up to another floor. The butler looking guy asks us to follow him. He climbs the staircase, which leads to a large room that could be a ballroom in a hotel. The room is set for dinner with a table covered in crisp linen off to the side and a large bar directly ahead. The butler informs us that the bartender will take our drink order, and one of the staff will offer a selection of hors d oeuvres once we have a drink.

Winther bows slightly and suggests ladies should be first. Sarah returns the bow and walks to the bar. I follow her with Winther.

"Excuse me, John—a word to the wise if I may."

Did I hear him correctly? "I'm sorry, what did you say?"

"All the rooms are wired for security. We have microphones and cameras everywhere."

"Oh," is the most I can think to say. Then I add, "I understand. Thanks for your observation."

He smiles.

Sarah has ordered a glass of white wine, and the bartender delivers it just as Winther and I arrive.

"What sounds good to you tonight?" The bartender asks.

"Well, I think I'll have what sounds good to me every night." The bartender gives me his full attention. "Tanqueray on the rocks with two olives, please."

Winther says, "I'll have the same."

The bartender turns away to make the drinks. I ask, "I thought you Muslims didn't drink."

Winther laughs. "I pray to be forgiven every night."

"What's on the agenda for the evening?"

"Mr. Jacobs enjoys having dinner with different types of people. Tonight, he is entertaining the President of Ecuador's special assistant and one of the army generals and their spouses. He is sure you will enjoy meeting them as well. You look quite lovely, Sarah. You have a nice glow."

Sarah stiffens at the complement but remains under control and thanks Winther. My drink arrives along with the same for Winther. He holds his glass up. "I propose a toast to the success of your broadcast and your safe return to the US."

"I can't drink to your objectives, Winther, but let me offer a toast as well. Here's to a Patriot missile that I hope will have you and Jacobs' names engraved on the warhead."

Winther laughs loudly. "Let's drink to the warhead then."

We take a sip of our drinks and Winther comments on how good the gin tastes. I nod in appreciation, and we don't say anything for a minute. I take another sip and wonder where all this is leading. Jacobs doesn't just do dinner without an ulterior motive. I can't see a tie into Ecuador, except that it's not part of the US and not bound by US law. There must be some other reason for coming here. The so-called broadcast could originate from anywhere, including within US borders. There would be nothing illegal with spreading lies, at least as far as I know. I'm no nearer to a possible reason when a young woman asks if I would care to choose something from her tray. I look and see she has a tray of canapés ranging from stuffed mushrooms to sushi. "I think I'd enjoy a little assortment if you don't mind." She smiles and lets me know she'll be right back. I turn to Sarah and ask if she would care for something.

"While you were deep in thought, the server took my order. I did the same as you and ordered an assortment."

"Let's go over to this little seating area," Winther says. He then proceeds to a small round table surrounded by four chairs. After he pulls one out, he motions to Sarah to sit. Sarah meanders over and takes a seat. I follow and sit next to her. Winther sits in the chair closest to me. As soon as we sit, the server comes back and presents each of us with a pleasing assortment of appetizers. We have Meguro Tuna sashimi, some lobster pieces, and a few crackers with hummus, cheese, and spread. It all looks delicious. The girl also places a napkin, silverware, and chopsticks by each plate.

I have an unusual ability to eat during times of stress, so I dig in. Sarah moves her pieces around with her fork. Winther has no reason not to dig in, but sits back and sips his drink. Maybe they've put drugs in the food, and that's why Winther isn't eating. Then my mind comes back to reality. If drugs are in the food, there'll be a way to target those who are to get it. Winther would be directing who got it and certainly not himself. So, I conclude, he's not eating because he doesn't want to eat. I continue to eat, as the food tastes good.

"When is Jacobs arriving with his guests?" I inadvertently spit out some crumbs when I ask the question, so I use my napkin to cover my mouth.

Winther doesn't answer me right away, and I assume he didn't hear me, but then he speaks up. "He should be here in a few minutes. He has a meeting with the special assistant to the President first. You have somewhere you need to be?"

I'm a little taken back with Winther's shortness but ignore it. I'm about to tell him I was just making small talk when I hear the arrival of Jacobs and his guests. Winther gets up and goes over to Jacobs, who stands with an attractive woman and a man in uniform. She looks stunning and reminds me at this distance of Angelina Jolie—thin with long brown hair and an engaging, warm smile. The General stands next to her, and looks as if he's from a booking agency. He wears gold braid, and a red sash wrapped around his large belly. Another woman stands with them and could be either the special assistant or the general's wife. She looks matronly and seems to stay in the background. I'd say she's the wife, as she makes sure she doesn't take away from his presence. So the stunner is the special assistant.

Jacobs talks expressively with the assistant, and she seems attentive to his every word. I don't see an escort for the assistant, so I think she came alone. It seems Jacobs is a bit too attentive, but who am I to say? Now he directs the special assistant's attention over to Sarah and me. "Looks as if we have company," I say. Sarah looks at me, and I nod toward Jacobs. She gives me a sarcastic-looking "how great," expression and rolls her eyes.

Jacobs, the general, and slightly behind him, his wife approach, and I get out of my seat with a frown. "I want you to meet the special assistant to the Ecuadorian President," Jacobs says. "Mrs. Bastrop, this is the famous John Cannon."

"I'm so very pleased to meet you, Mr. Cannon. You're quite famous in our country, and we are very pleased to have you as a visitor." She extends her hand, and since my mother would slap me a good one if I didn't, I accept it.

"I'm pleased to meet you as well. May I introduce Sarah Barsonne, who is also a visitor to your beautiful country?" Sarah doesn't get up, which makes for a little clumsiness, but does take Mrs. Bastrop's hand.

"Also," Jacobs says. "I want to introduce General Torres and his wife, Mrs. Torres."

When I shake the general's hand, I feel he has a strong grip. He smiles, but I'm not so sure that he enjoys this diplomatic chore. He'd be happier out with his men on some maneuver. I reach out for Mrs. Torres' hand, and I feel like I'm holding a baby bird in mine. Her oh so delicate fingers seem to twitch at my touch. The server approaches.

"Mrs. Bastrop, would you care for a drink?" Jacob says. She orders a glass of white wine, and Jacobs asks the General and his wife. They order wine as well. Jacobs goes over to the bar with the server.

"So, Mr. Cannon," Mrs. Bastrop says. "Mr. Jacobs tells me that you have an interesting story to tell, and you're going to broadcast it the day after tomorrow."

"Not sure it's all that interesting, Mrs. Bastrop."

"You can call me Connie. Why do you say *not all that interesting?*"

"What has Mr. Jacobs told you already?"

"He just said you had some facts to share on the terrorist threat against the Annapolis midshipmen."

"Well, I think you'll need to wait for the broadcast because you have all the information available right now."

Mrs. Bastrop gives me a funny look. Sarah looks pleased with my answer. I shrug to indicate that I'm helpless to say any more. I want to tell her the information is private but don't want to insult her. Before I can say anything, Jacobs comes back with a tray and the wine. He is gracious, and I wonder why a billionaire needs to bother with these two. It may be that he has some designs on Mrs. Bas—er, Connie, and is trying to be a good host.

An awkward moment follows after the first sip of wine where no one knows what to say. Jacobs breaks the silence with a description of the menu for tonight's dinner. His guests all seem to be interested in what he says, but for me, I could care less. I'm still trying to figure out the whole situation and am somewhat distracted.

Dinner is ready and we all sit-down. We are more or less seated boy and girl, except for Winther being next to the general, who sits next to Jacobs. The meal is good and moves along well enough. Jacobs acts the charming host and involves each of the people at the table in the conversation. No controversial subjects come up. The talk moves from the weather to suggestions on what to see while in Ecuador, as if we are a bunch of tourists. I mention Mrs. Bastrop's question on the broadcast, which brings a halt to the discussion. Jacobs quickly changes the subject and shoots me a dark look. I say little else.

Dessert is served along with coffee and after-dinner drinks. I pass on dessert but order an amaretto and coffee. While the group finishes, Jacobs tells a story involving his childhood. He relates how a Muslim holy man raised him and that he didn't know his father and mother. His older brother was in charge of the family business since his parents died during a bombing raid in the six-day war. This brother arranged to have him placed where he would be trained and educated in strict orthodox Muslim doctrine. Once he became of age, he joined his older brother in the business, where he seemed to have a knack for making the business grow. He moved the small pipeline business into a major multinational company, including one of the most successful worldwide suppliers of telecommunications equipment. I thought it interesting he made no mention of his wife and children.

While he talks, I think about how I met him through his telecommunications division. I'd been working for a competitor as their litigation attorney and had brought suit against Jacobs for patent infringement. Jacobs lost the case, and unfortunately, I embarrassed him, which he hasn't forgotten. I'm deep in thought when it becomes obvious Jacobs has asked me a question.

"I-I'm sorry; I was thinking of something else."

"I wondered if you would care to join us in a game of bridge."

"Oh, I'm sorry, but I don't play."

Jacobs smiles and looks pleased, and I'm sure he wants to spend a little time with his new Ecuadorian friends. He rises, and the rest of the group follows suit. He turns to Sarah and me, "We will meet for rehearsal tomorrow, and Sarah is free to join. If not, lunch will be at twelve-thirty." Then he turns to Winther, "Please, show our guests back to their rooms."

We bid our goodbyes to the General, his wife, and Connie Bastrop, and follow Winther to the hallway.

Once out of the room, I ask Winther, "What's going on between Jacobs and Connie?" Sarah gives me a shocked look, which reflects my audacity in asking. Winther chuckles and says that he knows nothing. "Besides," he says. "Even if I did know anything, what makes you think I would tell you?"

"Aw, come on. You know I'm doomed, so what's the difference?"

"John, you're a strange person. You never seem to know when to give up."

"I guess it's what keeps me going. You and I have been enemies for only a month, but it seems as if it's been years."

Winther laughs out loud but doesn't say any more. I'd half hoped he felt ready to engage in a little discussion that would give me some details of what will happen, and then I could prepare some defensive move. It's clear that won't happen.

"Here we are," Winther says.

We stand outside my room. "Well, good night," I say. I look at Sarah for any signal from her on what the rest of the night will bring. She remains expressionless as if she doesn't even know me. I open the door, go in, and turn around for one last check. Winther and Sarah have already begun to move down the hall. I close my door, but don't deploy the latch in case Sarah decides to come back. I have a feeling I'll be spending the night alone, however. Perhaps just as well, as there are cameras in the room. Why didn't I mention them to Sarah? Maybe I didn't want her embarrassed by this afternoon's activity. A darker motivation might be that I don't want to scare her off from coming back for more. Since the latter seems more accurate, I reckon I'm a bit of a bastard.

With a smile, I kick off my shoes and sit in one of the lounge chairs. I need to locate those cameras so that, if I ever come up with a plan to get out of here, I might be able to avoid or deactivate them. However, seated in the chair, I can't see anything. I don't want to look too obvious to whoever is watching while I start my search. It's a good assumption that they'll be up high in the room. I look in each corner, and all I can see is an infrared motion detector. When I get up, the little red light comes on and stays on as long as I'm moving. Why is a motion detector in the room? I don't recall seeing a security keypad near the door. In case I missed it, I walk over to the door—nothing even remotely resembling a security keypad. Obviously, this motion detector is here to make certain that when the occupant of this room moves, the observation personnel is aware of it.

Is a camera in with the detector, like in the last room Jacobs supplied? It could well be that the detector is a dummy, and the camera is part of the detector apparatus. If there is a camera in the corner, the whole room will be visible. The only part not visible is the closet and the bathroom. I walk into the bathroom but don't turn on the lights. After I shut the door, I sit on the commode. If there is a camera here, it'll be impossible to see anything in the pitch-blackness. Of course, they might have night vision technology, and then the blackness wouldn't hinder observation. When I get up from the commode, I see a red glow in the opposite corner. A detector is in the bathroom as well. Damn.

I open the bathroom door to see if I can detect any reflection of a camera lens. I open the door slowly, wider and wider while looking back into the bathroom. Nothing reflects the light of the bedroom. The guys watching me probably think I've lost it—sitting in a dark room and then opening the door as I did are not normal things to do. I'd better knock it off before they send in a pack of goons.

I'm forced just to be satisfied with knowing there are cameras and let it go. I can't see how knowing the location is going to benefit me. Short of carving a hole out of the rear of the closet and going through it, I don't see how I can avoid being noticed if I try an escape. This idea of planning to escape seems so fruitless. If I did escape, Winther and Jacobs would just eliminate Stephanie and all those innocent people at the hospital.

In frustration, I fall on the bed and call it a night. When I pull my clothes off, I leave them on the floor. Then I get up and turn off the lights, and ease back into bed. I watch the infrared detector, and once I'm still, the red light goes out. How much movement sets it off? I raise my arm, and the light comes on. I move my feet under the covers and nothing. With the position of the motion detector, there could be a blind spot low on the left side of the bed below the mattress level.

I'll try to slip over the left side of the bed and onto the floor to take advantage of the blind spot if it's there. I won't be able to see the light, but hopefully I'll detect its reddish glow if I trip it up. When I turn over onto my stomach, the glow of red indicates that my movement has activated the camera. I wait until the red reflection goes dark again, then put out my arm and place my hand flat on the floor. I wait, but no red reflection. With my right hand, I push myself head first over the side of the bed and leave my legs and feet still on the bed under the covers. No reaction comes from the motion detector.

My breath comes heavily, and so I wait a moment to calm. Gently, I pull myself forward until my legs lay at the edge of the bed. I wish I were on my back because I would have more control, but I need to finish what I started. To keep noise and movement to a minimum, I'll try and drag my feet down the side of the bed. I pull my body forward and then, before I know it, my legs have dropped to the floor with a loud thump. I wait for the red glow of the detector. Nothing happens.

I'm out of the bed on the floor, and the detector hasn't picked up the movement. I'm totally amazed. Flat on my side, the bed shields me from the detector. Could I make it to the closet without being detected? Once in there, I could move all I wanted to prepare whatever I figure out needs preparing. The best way to try and cross the room would be to slither like a snake on my belly. Despite feeling a bit silly, I roll onto my stomach and pull myself across the floor. I move carefully and use my elbows to act as the propulsion vehicle. It's what soldiers do when they go under barbed wire. If I move too much, I'll know when I see the red glow hit the floor. I'll keep going until it shows up. Sweat drips down my forehead. It doesn't take long to enter my eyes and sting. I wipe my eyes on my upper arm, but it doesn't help much.

Finally, I reach the closet door and am thankful I left it open. With a last effort, I go through the door by bending my upper body and sort of jack-knifing through the entrance. I roll onto my back and pull my legs up to my chest. I'm now fully out of the range of the motion detector. To let my breathing catch up, I pause for a moment. Then, with a roll to my right, I get to my knees and stand by putting one leg at a time under me. The pitch black of the closet doesn't give me any clues as to where things are. I reach out and touch the clothes, and remember the layout. Then I push some of the clothes aside and place my hand on the rear wall.

The wall seems to be hollow. When I knock gently, the sound tells me that the wall is one-half inch drywall and would be no problem breaking through to the other side. The question is, what's on the other side? I believe it's the hallway, but can't be sure.

Tomorrow will be soon enough for checking. I'll not be able to escape, but there might be an advantage in being able to move out of my room without anyone knowing. The drill's over for the night, and I should get back in bed. It won't matter if the detector goes off when I step out of the closet. With the lights out in the room, the goons won't know if I set it off getting out of bed or if I'm on the other side of the room. I step out of the closet and go to the bathroom. After I turn on the light, I run the water, take a face cloth, and put it under the faucet. With all the sweat, a nice cool cloth will feel good. I squeeze it to remove the excess water and wipe my face. That feels so much better. With the light out, I drop the cloth into the sink, and then return to the bed and lay down with a sigh. Although I still have no plan, I feel like I've accomplished something. I'll be able to sneak out of the room undetected, at least. In no time, I fall asleep.

Chapter Twenty-One

I wake and immediately look at my watch—seven o'clock. Given the deepness of my sleep, and the darkness of the unwindowed room, I hope it's in the morning and not at night. If I had a phone in the room, I'd be tempted to call the operator and ask for the time. The room does have drapes looking as if they cover windows, but they're just decoration like the last place.

With the assumption it's the morning, I decide to take a shower and get ready. While I head to the bathroom, a light knock sounds at my door, and I divert to open it. A guy, who looks like a waiter, stands and holds a covered tray. "Room service," he says. He doesn't wait for me to let him in but just moves by me as if he does this all day. He steps over to the coffee table by the couch, places the tray on the table, and removes the cover. An assortment of toast and muffins and, most importantly, a silver pot of coffee sit on the tray. The waiter pours from the pot, and I smell the special blend of coffee Jacobs favors. He sets the pot down and says, "There is also juice and some yogurt in a bowl filled with ice."

I'm not sure if he expects a tip, but I thank him, and he turns to leave. "Will there be anything else?"

"Is it morning or evening?"

He looks a little confused, but finally tells me, "It is morning, sir."

"There will be nothing else," I say. He leaves. Hungry and groggy, I could use a big gulp of the coffee. I move to the table and am pleased to see cream and Splenda along with the coffee. After I pour the cream, I add the Splenda and take a sip. I can't get over how delicious the coffee tastes. It is truly the best on Earth. I take another sip and walk to the bathroom with the coffee. A hot shower will do me good, and I turn it on. While it heats, I think of when Winther plans to pick me up. I don't recall him mentioning a time last night, so I guess I'll get dressed, have some breakfast, and wait for his knock. The water is ready, so I set the cup of coffee on the vanity with reluctance, drop my robe and step into the hot water. I adjust the temperature to a more skin-friendly level. Once there, I put my face into the stiff stream of water. Then I open a bar of triple-milled soap and lather up. I cover all of me with the sweet-smelling lather, and then rinse. The effect causes my skin to tingle and my mood to lift.

After the shower, I dress and finish a second cup of coffee. I also try one of the pastries and find it to be one of the best I've had. As I contemplate another, a small knock interrupts my thoughts, and I go to the door and pull it open. As I suspected, Winther stands there. I invite him in, and to my surprise he takes me up on my hospitality.

"Care for some coffee?"

"No, thanks. I've already had mine, but you go ahead and finish." He sits in one of the easy chairs and crosses his legs. He looks much younger these days, and I wonder if he uses makeup or something. He smiles then asks a question that causes me to wonder why the concern, "Did you sleep well?"

"Yes, very well." I'm still a bit cautious giving Winther any information. "It's not like you to show concern."

"You know, John, under different circumstances, you and I could have been good friends."

"What makes you say so?"

"Well, think about it. We're both successful and driven by our passions. You were in love with your boat, and I love my quest. We're also intelligent and know how to make things work. Am I right?"

"I'm not sure you're right in making things work, but I'll have to agree on the intelligence."

"This is why I can't figure out how you managed to get yourself into this mess. I mean, look at you. We have you by the short hair, so to speak, and you have no hope of getting out of this situation. Well, there is hope, but I don't think you're wise enough to do what's necessary to be free of all of this once and for all."

"You've lost me. I don't know what you mean by, *do what is necessary.*"

"Let me be clearer to you, then. We've coerced you into making a broadcast that will cause a tremendous amount of upheaval in the American political scene. This broadcast will take place and then you'll have to face the consequences of your actions. Sure, you'll have the knowledge that you did what you thought was best for all those innocent people we hold as hostages, but the result will be that you'll find no peace or justice in your system. You'll be an outcast, and the government will figure out a way to charge you and put you into a torturous situation for the rest of your life. You'll be lucky to survive."

"Yeah, does sound grim. Thank you for retelling my future for me."

"It doesn't have to end the way I describe."

"You have a better way?"

"Why don't you join us? We can protect you from your fate. You can be part of a movement that one day may, in fact, rule the world. I'd even bet that you could become one of the leaders and have a following of millions. Wouldn't this be better than rotting in Guantanamo Bay with no fingernails?"

"What makes you believe I'd seriously consider this proposal? Even if I accepted, what makes you think I'd live up to my end of the bargain?"

"We think you have a tremendous amount of political credibility already built with your heroic save of the Annapolis midshipmen. We think that squandering political credibility on a government that won't appreciate you shouldn't happen. Our movement can not only use the credibility wisely, but it can also build on it to make you into a world leader."

"You're telling me that Jacobs would approve a plan that would put me in a world leadership position?"

"He's already blessed the plan. He was impressed, by the way, with how the world press took a liking to you. He hates you, as you know, but he didn't become a billionaire by allowing personal feelings to stand in the way of sound judgment."

"So what would I have to do?"

"Not much, really. Once you finish the broadcast, you simply join us rather than going back to the US."

"That's all? Stephanie and those people in the hospital?"

"All set free. You have my word."

"Your word? Isn't there another form of guarantee?"

"Well, if you truly join us, there won't be a need for a guarantee. In time, you won't care for anyone or anything but the movement, and I know you'll become a true believer, just like me."

"What happens to Sarah?"

"I think she'll make a fine first lady, don't you?"

"What does she think?"

"She doesn't know anything. It would be your job to explain it to her."

"What if she doesn't agree?"

"She'll be free to go just as you're free to go. Her life won't be as wretched as yours since her defense team could argue she was an innocent pawn. I don't think her participation in the original scheme, plus the fact she has a body double under surveillance, will be something easily explained away. She may take the entire fall, given they have no one else to blame. You might just point this out to her as you explain her options."

"How long do I have to decide?"

"I would say you have up to your broadcast to decide. All you have to say after the broadcast is that you want to stay with us, and it will be a done deal."

"Either way, though, Stephanie and the others go free?"

"That is correct."

Now I have something to think about more seriously. I'm positive I don't want to join this pack of pirates, but this may give me some leverage while I try to figure out what to do to stop the execution of their plan. Winther sits and looks rather pleased with himself. I'm sitting with a cup of cold coffee in my hand. Neither of us seems to want to break away from the moment. I clear my throat.

"Okay, I'll think on it."

"Also, John, it will give us an opportunity to understand each other further."

I have no real desire to understand Paul Winther in any additional detail I don't already have. He is a cold-blooded killer willing to do anything for his cause. Winther's motivation is all I need to understand. I let it ride. "Yeah, I guess we could use further understanding."

Winther gives me a smile, and I can tell he doesn't believe I meant what I just said. I want to tell him I don't believe what I just said either, but then why give him anything? "Okay," he says. "I can wait for your decision. We have plenty of time. Are you ready to go to the broadcast studio and rehearse, or do you want more breakfast?"

"No, I'm ready to go. What's Sarah doing?"

"We'll stop by her room and see if she wants to go with us or come later."

"It would be a lot easier if you guys had telephones."

"Oh, sure, so then you could call your police and FBI friends? I don't think so."

We both get up, and I can see Winther liked my comment on the telephones—it gave him an opportunity to crack a joke. He loves to joke. He holds the door for me, and we leave the room. We walk to Sarah's room without saying anything. Winther knocks on the door lightly, and I hear Sarah coming to the door. She opens it, and it's obvious she won't be joining us. She looks out the door but keeps her body behind it as if she doesn't want us to see her nightclothes.

Her face has the appearance of just getting out of bed. Her hair is messy, and she has mascara under her eyes. She may have been crying, but I can't tell for sure, although her eyes seem puffy. Her skin has a ruddy look. In a husky voice, she says, "I didn't sleep well and will catch up with you later."

Winther and I tell her it isn't a problem and leave her. I look back and see her door close slowly. For a second, I have a flash. Maybe she wasn't alone in the room—she acted as if we'd surprised her, although she must have expected that we'd come to pick her up sooner or later.

A picture forms in my mind of someone partying the night before, who simply forgot to set an alarm. I don't know how to verify my assumption, and what Sarah does or doesn't do is none of my business. There's no commitment to a relationship, and for all I know, what happened yesterday will never happen again. The thought leaves me with an empty feeling that's hard to explain. Rationally, I know lovemaking with Sarah may have been a one-night stand, but I wish it weren't true. I think back to Stephanie as well. I truly enjoyed being with her, but if we never get together again, I don't have the same hopeless feeling. The lack of hopelessness makes Winther's idea about Sarah as first lady more appealing, which is a sad commentary on my mental state.

Could it be that I've fallen in love with Sarah? It could be possible. When we went out back on Mustang Island, I'd felt attracted to her instantly. I wanted to get to know her better and even told her so. I'd had no idea that she'd only gone out with me because Jacobs ordered her to do so. Yesterday's session led me to believe she has feelings for me. It could be that she's still working for Jacobs, and he ordered her to make love to me, but I doubt it.

If she does have someone in her room now, it will provide some evidence that she did, in fact, only make love with me for some ulterior reason. This thought makes for a depressing feeling. It seems I'm going to have to believe in Sarah and the fact she only did what she did because she was being intimidated. If I think or believe otherwise, there can be no possibility of a relationship with her, and the thought makes me sad to the point of tears.

"Take a left," Winther says. I pop out of my daydream and see we've reached the studio. We stop at the double doors, and Winther opens the right side and motions for me to go ahead of him. "We'll use Studio A. Follow me." Winther brushes by and takes a position in front of me. We walk down the hall until we come to a door marked Studio A—Authorized Personnel Only. This is the back entrance to the studio. Winther holds the door again, and I go through to a pitch-black room. "Hold on, John, let me get the lights." I stop until light floods the room. We've entered a control room.

Through the glass, I notice a studio made to look like someone's living room. Two comfortable chairs have a low table between them. My guess is that I'll be asked to broadcast along with an announcer. Will I have a script? Maybe the format will be question and answer. In any case, the set looks as if it's right out of a late night talk show.

"Is there a script?" I ask the question out of the blue, so I'm not surprised when Winther has no idea what I'm saying.

"Script?" He pauses then gets what I mean. "Oh, a script. Yes, there will be a script. We have a moderator who will kick off the session, but after, your comments will be scripted. We'll need to spend some time with the teleprompter, so you're comfortable with it."

"That's good because I'm not too hot at memorizing."

"Yeah, you won't have to worry. You'll have three teleprompter screens so, no matter where you look, your script will be visible to you. Let's get a cup of coffee, and I'll introduce you to the producer and the moderator."

We leave the studio and go across the hall to another room. When we enter, a couple of people excuse themselves and leave. Four comfortable-looking chairs surround a low table. Two men sit in a deep discussion and look up as we approach. They both stop talking and rise from their chairs.

"I want you to meet your producer and moderator," Winther says. "Gentlemen, this is John Cannon. John, this is Sammy Speale, your producer, and Clive Gibbons, the moderator."

We shake hands as if this is a business meeting, and Winther asks us all to sit. He pulls up a chair from a table across the room and joins us. He looks around, gets back up, and goes over to a sideboard, which holds coffee and muffins. "Anyone want a cup while I'm here?"

I thank him but decline. The others decline as well. He shrugs, and then fixes a cup. He comes back to his chair, sits, and takes a sip of coffee. He looks at Speale and Gibbons and asks, "What's the plan?"

Gibbons speaks up, "The script is ready, and we thought there would be a first run-through before lunch."

Winther seems pleased. "So where is the script?"

"It's in duplicating right now," Speale says. "It should be here any moment."

"Ah, good." Winther sits back and enjoys his coffee. "You two are familiar with John's exploits, are you not?"

Gibbons and Speale look at each other and nod to the affirmative. They don't have a lot to say. It might be that they're a little intimidated by Winther. Finally, Gibbons speaks, "You're the one who messed up the Midshipman mission, aren't you?"

"If you mean I messed it up, so your band of cutthroats didn't rule the day, then yes, I messed it up."

"Whoa," Gibbons says. "I'm not part of this group. I'm being held here the same as you. I have a family back in LA, living under the fear of death if I make a mistake."

I'm speechless. I turn to Speale and ask, "Are you a hostage as well?"

"My family was taken from my home a week ago, and I've been told to produce this show or else."

I look at Winther, who has somewhat of a self-satisfied smile on his face. "Will you people go to any end to get what you want?"

"Well, you've finally figured us out. Bravo."

Gibbons and Speale have the look of two guys scared to death. They have that caught-in-the-headlights stare. "Don't you two worry. Winther and I go way back, and he won't hurt you or your family as long as you do what he says."

Chapter Twenty-Two

Winther doesn't get my sarcasm. "Why, thank you, John. I couldn't have said it any better."

I ask, "What do you guys do in real life?"

Gibbons says, "I'm an anchor news person for an LA television station. I suppose they chose me because I'm familiar with how to deliver a news broadcast. I don't know why, specifically, they want me." I turn to Winther, and he has no comment.

Speale says, "I'm a producer of documentary films and some live television. I did an exposé of some nasty drug folks and got put up for a journalism award."

"Do you know who Winther represents?"

"I don't," Speale says.

"Winther and his cohorts are out to destroy the West and will stop at nothing."

Speale nods. "I figured out their objective. Wait until you see the script."

"How bad is it?"

Winther says, "You'll see it soon enough." He gives us a hard look. "In the meantime, you all need to work together, so I hope you'll keep the nonsense down for the sake of those you hold dear."

We each look at Winther as if he'd just thrown up on a buffet table. I sit back and fold my arms. It's silly to try and have a conversation in front of him. These two guys don't know anything and will, in all probability, be useless in helping generate a plan to get out of here. Will they be free after they finish their work? I want to ask, but need to wait for a more private time. It occurs to me that with this many people being held hostage there must be a plan that we can all work out. Maybe if I concentrate on a way to capture Jacobs and turn the tables on him, I might be able to get something cooking. I'm in deep thought when a sound behind me causes me to turn and look.

The door opens and in steps a youthful-looking girl with a few scripts in her hands. Winther tells her to leave them, and she puts them down in front of him. He picks one up and pages through it. He mumbles compliments while he goes from one page to the next, and looks pleased with the result. Winther says, "This script is the product of our youthful training corps. All college students with the task to research the background for this script. I believe you'll be impressed when you see the fine work. So, without any further delay, here is your copy."

I reach out and take it from Winther. The others take a copy as well. I turn to page one and see the stage directions have me sitting in one of the chairs with Gibbons in the other. Gibbons has the first line, which gives an introduction of the subject matter and me. I turn the page, and the next section has me making a statement to the effect that the government forced me to lie regarding saving the midshipmen. It also states that I've come across some information I want to share on oil prices. Gibbons has a few questions about the false terrorist attack, and then brings up the subject of the price of oil.

Further into the script, supposedly a high official in the Saudi government gave me a document. This document has a copy of a string of e-mails where the Saudi government asked permission from the US to lower oil prices to stimulate demand. The e-mails supposedly go on to say that the US government refused to grant the Saudi's request to do so. The reason given was that as long as oil prices remain where they are, the current administration always has the opportunity of making a big deal out of getting them lowered later. The option of lowering prices later will be especially true if there are any domestic issues coming up which are potentially embarrassing to the President. The announcement of lower priced oil will bury any embarrassing issues.

The impact of the knowledge that the Saudis had to ask permission to raise or lower oil prices will hit the commodity community like a ton of bricks. The assumption has always been that the oil cartel operated independently from US influence. Exposing these e-mails will put the entire world oil pricing structure under question. This is why these guys are using me. By the time anyone figures out that the information is false, my plausible delivery will have already done the damage. My stomach rumbles in protest to the fear I feel. My status as a hero will be twisted to meet the ends of this group. Since the vast majority of the people seeing and hearing my broadcast believe I'm an American patriot, they'll fall for the ruse, and raise hell with their elected officials. The President's word will mean nothing until the lie is finally exposed. The Saudi's will no doubt deny any involvement and just may up production and drop the price of oil just to prove how independent they can be. This would have a negative effect on the dollar which is tied to oil. Cheaper oil would be a good thing for the consumer but would raise hell in the energy sector. Stock prices would fall and with them a lot of money lost. Of course, they could also elect to raise prices to show independence. This would put additional pressure on the consumer household with the effect of possible contraction of discretionary spending and resulting declines in stock in that sector. No matter the reaction of the Saudi's there will be turmoil as a result of the broadcast.

The financial impact is only one piece. I can't imagine what the government and President will do with this information. Congress has such a low standing in the American population that I can imagine the cry for justice. Congress will, en masse, blame the President, but it will still need to come to grips with the idea that it's being accused of misleading the public. I'm not sure what the President will do, as the e-mails state that the actions are being taken on behalf of the President. The e-mail looks as if it came from an office in the White House, but shows no identity of the author. It doesn't matter, though, as the first hour after the broadcast will be the most damaging, and any investigation will be too late to correct the ensuing problems.

Can I go ahead with this broadcast even though if I don't, it will mean the death of Stephanie and several thousand people? What will be the social consequences of the two directions I could take? The first direction is to go ahead with the broadcast and cause a the results I think will happen and even if temporary they will be severe. The other direction is to refuse to do the broadcast. To refuse will cost Stephanie her life and the lives of the innocent people at the hospital. The limit of the carnage will be to that one event. I can't quite bring myself to come to a definitive decision, knowing I'll be responsible for her death. She is a real person to me, and all the others are abstract points of information. To decide life and death over others is a terrible position. To be forced to have life and death decision ability is probably the cruelest form of torture. Jacobs must have taken his time to think this one up. It is so totally diabolical in its construct that it's genius. He hates me and is getting true revenge.

I finish reviewing the script and toss it on the table. "What's wrong?" Winther says.

"I can't do this. Your plan will create havoc in the financial markets and lead to an unstable situation in world politics."

"Yeah. You're right. Isn't it beautiful?" Winther says.

"Go to hell." I sit back, look down at the table, and wait for someone to say something, but all I can hear is Winther continuing to chuckle at my pain.

"No one said this was going to be easy, John. You have a lot of credibility out there, and we'll make sure everyone far and wide hears your story."

"What if I refuse?"

"You know what happens. Stephanie and two thousand people find their way to heaven."

"How about you two? You have anything to say?"

I don't expect an answer but am tired of shouldering this responsibility alone. To my surprise, Speale speaks up, "I can't tell you how much this sucks. I didn't realize the full scope of this thing when I first got here. Now I see we're being asked to disrupt America and world politics in order to save our loved ones. I'm not sure our families would want us to behave in such a way."

Winther stops chuckling. He moves his chair closer. "So, are you willing to let your people die for your principles?"

Speale does some serious thinking before he answers. He stands up and looks as if he might punch Winther. "You give us no choices. If we do what you want, America suffers. If we don't do your bidding, our people suffer." He trembles with rage. Since he doesn't look the part of a rebel, I'm impressed. "You and your boss should be in jail and labeled what you are: criminals."

Winther stands and squares up to Speale. "Sit down, before I call a couple of people in to give you a lesson in discipline."

Speale becomes emotional. "You sit."

Gibbons gets up and puts his arm around Speale to protect him from doing something foolish. Speale takes the hint from Gibbons and seems to relax a little. Quietly, Gibbons says something to him, and he nods.

Gibbons helps Speale back into his chair, and then turns to Winther. "You can sit down now. The outburst is over."

Winther smiles and takes his seat. "You were wise to help Mr. Speale. I don't think he was fully rational. I'm sure he would regret the loss of his folks, especially after we went ahead successfully without him." Winther turns to Speale. "We're a powerful organization. If you elect to be a disruptive factor, we can eliminate you and your loved ones. Your behavior will have no effect on the mission outcome. We'll be successful with or without you. It's your decision, but I wouldn't get wrapped up in the America-the-Beautiful crap as it relates to you. You're expendable, and if we have another episode like this, I'll order your elimination. Do I make myself clear?"

Speale looks at his shoes and mumbles something that sounds as if he understands. At least he spoke out. Gibbons seems to be a logical person, and I don't know what he said to Speale to get him to calm down, but I suspect it was close to what Winther just ran through. I get the feeling Gibbons has already considered all the options and has come to the conclusion that he's powerless over this situation. I've come to the same summary, although as Speale does, I want to rage at the machine. The only thing holding me in check is the futility of it all.

"Shall we get back to work, gentlemen?" Winther says. "Let's have a read through, starting with page one."

An audible sigh shows how the three of us feel. We begin the run through and conclude forty minutes later. Because a number of corrections in grammar and sentence structure are needed, the first reading takes a lot longer than the actual segment will take. I estimate the entire broadcast will take no more than twenty minutes. Before we go through it again, I need to visit the restroom. "Excuse me, Paul, but can we take five minutes for a bathroom break?"

"Yeah, that's a good idea. We made some nice progress, so let's take ten. Coffee's over on the buffet if any of you would care for some."

We get up, and Speale stretches. I'm sure his standing up to Winther took a lot out of him. The three of us leave the break room and go into the men's room next door. We get into the room and Speale signals with his finger on his lips to be quiet. I look with amazement while he lifts his shirt to expose the handle of a knife in his waistband. He drops the shirt immediately, so I'm not sure if Gibbons saw it as well. I hold out my hands and shrug with a gesture I hope he takes to be, *what are you going to with the knife?* He smiles and taps his watch, and I take that as a "later" signal.

I'm sure this room is bugged and probably on camera as well. I look around but don't see anything in plain sight. The silence is not good, so I speak up. "What do you guys think of the script?"

Gibbons looks surprised when he turns from the urinal and moves to the sink. "Well, we helped clean it up, but I think it sucks," he says.

"Yeah, and I can't imagine the fallout once the broadcast is over," Speale says. He then moves to a urinal and seems to take forever emptying his bladder. Gibbons and I end up at the sinks together. I turn on both faucets of water, and he does the same. I hope the noise of the water will distort our conversation. We whisper together.

"Is there any way out?" I say.

"Not one I can figure out," Gibbons says.

Speale finishes and joins us at the third sink. He turns his water on as well and whispers, "We need to get together on a plan. Right now isn't the time, and I think we should shut this water off before those guys come in here."

I laugh out loud at the ridiculous nature of the three of us making noise with water. The goons will know what we're up to and put a stop to it. I turn off my faucets, and the others do the same.

"All right then," I say. "We can do this again sometime." When I look at their faces and their expressions, I believe they understand, and we share a smile as we walk out of the restroom.

"So, you ready for another run through?" Winther says.

I look at Speale and Gibbons, and then make a stand right here, "I want to talk to Jacobs before the broadcast," I say. Speale and Gibbons look as if they might pass out. I guess I took them by surprise.

"Why do you need to talk to him?"

"I think the subject will be between Jacobs and me."

"I'm sorry. He's not here."

"Where is he?"

"None of your business, but for the record, I have no idea."

I'm surprised Winther doesn't know where Jacobs has gone. Is he just saying it so I'll stop asking about talking to Jacobs? I press the issue a little more, "Can you get a message to him?"

"Yes, of course—we're in constant communication. I can text him. You'll need to tell me what you want to discuss, as he *will* ask."

"Okay, just tell him I don't want to do the broadcast and want to work out a deal."

Winther looks at me as if I've lost my mind. "Work out a deal?" He laughs. "With what do you have to deal? You have nothing he wants, and he holds all the cards."

"Just deliver the message, please."

"I'll deliver it, but there's no guarantee he'll talk to you."

"If he doesn't talk to me, then I'm not doing the broadcast."

"I would think over your position carefully if I were you, John. You're playing with fire, and your folks are going to get burned."

I look at Winther. "I understand your concern but would appreciate you delivering the message." He agrees to do so, and I believe him. I get a tight feeling in my stomach because there's no turning back now. I've thrown down a challenge, and it will be a matter of time to see if Jacobs will take me up on it. Now I just need to figure out what kind of deal I can invent. Perhaps I could offer to join their group, as Winther suggests, which is a zero sum game. I'd still have to do the broadcast and wouldn't be ahead of where I'm at now. The plan will require some thought. Hopefully, Jacobs won't want to talk until tomorrow, which will give me time tonight to figure something out.

"I'm ready for the run through," I say. Speale and Gibbons look at me and nod. Winther looks surprised, but at the same time also pleased. We take our places in the studio, and Gibbons and I get mic'd up. Crew members stand behind the cameras and at the production control board. Are they here voluntarily? I don't ask—I've enough to deal with right now, let alone taking on their problems.

Speale takes his place in the control room, and I hear chatter in my earpiece. Speale says, "Quiet on the set; we begin in three, two, one." When he reaches one, music plays in my ear, followed by an announcer describing the broadcast as a special report from the studios of the Desert Wolves. Then he begins an introduction of Gibbons. Speale talks over the announcer, "Gibbons on three, two, and one."

Chapter Twenty-Three

The broadcast run-through goes well. We had a few mix-ups and miscues, but, all in all, an audience wouldn't notice. Speale speaks from the control room and advises everyone that we'll take a lunch break, and will do one more run through after lunch. I pull the earpiece out and unclip the mic. Winther comes into the studio and puts a hand on Gibbons' and my shoulders. "You guys were great. You gave a smooth and convincing performance. Congratulations."

Gibbons and I don't say anything. We don't feel as if this is work deserving of praise. I think we both feel this is the devil's work, and would rather not be part of it. Purposely, we wander away from Winther.

Gibbons says, "I'm in your corner on not doing the broadcast unless you talk to Jacobs. What kind of deal are you going to propose?"

"I haven't figured that out yet."

"You what?" he says.

It's reasonable that he assumed I had a trump card in the hole before I opened my mouth. I explain, "I don't have a trump card but will figure something out before tomorrow morning."

He doesn't look comforted. I say, "Everything will be okay." But I can see he's upset.

"We're playing with people's lives, and we need to be careful," Gibbons says.

We walk into the break room, and Speale stands by the table of sandwiches and fruit. "He doesn't have a plan," Gibbons says. "He's shooting from the hip."

"Calm down," I say. "We don't need to let Winther know all our business."

"What do you mean you don't have a plan?" Speale says.

"I wanted to get on Jacobs' schedule, and I spoke before I had a plan together, is all."

"Is all?" Speale says. "If you don't do the broadcast, then a lot of people are going to die. If Jacobs gets the idea you're just playing with him, he may make you do the broadcast and kill them anyway. Did you ever think that might be possible?"

"Of course, I've thought of the possibility. What do you take me for, an idiot?"

"Well, you sound as if you're one more and more," Gibbons says. "Without a plan, Jacobs is going to have you for dinner. He might not talk to you out of spite. What will you do then?"

"I haven't come to a decision yet. If he won't talk to me, then I don't know what I'll do—"

Gibbons says, "This all seems way too up in the air. You don't have a plan for the discussion, and you don't have a plan if the discussion doesn't take place. You're bluffing at the highest level."

"Yeah, it certainly looks as if I'm bluffing. It's just that I couldn't take it anymore and wanted to slow things down a bit." I have to admit I sound as if I don't have a brain. "I need to think this out if I'm going to be of any value in solving this problem. A food break might help."

The three of us go over to the buffet and look it over. I could use some coffee, but I don't seem to have an appetite for sandwiches. At the coffee machine, I see it's one of those kinds where you select a flavor out of a number of colorful and descriptive offerings in little containers. I grab one for a mountain-grown blend. The fresh coffee pours out of a spigot, and the aroma causes my mouth to water. I take a sip and know I made the right choice.

Speale and Gibbons have helped themselves to a sandwich and some salad. They are sitting at a round table, and I join them.

"Not eating?" Gibbons says.

"I don't care for any food right now. I think my stomach is trying to rebel against this uncontrollable situation. In any case, I'm not hungry."

"Yeah, you should eat something."

As Gibbons finishes his advice, Winther comes over to the table. "John, may I have a word with you, please?"

I get up and follow him to the hallway. He stops and faces me. "I got a message from Jacobs and he wants you to know the only way he'll talk to you is after you deliver the broadcast."

I don't say anything and try to have a reasonable-sounding reply, so I take some time to think. Winther stands with a look of confusion on his face. "John, did you understand what I just said?"

I need to say something. "Yeah, I understood what you said. I just don't understand why he won't talk to me."

"Simple. If you and he talk, and you've somehow come up with a magic formula that will please everyone, we still have no guarantee that you'll follow your end of the deal. He believes your end is doing the broadcast. He knows you don't want to do it, so he believes you'll offer something other than that. Jacobs commits to this mission, and whatever you ask for as a substitute for the broadcast, he'll be forced to deny. Also, he will be more willing to grant your request if you're already fully committed, which you would be after finishing the broadcast. You understand?"

"Yeah, I get it. So, after the broadcast, he'll talk to me and hear what I propose?"

"Well, yes, but if you think your proposal has any merit, I'll be happy to transmit it to him before the broadcast with no guarantee he'll entertain your idea."

"Seems fair. Let me think on it. In the meantime, is Sarah going to come down for lunch?"

"Nope, she said she doesn't feel well and wants to catch up on her rest. I'll make sure they deliver something."

Obviously, we're finished talking, so Winther goes back into the break room, and I follow and take up my chair next to Gibbons. Winther leaves the room after telling us we will resume in fifteen minutes. My coffee has gone cold. Maybe I'll get a little something to eat after all. On the way to the buffet, I replay the discussion with Winther. The conversation felt strange. Why did Winther offer to send a proposal to Jacobs as he did? He must have some information that Jacobs is willing to see what I have in mind before the broadcast. He wouldn't go against Jacobs in any way, so perhaps Jacobs was doing the diplomatic shuffle by saying "no" when he means "maybe." It could be he knows that without me the broadcast would flop and the intended result would never take place. The population is not gullible enough to accept the word of just anyone. My hero status has credibility and so I think Jacobs knows it needs to be me or scratch the broadcast. I hope this is the case since it gives me some level of a bargaining position.

I'll offer to join Jacob's team if he doesn't require the broadcast. No, wait. No way will Jacobs accept those terms. If I join his team, he'll insist I do the broadcast as a show of good faith. Maybe I can offer to do the broadcast only with an announcement up front that I'm being forced to broadcast in exchange for saving others' lives. But I reject that thought, as he'll never go for it. If I make any such announcement, it will take the teeth out of the whole message.

I pick over the salad and take a plate back to the table. "What did he say?" Speale asks.

"He won't talk until after the broadcast."

"Whoa," Gibbons says. "That takes care of that."

"I'm not sure," I say. "Winther said he'd transmit my proposal to Jacobs before the broadcast."

"A proposal you don't have," Speale says. "What are you going to do?"

"I need to come up with something. I've toyed with a couple of ideas, but I don't think they'll work."

"What ideas?" Gibbons says.

I hold up my hand and signal we should all go out in the hallway. We get up and leave the break room. My look up and down the hall satisfies me that no one is around. I answer Gibbons' question in a low voice.

"Oh, like making a statement before the broadcast about how I'm being forced to do it."

Speale shakes his head. "Good call on that not working."

"Wait a minute," Gibbons says. "You gave me an idea. Let's just say you ask for the statement, and Jacobs says 'no.'"

"So far, I think I follow," I say

"Well, then you counter with Jacobs to the effect of allowing you a second broadcast where you can explain being forced. It could air after the original and might serve to blunt the message of the first."

"Why would he agree?"

"He won't think it'll matter by then, and will figure there's no problem since the damage is complete."

"Don't you think he'll be right?"

"Yeah, I guess he would be."

"So what's the percentage?" Seale asks.

"We're going to tape the broadcast, right?" Gibbons says.

"Yes, it is my understanding that we are," I say.

"Well, what do you think would happen if the tapes somehow get mislabeled and the second broadcast went on the air before the first?"

"Wow," I say. "Very cool. Could you make it happen?"

"Yes, but the only question would be what would Jacobs do to the people he was planning to kill if we didn't do what he says?"

"I could make a deal that includes letting all the people go after the two broadcasts are in the can. Letting them go would guarantee we could pull this off without hurting anyone."

"Would he go for it?" Speale says.

"Since the tapes are already made and I assume Jacobs will want to be as far away as he can get from the broadcast site when they air, I'll bet he wouldn't object. Besides, he's arrogant enough to believe we're powerless and that his team will take care of things at the studio. So he has no reason not to agree, other than being an ass."

Gibbons, Speale, and I stand in silence for a few moments. I assume that they're analyzing the plan to find any weak spots, just as I am. Gibbons speaks, "I think the plan will work." Speale nods his agreement.

I finalize the next move. "Okay, so this is the plan. We need to think some more about loopholes. When I talk to Jacobs, I'll tell him I want to make a follow-up broadcast and to release the hostages before the tapes air."

"How will we know they're safe, though?" Speale frowns.

"Good question. Any ideas?"

Gibbons pauses to think, and then says, "We should ask for three cell phones and our folks could call us."

"Good idea," Speale says. "I still don't know what will motivate Jacobs to do all this."

"I do," I say.

"What is it, then?" Seale asks. "I don't see it."

"If we all offer to join his team, I think he'll do it."

"Join his team. What the hell do you mean?"

"I mean we would be part of this pirate band at least until Jacobs figures out the tape swapping scheme."

Gibbons frowns, and then says, "What happens then?"

"I suspect he'll kill us." I look at Gibbons and have to laugh at the way his jaw flops open. He probably never thought it would come to this, but I don't see any other way Jacobs will react.

Speale also looks surprised, but says, "I guess my life to thwart the plan is not such a bad deal."

I turn to Gibbons, and he nods somberly. The two of them are okay with giving up their lives to save their loved ones and the American system as we know it. I want to make sure. "You guys okay with giving your life for this?"

They look at each other and then back to me and nod yes. Each has come to his conclusion, and I have a huge amount of respect for these two. I reach out to take their hands, and they surround me in what could pass for a group hug. "Okay, we're committed," I say. Gibbons wipes his eyes, and I get a warm feeling from his and Speale's sacrifice. If we can pull this off, we will have saved a lot of lives and, hopefully, parts of the system as well. We remain silent as we go back into the breakroom. We sit at the table and go through the motions of finishing lunch. Winther comes through the break room door and asks if we're ready to resume. We all get up and go into the studio. It takes another three hours to get all the mechanics of the broadcast down. We finally take another break, and I ask Winther if Jacobs will be talking to me. "Jacobs has agreed to a meeting tonight at six o'clock. There will be a video hookup arranged in the studio next door. Until then, I think we can do another run-through of the broadcast. You guys have done a nice job, and I think one more time is all we need before the taping tomorrow."

We finish a cup of coffee and go back to the studio. The run-through session takes two-and-a-half hours, and we finally wrap. I look at my watch and see it is five-thirty-five. We only have twenty-five more minutes until I put our plan into action. My heart gives an unusual flutter, and I get nervous at the prospect of talking to Jacobs. Winther comes up behind me, and I jump when he speaks, "You ready to go next door?"

Chapter Twenty-Four

I get up, and Winther leads the way as usual. We go into the studio, and Winther hits the lights. The studio feels unusually cool. I ask, "Why so cold in here?"

"When the lights are off, the room gets cooler since the air conditioning is set to a lower temperature to offset the heat of the bulbs."

This studio has a large screen on the wall opposite the control room. I assume the video uplink will be on this screen. While I'm thinking, Winther asks me to get a couple of chairs, and he goes to a phone on the wall. A couple of guys stand in the control room, and I believe Winther is talking to them. He hangs up just as I bring the last chair and position it to face the screen.

"The control room says we'll start at six. I'm going to get something to drink. Can I get you anything?"

"I'd appreciate some water if you don't mind."

"Not at all." Winther goes toward the door and then disappears. I check my watch, and it is ten minutes to six. Some flickering appears on the screen. They must be setting up the call right now. The flickering ends and the image of Jacobs pops into view. He isn't paying attention and seems to be talking to someone off camera. The sound is off, but he smiles and carries on a lively conversation.

The person to whom he is talking comes into the camera view and has her back to the lens. All of a sudden, she leans in and gives Jacobs a kiss. Then she rises and walks with her back to the camera and out the door. Although I couldn't catch a view of her face, I managed to see her diamond stud earring as she leaned in to kiss Jacobs. There's no mistaking the earring: it belongs to Sarah. My heart skips a beat, and my mind races to understand what I just saw. I'm taken aback and can't seem to concentrate. The idea of Sarah kissing Jacobs has ramifications I'll need time to digest. I try to keep my current objective with Jacobs in mind, as its clear the call is about to begin.

"Can you see and hear me, Cannon?" Jacobs says. He sounds as if he's on a satellite phone.

"Yes, I can hear you, although the connection seems a little shaky."

"Yeah, that's always the case when the call first starts. It will clear up shortly. So, you wanted to talk?"

"Yes, I wanted to see if we could work out a plan, so the broadcast doesn't need to take place."

"Not a chance. I've invested my time and energy in this broadcast, and I'll not change my mind. Besides, I don't see any upside in it for me."

"What if Gibbons, Speale, and I join your team?"

"You all want to join my team? Why?"

"To be clear, we're not overjoyed to join your team, but the alternatives aren't that appealing. We think we can aid your cause with our talents."

"What talents would those be?" Jacobs isn't going to let me off the hook easily, and he appears to enjoy this charade.

I say, "Gibbons is a highly talented broadcaster. Speale knows broadcast technology, and I'm a damn good lawyer and national hero. We could make your cause sound like it's a charity."

"Real tempting, but the broadcast goes on as planned. Once it's over, you three won't have a pot to piss in anywhere. You'll be soiled goods then."

"Okay, we make a separate statement before the broadcast about the three of us being forced to co-operate with forces intending to harm America, and that we're innocent. Then we'll still be worth joining your cause."

"You must think I'm so gullible. I'd never let you do any such thing. It would invalidate the message I intend for you to deliver."

"I thought you'd say that, so here's another proposal. You let us make another broadcast tape where we try to explain the first, which we can broadcast after the original. The reason we think it's important is we want our loved ones to be free of the burden of trying to defend our actions. We would apologize to the American people for being duped by the government. We would say we had no part in the lies and deception, and that we feel there are very few people responsible for it. We tell the public we're being forced to make the broadcast, but are joining the group doing the broadcast since we think their cause is right. We ask that everyone remain calm and appeal to Congress to get to the bottom of the situation. We join your organization after we're sure our loved ones are okay."

"What do you mean, *after you're sure your loved ones are okay?*"

"We want to get three cell phones to be able to reach our loved ones. All we ask is that after we make the original broadcast tape and before it airs, you release our loved ones, and we verify they're okay."

"If I don't?"

"We're not going to make the broadcast tape."

"Yeah, right. I could kill one of your so-called loved ones and throw the body in the street, and I guarantee you would make the broadcast. Maybe I'll select the smallest one. I think Gibbons has a little kid. Speale has some kids as well. You're a different matter. I'd probably have to have someone go into the hospital and hunt for some child. I could have the videos sent to you for souvenirs of your disrespect and poor behavior."

"If we're your followers, I don't see why you wouldn't let us be free from our current obligations. By assuring they're all well, we would be able to concentrate on your cause while forgetting our past lives."

"I see why you beat me in the Taft Avery lawsuit. You're persuasive. All right, I'll think on letting you know your loved ones are okay before the broadcast airs. I like your idea of the second broadcast. It adds some flavor to the original. Also, whether you know it or not, it sets the stage for further broadcasts using your hero status as a spokesperson for the Desert Wolves. You can go ahead and make the second broadcast tape. I'll want to review it before it goes on air, and anything I don't approve, I'll cut. I'll let you know about getting in touch with your loved ones before the taping of the broadcast tomorrow morning."

"I guess I can't ask for anything more. I appreciate your consideration."

The screen goes blank when Jacobs shuts down his side of the call. I sit back in my chair and realize that I've been sitting on the edge of the seat. The session with Jacobs felt more stressful than I thought it would be. When I talked Gibbons and Speale through the proposal, it seemed as if it would be an easy proposition. I realize now that Jacobs doesn't have to accept any of my terms, and there isn't anything we can do if he doesn't.

I think of Sarah and Jacobs, and I want to scream. Why would she take up with a murderer? She knows what he did to her best friend and what he contemplates doing to her sister. My last thought may be the reason she is so accommodating. An overwhelming feeling of sadness replaces my rage because she feels she must give of herself to save her family.

I turn to thinking of the idea of making a second tape. If Jacobs is going to review it, then we'll have to keep it more or less on message. Do Gibbons and Speale have a way of producing one for Jacobs' review, and then another for the actual airing?

Winther walks into the room. "I just got off a call with Mr. Jacobs. He told me to set up some studio times for another taping session. He wants me to supervise what you're doing but outlined that you're joining our organization. Congratulations."

"Did he also tell you we want to speak to our loved ones before the broadcast airs?"

"Yes, he did, but I'm a little confused."

"Confused? How so?"

"Well, let me see. You guys are going to pre-tape the broadcast, right?"

"Yes, that's right."

"What's to stop us from using the tape even if you don't get to talk to your precious girlfriend?"

"I convinced Jacobs that if he lets us make sure our loved ones are safe, we'll be better followers of your cause. I also told him the extra broadcast should enhance the overall effect. I think he agrees."

"Okay, I just want to make sure you don't think you somehow have an upper hand. I'm sure you know you're expendable, and I would behave accordingly. What time do you guys want to do the other taping?"

"We could do it now, after we've had a chance to work up a script."

"Well then, follow me and you guys can get to work."

Winther leads the way out of the studio and back to the break room. Gibbons and Speale, seated at a table, wear anxious expressions. I break the tension. "Jacobs has authorized the second tape. He's not sure he'll allow the call to our loved ones but seems to be in favor of our concept of the second broadcast." They look uncertain what to say next, so I help them out, "We will need to script the broadcast along the lines we discussed. You know; first an opening, then an explanation of how the government let the public down. We will follow with the fact that we were forced to do the broadcast, and finally how we're joining the group." I let it sink in as an outline.

Gibbons says, "So, the first thing we need is a script."

"Yes, that's right," I say. Speale sits silently. "Do you have any ideas?" I aim the question at both of them and hope Winther will be bored enough to get up and let us talk together.

Speale speaks up, "I think we should be alone for a while and work out a script."

Winther looks up with an expression that could pass for reflecting a stomach ache. "Oh, by all means, you should work independently. I was just leaving." He rises from the chair and walks toward the door. "You give me a call when you're ready to tape."

"It may be an hour or two," I say.

"Well, just lift the phone on the wall and I'll answer." He goes out the door.

I motion for the two of them to be quiet. I grab a pen and legal pad. I write out a message, *there are cameras and microphones everywhere. Be careful and follow my lead.* I clear my throat. "Come over here and read what I've outlined." They gather around, and I show them the message. "Now, I think we can open the second broadcast much as we did the first," I say. I write, *Jacobs wants to review the tape before it airs. Is there a way to give him one version and then air another???*

Gibbons picks up the need for role-play and answers, "Yes, I think a similar opening will work."

"Do you think we can blame the government?" I say. I write, *how are we going to shoot two versions with Winther watching the whole time?*

Speale says, "The interesting thing on blaming the government is that when we record the words, we can always change them if need be to meet the condition. Whoever is on camera will be mouthing some words, but they could be different in the sound loop."

"Oh, I get it," I say. "We could change the script at the last minute without reshooting the video. For instance, if we know something has changed between the first broadcast and our second, we can change the sound loop to accommodate."

"Exactly what I'm saying." Speale wears a smile.

"The next element is to explain our involvement," I say, and then write, *okay, so we only shoot one version and then dub the sound to fit our need. Right?*

"I think so," Gibbons says.

"Okay, let's get the script written then. How do you want to divide it up?"

"I'll take the opening," Gibbons says. "I think it will be standard. You know, welcome to our broadcast with an introduction as to what we'll cover."

"Sounds good. I'll take the basic story and lay out the facts. Speale, you want the closing?"

"Yeah, I'll take it. I would rather do the opening, but what the hell."

"You'll do a great job. So, let's get to work and share our notes in an hour. Will it be enough time?"

Both mumble affirmatives. They move to different parts of the table and dive right into the task. I look at my blank sheet of paper and wonder where I'll start. I need to make both versions as close to each other as possible, so I start writing the first version. In it, I explain to the viewing public that the previous broadcast was designed to cause everyone to turn on each other. Then I outline the two points of the broadcast: One, the terrorist attacks on the Intrepid Museum and the Annapolis midshipmen were made up by the government to have some good news to give the American public to take their minds off the economy and healthcare. Two, the government has been fixing the price of oil and has denied the Saudi request to raise prices. Next, I go on to assure the public that only a few in government are responsible for this fraud. The real culprits are the members of the government who are responsible for setting policy, and the public should not panic, but call upon Congress to launch an investigation. The calling on Congress for help is the part Jacobs will love because he knows Congress is powerless to come to any conclusions, not along party lines. The Democrats will blame big business for the problem, and the Republicans will blame the President and other Democrats. I wrap up my first version and hope Speale has the part where we declare we are now part of the movement.

The second version, I begin right at the point where I outline the principles of the broadcast. Instead of outlining the broadcast, I write out the fact the public will be seeing a second broadcast after this one, and that the second broadcast will say that the terrorist mission was a hoax, and the US government is manipulating oil prices. I conclude with the following: *My fellow Americans, there is no truth to anything I say on the other broadcast. This broadcast is being put on air ahead of the other. The first broadcast will let the American people know a group of terrorists named Desert Wolves have held members of our families, and in my case, Jason Savard's sister, and forced us to make the tape you may see next. These people need to be brought to justice. There are three of us who will be giving our lives to make sure America is safe. People, do not believe anything you hear in another broadcast. It is all lies. The two others who have helped me are Sammy Speale and Clive Gibbons. They are heroes whom we should not forget. So, goodbye America and God bless the United States.*

I lean back and re-read what I have written. Satisfied that I've covered the subject adequately, I pause to think of what Jacobs will do when he hears this form of the broadcast. Winther will most likely jump in and try to stop it. We'll have to figure out a way to lock the control room door. Jacobs will take the three of us out and shoot us. I have to hope he does just shoot us rather than do some weird torture thing. I shake off this kind of thinking. It doesn't add to my confidence, and I need to be resolute. I can't allow these guys to be victorious in their quest to harm my country.

I look up at Sammy and Clive to see how they're coming along. They seem to be still writing. "You guys finished?"

Sammy holds up his finger. "One more minute. I need to finish this last paragraph."

Speale sits back in his chair, finished. "Want to read it?" he says.

"I think we all should trade our papers around. Here, take my middle and I'll look at your closing." Clive smiles and passes me his paper. I give him my two versions. Sammy gives us a hurt look. "Don't worry; we've got enough time. Why don't you finish up?" Sammy nods and goes back to his writing.

Chapter Twenty-Five

When I look Clive's paper over, I see that he's correctly summarized how we will join the Desert Wolves. All in all, his first draft looks like a keeper. "Nice work," I say.

"Yours looks good. I like the hero part. I must admit that I didn't give that eventuality a thought before now." He speaks in code and is referring to the fact that we may die.

"Yeah, I know what you mean. It's not easy being a hero."

Clive laughs, and I join him. We must have weird senses of humor. "I think yours is perfect," Clive says.

"Thanks." I look at Sammy. "How about you? Done yet?"

"Yes, I'm finished. Here's mine. Give me Clive's. He can sit out for a while."

I read over Sammy's introduction. He takes the task of explaining that a previous broadcast exists and that this is a follow-up. In it, he sets Jacobs up and provides some background on the original terrorist mission, and how Jason and I were responsible for thwarting it. Then he adds a small teaser on the mission and introduces me. It will be a good introduction.

"This looks good to me," I say.

"Looks like Clive has a good ending as well," Gibbons says.

"Yeah, I thought so too." I hand Gibbons' introduction to Clive. "Why don't you weigh in on Gibbons' intro."

"Better like it, Clive," Gibbons says. Clive looks up and sees that Gibbons is kidding him. He smiles and looks back at the paper.

After five minutes, Clive says, "Yeah, this will work. Why don't we go into the studio and record the first version."

"Winther wanted us to call him when we were ready," I say. Clive looks at me as if I just joined the other side.

"What the fuck do we need him for?" Clive sounds stressed.

"We don't need him, but Jacobs warned him to supervise the taping."

Gibbons holds up his finger, writes on the back of his script, and then shows it to Speale and me. *Why don't we go in and record the dub and then call him?*

I look at him with a puzzled expression. I take the script and write, *what do you mean "dub?"* I think he means the second audio recording, but want to be sure.

Gibbons takes the script back and writes, *a dub is a piece of the audio portion of the video. Usually, it's some off-camera dialog or narrative, but in this case, it's the alternate audio that will tell our story.*

"Yeah, I thought so," I say, then write on the script, *I'm okay with doing it right now and then calling Winther. Let's go.*

We all get up and go down the hall to the studio. When we go in, and before we can turn on the lights, we see Winther sitting in the control room, studying his phone. He looks like he's in a fishbowl because of the contrast between the brightly lit control room and the totally dark studio. "What do we do now?" Gibbons says.

"Let me handle this." I walk to the control room door and open it. "We were just going to call you. We're ready to record our broadcast."

"Just going to call me, huh? It looks like you guys were going to go ahead without me."

"Naw," I say. "We were going to rehearse a little and then call you."

"Yeah, okay. I'll buy it. In fact, I think I'll let you do your thing. I'll be right back. Jacobs wants a report."

"We'll be right here."

Winther gets up and leaves the control room. I hold the door and let Gibbons and Speale come inside. "We don't have much time. How can we do the dubbed tape from this booth? We have no camera operators."

"It's easy," Speale says. "I can put one of these microphones up, and we'll just record it. The cameras are automatic. Speale will operate them from the booth."

After he throws a couple of switches, Speale puts on a pair of earphones, and I do the same. He gives me a three sign. I indicate my understanding with a nod. He lowers each finger in turn, and then points to me. I'm on. Quickly, I go through the dialog and finish in three minutes.

Speale looks up and says, "A little rushed, but I think we can make it work. I'll pull the disk on this and put in a fresh one."

While he works, Winther comes back into the control room. "You guys ready for your broadcast?"

"Yes, I think so. We've finished rehearsing, so I guess we can do it."

"Well, let's get to it."

Speale mans the control booth. Gibbons and I get up and go out into the studio. The lights come up, and the automatic cameras come to life. Speale gives us the countdown, and then we record. Gibbons opens the broadcast and follows the script closely. When my cue comes,

I jump into action. I try to keep a sincere look and deliver the message, at a slower speed this time. It seems like only a few minutes when I hear Speale say "cut" in my ear bud.

Gibbons and I go to the control room. "How does it look?" My question is to Speale, but Winther speaks up instead. "I think it looks believable. You guys should get a lot of folks to believe you're telling the truth."

"Well, coming from you, that's a rave review. We can call it a night."

Gibbons and Speale close down the electronics in the control room. As they work, Winther speaks to all of us. "I talked to Jacobs, and he's agreed to arrange for you to talk to the people who you want to ensure are safe before the broadcast tomorrow. He'll give you each a phone tomorrow just before the broadcast. You can call and assure yourselves all is well."

"That's good news," I say. "I'm glad Jacobs saw the reasoning to do it."

"I think Mr. Jacobs would rather have committed people on his team rather than simply being under duress. So, however you sold the idea, I must commend you. I wouldn't have gone for it, but what the hell. If it's good enough for Mr. Jacobs, it's good enough for me."

"In any case, I'm sure we'll want to thank Jacobs in person."

"Yeah, that's not going to happen. He'll be busy, and his last words to me gave the impression I wouldn't see him until well after the broadcast."

"Well, if you do talk to him, tell him we're grateful."

"You guys ready to call it a day?"

All of us give Winther a nod. I'm so glad we decided to do the dub early. Now it will be a matter of controlling the broadcast booth long enough to switch the recordings and put ours on air first. It shouldn't take any longer than the few minutes of the broadcast to discredit Jacobs' broadcast completely and ruin his plan for chaos. When I think of how disappointed Jacobs will be, I want to laugh.

Winther gets up, we follow suit. "You guys can order room service if you're hungry. Oh, and I'm going to let Mr. Jacobs review your second broadcast. I'll need a copy."

Speale says, "No problem." And he and Gibbons punch some buttons, and the playback comes up on the monitor. "Copying now," Speale says.

"Can we all eat together?" I say. "We want to share a meal after such a hard day."

Winther looks at me with some suspicion. "I don't think that will be such a good idea. You all have nothing more to say since your second broadcast recording is in the can. So, no."

I had anticipated the answer but thought I'd give it a try. It would certainly make planning a lot easier if we could run through it first. I'll have to leave it up to Speale and Gibbons to pull off the switch on the audio dub. I want to say something to that effect but can't think of a way to say it without raising some alarm with Winther.

"All set," Gibbons says. He hands Winther a disk. "I'm sure Mr. Jacobs will approve."

"I'll let you know after he sees it. If he doesn't approve, you guys may have to do another one."

"We understand," I say. I want to cut the communication and get out of the control room.

Winther holds the door again, and we all walk out of the room. We reach my room first, and I stop by the door. I turn to Gibbons and Speale, "I'll see you tomorrow." I then turn to Winther, "What time are we meeting tomorrow?"

"We plan to tape the broadcast at nine o'clock for a ten o'clock airing. I'll come to your rooms at eight-thirty."

"Okay then, I'll see you guys at eight-thirty. When will we be able to make our phone calls?"

Winther doesn't pause, "I'll have the phones with me. As soon as the broadcast recording is complete, you will be able to make the calls."

"Sounds good to me." I open my door and go into my room. I'm totally exhausted. The meeting with Jacobs, followed by the tension of getting the dub done before Winther showed up, has left me feeling weak. When I sit on the bed, I realize I need to get some sleep to be ready for tomorrow. It'll be hectic with finishing the recording, and then making sure Stephanie's okay before the actual broadcast. Also, making the switch and somehow defending the control room will take all of our energy. I had thought that I might try to sneak down to Speale or Gibbons' rooms to do some final preparations, but I now see I'm way too tired and not that alert. I could make too much noise or something, and cause someone to see me in the hallway. Instead, I take off my clothes with the intention to go to sleep. Even the idea of brushing my teeth is painful. I throw my clothes on the floor and, before long, fall into a deep sleep.

The alarm goes off at eight o'clock, and I don't even remember setting it. That gives me a half hour to have a shower and get dressed. I could go for some coffee for sure. With a stretch, I ease out of bed and move into the bathroom and start the shower. I need to brush my teeth, and regret not brushing the night before—the morning brings me the mouth of a lion. Some extra time with the brush and before long, I eliminate morning mouth.

When I step into the shower, and the lukewarm water hits my skin, goose bumps raise. The shower feels good and tingly. I add some more hot water, and soon it's at a soothing temperature. This would be the way to avoid all troubles—staying in the shower and having no opportunity for a problem to arise.

Unfortunately, real life interferes with the fantasy, and way too soon the time comes to face the day. I pull the handle over to off, reach for a towel, and remain in the heat of the shower stall as long as possible to dry off. Even this delaying tactic runs its course, and now it's necessary to step out of the shower. The cool air makes me shiver. I'm not totally sure it *is* the air, but don't want to contemplate that I might be afraid of what I need to do today.

Just as I finish dressing, I hear a knock at the door. When I open it, Winther stands with a shit-eating grin on his face. "Morning, John," he says.

"Yes, good morning, Paul."

"You ready?"

"I am." Got to wonder what's on his mind, as he hasn't stopped grinning. I say, "You sure look chipper today." Then I pull the door closed and step into the hallway.

"I just got some fabulous news." Winther walks toward the studio.

"Where are Gibbons and Speale?"

"Already at the studio. Apparently, they wanted to set everything up ahead of time so there would be no delay with the phone calls. Aren't you curious about my good news?"

"Oh, yeah. Sorry, I was concerned about the guys. So, what's your news?"

"Mr. Jacobs is leaving me in charge of the mission. He and Ms. Barsonne are to leave early. It looks like they're off on a little vacation."

"So the good news is that you're in charge?"

"Well, maybe it doesn't seem like much to you, but since the mess with the midshipmen, Mr. Jacobs hasn't been particularly convinced I can finish an assignment. We had a long talk on the phone, and he tells me he fully trusts I'll complete it today."

"Did he tell you where he and Sarah were going?"

"No, and I didn't ask. What is it to you?"

"Just curious, I guess; although I'm confused as to why Sarah is going along with him."

"It might be that he's making sure it'll be worth her while."

"What do you mean *worth her while?*"

"I don't know anything specific, but I get the impression Mr. Jacobs has hired Ms. Barsonne as an escort."

My mind races. To do Jacobs' bidding to save a loved one is one thing. To go along with him for money is quite another. I still don't understand why she slept with me, not seeing she had anything to gain, and I don't think she was doing it because of some direction from Jacobs. I want to believe she was there because she wanted to be. Maybe it was her way of apologizing for the deception that had occurred in the past and may occur in the future. In any case, Sarah needs to be off my list of people over which I have a concern. She now needs to be dead to me, as I have no more energy to place in her corner.

"Here we are," Winther says. He holds the studio door open, and I go in. The lights are all up, and the set looks ready for the recording. Speale and Gibbons work in the control room along with two other technicians. We step through the door and go in. Gibbons looks up from the control board and gives me a smile. I'm excited, as I take his sign as all will go according to plan, and he and Speale have had enough time to set everything up.

"Hey, guys," I say. "Are we ready to roll?"

Speale speaks up, "We're ready. Why don't you and Gibbons go into the studio and we can get started."

Gibbons gets up, and we both go into the studio. When the control room door closes, I whisper to Gibbons, "We all set?"

He whispers back, "Yup, and no need to say more."

Hint duly received, I stick to the business of recording the broadcast and say no more. We put on our microphones and take our places, and the next hour is a blur of activity. A simple table with two glasses of water and two comfortable-looking chairs make up the set. Speale gives us the countdown, and I hear "you're on the air" in my ear bud.

Chapter Twenty-Six

I concentrate on the teleprompter while Gibbons makes the opening. His performance is flawless and, finally, he turns the discussion over to me. I follow the script closely and, in what seems only a few minutes, I hear "we are away."

I sit back in the chair and feel as if I have just run a race. It always amazes me how well the body adapts to stress when it happens. You get through it, and only after the situation is complete do you feel the results. I pick up the glass of water on the table and take a long, shaky drink, then I smile at Gibbons, and he gives me a smile in return. He looks spent as well. "The recording looks good," Speale says over the intercom. "Come on into the booth."

Gibbons and I get up and go to the door. Before opening it, he whispers, "Follow my lead today." I nod, and we go in. His comment seems strange, but I'll go along because it's obvious he and Speale have worked out a plan.

"Well done, John and Sammy," Winther says. "I think your performance will be real strong. Jacobs approved of your post-broadcast message, so he authorized the calling of your loved ones. As promised, here are your phones. You'll have less than fifteen minutes to place your calls. I'd like you to stay close, as I want the recording to begin at precisely ten o'clock. We programmed the phone numbers of your folks into the phones. All you need to do is look up contacts, and they will be there."

"Wait a minute," I say. "Our people were to be let go. Why the phone numbers?"

"They have been 'let go' as you say. You need to understand that they were always free to move around. We simply had them wired and could monitor what they did. We've removed the wires, and your people will be at the numbers in the phone. You will find that these are the same numbers you would have called on your own, but we wanted to make sure you had them."

I relax. Then another thought comes to mind. If these guys no longer have our folks wired, then they'll have to find a place to hide. Once our recording hits the air, Jacobs' people will be back at our people with a vengeance. I'll have to let Gibbons and Speale know as well. "Okay," I say. "Why doesn't one of us go into the studio, one into the break room, and one stay here?"

"Sounds like a good idea," Winther says. "I'm going to my room for a minute. I'll be back as soon as it's time for the recording to air." Winther gets up and goes to the control room door. With his hand on the knob, he says, "Who's going to the other rooms?"

Right now is not a good time to try to warn Gibbons and Speale, but I need to try. "I'll go to the break room," I say and follow Winther. Over my shoulder, I say, "You two should tell your folks to go under cover in case any citizens want to come and get them after the broadcast airs."

"What a great suggestion," Winther says. "After you, John."

Winther holds the door, and I go out, hoping Gibbons and Speale got my message. Winther didn't seem to catch it, so I hope those two did. I follow Winther as far as the break room, and then say, "I'm going to make my call now." Then I open the break room door and leave Winther in the hallway. I look at the phone and turn it on. A phone icon appears on the screen, I touch it, and then hit contacts.

One number displays, so I touch it, and the phone rings out. I step back into the hallway to check, and Winther has indeed gone. I'll make the call from here—less chance of being overheard in this spot as opposed to a room.

"Hello," Stephanie says.

"Stephanie, it's John. Are you all right?" I keep my voice low.

"Yes, I think I'm fine. Some guys came into my room at the hospital and told me I would be getting a call from you. How are you, and who were they?"

"I have no time to explain now. You're in real danger, and you need to get out of the hospital and go somewhere. Do you have any listening device on you?"

"What do you mean 'listening device?'"

"Any microphone put on you by people who may or may not say they are with the government."

"I had one on me up until this morning. They said they were with the FBI, and they thought I was in danger, and the microphone was so I could call for help if anyone tried to hurt me."

"You said until this morning."

"Yes, the same guys who told me you were going to call took it off. They said the danger was over."

"Stephanie, can you get up and out of bed?"

"I've been able to get up briefly. If I'm up too long, I get real dizzy."

"Can you get up now and get dressed?"

"I can, but I don't know how far I can go without help."

"Is there anyone there who can help you down to a taxi?"

"John, what is this?"

"I've been playing with the guys who tried to kill you, and I've bartered away my freedom for your life. If I go back on my agreement, they'll come after you. Is it clear what I'm saying?"

"No, it is *not* clear. What do you mean by your freedom for my life?"

"Stephanie, I didn't want to get into this right now, but I'll try to explain. Those guys who tried to use my boat to blow up the midshipmen, and who killed Jason, have captured me. They are the ones who shot you. They want me to make a broadcast to send the commodity market into a spiral and cause people to think our government is totally dishonest. I need to make sure you're safe in case anything goes wrong." I can't fully explain to Stephanie, as this phone may have a bug. I hope she gets it.

"Why did they let you call me?"

"I made a deal with Jacobs, their head guy. I told Jacobs that once I knew you were safe, I would join his terrorist group."

"So joining them is giving up your freedom."

"Exactly. I need you out of harm's way." She won't understand unless I lay out the whole plan. If the phone has a bug, I may give away the whole thing, but I can't take the chance that Stephanie won't feel the need to get to a safe place. If she's safe, I don't care what happens to me and hope I can execute the plan even if Jacobs knows what's going to happen. "Stephanie, listen to me. The schedule for the broadcast is ten o'clock, so there isn't much time. You have to understand. I'm not going to join them and will do everything I can to destroy their mission. We plan on making a switch so the recording that goes on the air won't be the one these guys want. Do you get it yet?" The thought of this phone being bugged makes my stomach turn over. If it is, I just killed Gibbons and Speale as well as myself.

"I think I understand, John. I'll just have to do the best I can to get the hell out of here in the next few minutes."

The sacrifice is worth it. "Now you're talking. Do be careful and try to determine if you're being followed or not."

"Yeah, okay. I'll do that. I just hope I can hold it together until I disappear. How will I get in touch with you?"

"I'm not sure. Do you have your cell phone with you?"

"Yes, but it's turned off. The number you called me on is the hospital phone in the room."

"Give me the number and don't turn your phone on for at least twenty-four hours. Hopefully, I'll be able to send you a text when all's clear. If you turn it on and don't have an all-clear from me, throw the phone away and change location. If I don't text, it means things didn't go well."

"Oh, John, please be careful. My number is 212-555-3135. Got it?"

"Yeah, I got it. You need to go now. Good luck and God's speed. Please, remember not to turn on your phone. They can track you with it."

"I'll remember. Goodbye, John. Thank you for everything. I'm sorry it's turned out this way. Thank you for thinking of me."

"Goodbye, Stephanie."

I end the call and will probably never talk to Stephanie again. At least she has a chance to get away. If the phone's bugged, these guys won't take my double-cross lightly, and I can imagine them being pissed off. To what end, I have no way of predicting. With nothing to do now but wait, I go across the hall to the studio and open the door.

Both Gibbons and Speale sit in the control room, which means they've finished their calls as well. I pull open the door and say, "So, how did it go?"

"Fine," Gibbons says.

"Yeah, went okay," Speale says. "I think our people will be safe."

"Good. Are we ready for the broadcast?"

Gibbons nods. "We are."

"Has Winther come back yet?"

"No, he's still gone. I think he'll be here shortly, as we have less than ten minutes 'til the broadcast."

As if on cue, Winther comes through the door, and with him come two guys who look as if they've spent some time on a SWAT team. Dressed in black, it's clear by the sidearm and automatic rifle each carries that they mean business. Winther looks at me, "I wonder if I could have a word with you?" His tone is not unlike a Vice Principal planning detention for you.

"Sure," I say. I keep a casual tone in my voice, although I have a knot in my stomach.

"Let's step outside," Winther says. He grabs the doorknob and pulls the door open. He says to the two guards, "You two stay here and don't let those two touch anything."

The door closes behind us, and Winther grabs my arm. "You planned to double-cross us. John, I'm surprised at you."

"What do you mean?" I say. I know what he means, but I need some time to think up a way to get out of this dilemma.

"Come off it. You know very well what I mean. Did you honestly think that I'd give you a phone and just let you call your girlfriend without some control? I would've thought you would know me a little better. We have the whole conversation on tape."

"Yeah, I guess I should have known better."

"So, what we're going to do is go back into the control room and switch the recordings. Our original broadcast that you so cleverly substituted with your own will now go out as planned. You, sir, will be a piece of meat in thirty minutes or so. Let's go."

"You can let go of me, Winther. I'll go with you and not give you any trouble."

"Yeah, now your ass is cooked, you decide to be a good boy. It doesn't matter, you know. You're not going to get out of this. It's too bad. I'd looked forward to working with you on future projects."

Winther opens the control room door and motions me inside. Gibbons and Speale sit where we left them. They don't turn around, and I suspect the two big guys with guns are the reason. "Okay, Gibbons and Speale," Winther says. "You two get up and turn around."

Gibbons and Speale rise in unison and turn toward us. Their expressions are as if they've been a witness to something terrible. The expression "white as a sheet" fits their skin tone. I get a little nervous, as I don't understand their current demeanor. It could be that they thought someone would shoot them, or are just truly frightened. Winther speaks up, "You guys thought you were real clever in doing a second tape and substituting it for the first. Your pal John, here, blabbed the whole thing to his girlfriend, and we're on to you. You'll need to take the recording you have racked up and give it to me. Then rack up the real broadcast. Once you do that, if you touch anything, I'll have these two gentlemen blow your brains out. Am I clear?"

Gibbons says, "Yes, we understand. We were—"

"Enough," Winther says. "You guys are lucky I don't hold you responsible. I know you were helping John with his foolish quest to save the world. So I don't want to hear any more. Just give me the disk."

Gibbons turns back to the control board, pushes the eject button on the audio and video playback module, and the disk slides out. He pulls it the rest of the way and holds it out for Winther. "How do I know this is the one you guys had planned to broadcast?"

"There's only one slot on the board, and this is the only disk queued up. Also, it has the name *John* written on it, which means it's the version John made for his broadcast."

"Okay, I get it. Where's the other disk?"

"Right here," Gibbons says. He holds up the disk for Winther to see.

"Hand it to me."

Gibbons hands the disk to Winther. "I see the label says 'Jacobs broadcast.'"

"Yes, sir. We wanted to make sure we wouldn't mix them up."

"Okay, put this one in the slot and cue it for broadcast. We only have a few minutes left. Not enough time for me to preview the recording. Let me tell you, though, if there's any mistake, you'll die. You understand?"

Gibbons looks shaken. "Yes, sir," is all he says as he puts the disk into the slot and sets the counter. Speale hasn't moved since he was told to stand, and now takes a seat at the console. He looks quite shaken and about to faint.

"So, what do you plan to do with us?" I say. "Now you've discovered our plot, I'd like to know what you intend to do."

"You know, you always act as if you're going to live forever. Once we finish the broadcast, I'm going to let these two guys take you for a ride into the jungle. I don't care who comes back, but I hope it's not you. You've disappointed me, and you're not all that inviting right now."

"Don't you think your boss might have something to say?"

"Yeah, I do, and he already said it. 'Kill the son of a bitch,' were his exact words."

"Well, I guess it makes it all okay then, huh?"

"Shut the fuck up. You two, get ready for the broadcast."

Gibbons and Speale turn to look at me as if they feel somewhat sorry for my plight, and then turn back to the control panel. I ask Winther, "What goes with Sammy and Clive?"

"What do you mean?"

"You going to kill them too?" Gibbons and Speale sit at attention, evidently interested in the answer.

"Hell no, we aren't going to kill them. We don't think they're worth killing. We'll free them like we originally agreed."

The two sets of shoulders at the control panel slump at the news. Of course, you can't trust Winther, but still, they must be glad.

Chapter Twenty-Seven

Two minutes to broadcast. How can I stop this from happening? The two big guys stand near the door, and Winther leans over Gibbons. I assume he'll watch every move the two make, so there'll be no slip-up. I could jump one of these guys and try to move him around so I could at least maybe use his gun to shoot out the DVR. Not sure it would work but might be worth a try. When the red *On the Air* sign comes on in the studio, I tense up to make a move. Winther asks to have the speaker turned on in the control room and watches the monitor with an intense focus.

From my limited view of the monitor, I can see that the recording on air right now is the one we made last night. I don't know how he did it, but Gibbons managed to get the disk away from Winther and put it in. But no, to get it away from Winther would have been impossible. Gibbons must have switched the disks before Winther came back to the control room. I want to laugh out loud. Winther won't know the difference for another thirty seconds or so—I must make my move now, or I'll lose the opportunity of surprise.

Just when I'm going to spring, Gibbons grabs Winther by the neck and pulls him down quickly, so his face hits the console. Winther screams, and the blood rushes from an obviously broken nose. The two guys with Winther spring into action, and Gibbons jumps up, picks up Winther, and makes what can only be described as a pinwheel spin, and hits the first guy in the face with Winther's shoes. He throws Winther onto the guy as he goes down. The other one raises his weapon, but too late, as Gibbons opens up with the captured automatic, which is still in the hands of the big guy. Gibbons sprays the wall and catches the other guy in the field of fire. His body explodes in a red haze. Gibbons wrestles with the guy he knocked over, and yells at me, "Grab his weapons." I go over to the mass on the floor, pull the automatic sling from around the body, and grab the pistol from the holster. "Shoot him," Gibbons says.

"He's already dead."

"Not him. This one."

Oh my God, I've never killed anyone before. The need to do it to help save Gibbons couples with the ethical question of killing a man. I have to shake myself free of the dilemma and do something. With a big breath in, I move toward the struggling Gibbons and the big guy, and then I place the pistol next to the big guy's head and pull the trigger. The explosion sounds deafening, and the kick of the pistol makes it jump up and threaten to fly out of my hand. Luckily, my grip is hard enough so it stays in my hand. The answer to the ethical question rings in my ears. I want to puke.

Time stands still. Time rushes to catch up. Gibbons no longer struggles and now lies under the big body, which is no longer moving. Gibbons is out of breath and panting heavily. It will be easier for him if I remove the thug from on top. I grab the arm, and the guy's hand brushes mine—I've never felt a dead hand before, but it doesn't seem any different from a live one—I pull the guy off Gibbons and he thanks me. His breathing comes easier now.

I go over to the frozen-in-place Speale. "You okay?" I say.

"Scared shitless," he says. He'll be okay.

Over at the console, Winther sits on the floor and looks as if he's in a trance. Blood runs from his nose, over his mouth, and drips off his chin. I go to him and look into his eyes. He seems to be unconscious with his eyes open. "Winther, can you hear me?"

He looks up and whispers, "You're a dead man."

"I just may be, but if you can hear the broadcast, I think Jacobs is going to want to talk to you, and it's not going to be good. It just may be you who is the dead man."

Winther gives me a half smile, and then looks down at the pool of blood on the floor. "I guess I better stop this bloody nose or Jacobs will have his wish."

"Stay there. I'll get you some ice and a towel."

I leave the control room and cross the hall to the break room, where I grab a couple of dishtowels and scoop some ice out of the ice bin. When I head back to the control room, I hear voices down the hall, and sprint through the door. "We have company." I meant to yell the warning, but it comes out in a sort of croak. "Gibbons, get up. We need to barricade this door."

Gibbons gets to his feet, and we pull some chairs over to the door and hook them under the knob. "Not going to stop them for long," Gibbons says.

"Yeah, I know, but at least we can hold out long enough for the broadcast to finish."

"If those guys were smart, they would just cut the power," Speale says.

I toss him my automatic rifle. "Take this and shoot anything that comes through the door. I'm going to take care of Winther. And for God's sake, don't give them any more ideas." I look up at the observation cameras.

"Yeah, as if they can hear me."

"There are bugs in the room, remember?"

"Oops."

"Hey, Sammy, back up Speale, will you?"

"Sure thing. You take care of Winther; we got this."

I lean down at Winther's side, place some ice in a towel, and put it on the bridge of his nose. "Lean your head back and let's see if we can stop this." Winther does as I tell him, and before long the bleeding slows down.

"Blood's running down my throat," Winther says.

"Just hold your head back and it will be okay. In fact, why don't you lie down?"

Winther pushes his legs out from under and lies back on the floor. "I didn't think Gibbons was so strong."

"Yeah, Gibbons, where did you get the strength for such a maneuver?"

"Well, not so it matters now, but I used to be a professional wrestler. My ring name was Mangler."

I can't help but laugh. Of all the people I get associated with, a professional wrestler is paired up with a nerd to save the day. "How did you guys know to switch the disk?"

"We figured all the phones would be bugged, and one of us would give the plan away. We knew the time was running out, so a switch was a last ditch effort. If nothing happened, we could always switch them back quickly. Good guess, huh?"

"I would say so. It looks like Winther'll be okay. We need to keep an eye on him, though, because he could be trouble when he feels better."

Winther coughs some blood. "I don't think I'm going to feel better soon, so you boys go ahead and have fun. Pay no attention to me."

When I stand, for the first time I notice the mess on my right hand and arm. The blowback from shooting the guy coats up to my elbow. The thought of pieces of brain and tissue cause me to gag, and I stop short. I grab one of the towels and wipe my arm as best as I can, and then throw the towel in the trash can. "I wonder why those guys haven't tried to bust down the door? Any ideas?"

Gibbons says, "They could be bringing in some heavy stuff to blow the door and the contents of this room."

"What kind of heavy stuff?"

"Don't you think they have grenades, rockets, and explosives?"

"Oh, that kind of heavy stuff."

"Yeah, but personally I don't think they'll rush us, given the fact that we have two automatic rifles and two handguns. It would be too much work. All they have to do is lay a couple of concussion grenades against the door and boom. We would be picking toothpicks out of our butts for a year."

"Well, let's continue to speak up and let them know what to do."

The loudspeaker in the control room comes to life. "ATTENTION, JOHN CANNON."

I want to ignore it, but that would be futile. So, I say as calmly as possible, "Yes?"

"YOU NEED TO LAY DOWN YOUR WEAPONS AND COME OUT."

I have this tingly feeling in my stomach like when a bully decides to pick on you, and you're going to haul off and hit him. "Not going to happen. I'm sorry to say."

"IF YOU DON'T LAY DOWN YOUR WEAPONS, WE WILL CALL YOUR MOTHER AND YOU WILL BE IN REAL TROUBLE."

Then I recognize the voice of Ned Tranes. How did he get here? "Okay, Ned, where are you?" Gibbons and Speale look around as if witnessing the arrival of a deity from the heavens. "It's okay, I think the FBI has arrived," I say.

"I'M IN THE NEXT ROOM."

"Okay, Ned, we'll open the door."

I go to the door and pull the chairs away, then turn the knob slowly, and over my shoulder I say, "Get ready for a trick." I pull the door open and, to my happiness, there stands Ned all decked out in his SWAT team gear. "Ned," I say. "You're certainly a sight for sore eyes."

"Nice to see you're still alive," Ned says.

We grab each other in a big hug. I don't think I've ever been so glad to see anyone in my whole life. "How did you get here?" I say.

"All in good time. We need to secure this booth." Ned says something into a microphone connected to his ear. "Who's that on the floor?"

"Paul Winther, Jacobs' leader of this mission."

"I mean to tell ya these guys sure know how to set up an operation. We had to fight our way in here past a bunch of armed men. Most gave up, but there were a few diehards. Paul Winther, you say. I thought they had him in Gitmo."

"Well, that's what the authorities think as well. He had a stand-in who looks enough like him to fool everyone."

"No shit. I better get this info to the section leader."

"You might as well tell them that Sarah Barsonne isn't confined to her house either. She has a stand-in as well."

"You're kidding."

"I wish I were. She and Jacobs have become lovers— they were here yesterday, but I think they left."

Two men rush into the booth and grab Winther, then put him in hand and ankle cuffs. They confer with Ned, and then take him away. "I would like you to meet two heroes." I guide Ned over to meet Gibbons and Speale.

Ned shakes each hand and says, "America is grateful to you boys. I must say, we thought we would be here quicker, but the guys out in the building put up one hell of a fight."

Gibbons says, "At least you got here. We're mighty glad to see you."

"How did you know how to find us?" Speale says.

"Well, boys, this info could be classified, but I think you've earned an answer. We figured the terrorists would try something with John, so while he was unconscious from his wounds on the first go around, we implanted a device under his arm. We've been tracking him since day one. The device stopped working after Stephanie got shot. We didn't connect the two events, but we were in a real pickle. There was no way to get it fixed. We got used to the fact that the device gave off John's exact location for twenty-four hours a day, so we became complacent. Not to turn a short story into a major novel, I'll just say that we got a phone call yesterday. The caller gave us John's exact location."

I look at Ned with, I'm sure, disbelief on my face. "Only two people knew where we were."

"Yeah, and I'll bet you can guess Jacobs wasn't the one who called."

"So you're saying Sarah placed the call?"

"Well, she didn't give her name, but we're fairly sure it was her."

"Well, that gives me some hope she's working on the right side."

"I'll bet she's under some pressure. I would bet that if Jacobs found out about the call, Sarah wouldn't last a minute."

"Also, you could have told me about the transmitter."

"If we told you, John, you would have somehow given away the fact, and we couldn't have that."

"Yeah, but it would have saved a lot of worrying."

"Oh, I don't know. If you were sitting around waiting for a rescue from us, you never would have taken the action you did today. I venture to say, and I won't know all the facts until you brief me, but you guys did something here to save the day, I'm sure."

"Well, you're right. The terrorists forced us to make a broadcast that would have brought the financial community to its knees. We made a different one that validated the strength of our government. It just finished broadcasting. Even if the terrorists broadcast the other one, it won't have much effect."

"I'll take your word for it. You say Jacobs was here yesterday?"

"Yeah, I talked to him."

"I wish we had an implant on him. It would make it so much easier to nail him."

"He's going to get away again, isn't he?"

"Well, I'm not sure. It would be nice to catch him in the act."

"How's Stephanie?"

"Last I heard, some local cops are watching her. She ran out of the hospital and into a police station. They didn't believe her story until she had them get in touch with me. I had to call there and get them to keep an eye on her."

"Is she at home?"

"Naw, they took her to a safe place. I'm not sure where it is, but when we get back Stateside we can go see her."

"I would be grateful if we could."

"Yeah, don't expect a warm welcome, though."

"What do you mean?"

"Well, she got a pack of photos of you and a woman making love, and I don't think she took it in a good way."

"When did she get those photos?"

"While she was still in the hospital. I know she got it because she called when it came in. She'd already opened the envelope. We picked it up to see if there was anything useful on or in the package."

"Did you look at the pictures?"

"No, of course not. None of my business."

"Stephanie told you what was in the package?"

"Unfortunately, yes."

Well, now I know the reason for Sarah's visit that night. I guess Jacobs wanted to make sure my life got disrupted as completely as possible. How am I going to work this out? I'll have to try. Could Stephanie and I ever have a relationship? Regardless, I need to tell her, at the least, that I'm sorry she got roped into this mess. It is too bad, though. I'd thought I loved Sarah, no matter what she'd done to me, and I got carried away. I need to take it a little slower, although I do care what Stephanie thinks about me. Maybe I'll bounce it off Ned when we get moving, and see what he says.

"You ready to Adios, John?"

"I sure am. I sure am."

End

ABOUT THE AUTHOR

John's main interests are reading and writing. He turned to writing as a full-time occupation after an extensive career in business. John writes thriller fiction novels and short stories. He also has a daily blog at **johnwhowell.com** where he writes about a number of subjects related to reading, writing, and life in general.

John lives on Mustang Island in the Gulf of Mexico off the coast of south Texas with his wife Molly and their spoiled rescue pets. He can be reached by e-mail at **johnhowell.wave@gmail.com**

John is also the author of the first book in the John Cannon series titled *My GRL*. The book is available in paperback on Amazon and in the e-book format wherever e-books are sold.

The third book in the series titled *Our Justice* will be available in the summer of 2016

www.ingramcontent.com/pod-product-compliance
Lightning Source LLC
Chambersburg PA
CBHW060526260626
47161CB00003B/782